WHAT REVIE\
PAT MESₜₑₖₙ ᴎᴏᴠᴇʟꜱ:

"Pat Mestern should be considered a national treasure. Her descriptive writing style gives a wonderful glimpse into past lives and times that are quickly being forgotten."

—Fergus Elora News Express

"In conversation with Pat, one senses that no reading of her works of fiction can take us into the deep, compulsive level of creativity that this novelist experiences and accepts as another strata of her life—a plateau as mysterious as some of the characters in her novels. And this deep level of creativity is what makes Pat's novels so compelling. They come from the heart and soul of the writer."

—Ryan Taylor, Book Reviewer, Fort Wayne, Indiana

"Pat Mestern's fictional works are among the most rewarding and most pleasing published today. Her historical novels conjure up a time long gone and characters long dead. They never fail to embrace the sorts of scandals, dreams and secrets that can haunt nearly every family in every walk of life for many tomorrows."

—J. Marshall Craig, screen writer and film director

RACHAEL'S LEGACY

PAT MESTERN

Canterbury House

an imprint of Dudley Court Press

www.canterburyhousepublishing.com

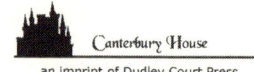

Canterbury House

an imprint of Dudley Court Press

Published in the USA by
Canterbury House Publishing
An imprint of Dudley Court Press
www.canterburyhousepublishing.com
www.DudleyCourtPress.com

Author's Note:
This is a work of fiction. Names, characters, places and incidents are either the product
of the author's imagination or are used fictitiously, and any resemblance to actual persons
living or dead, business establishments, events, or locales is entirely coincidental.

Publisher's Cataloging in Publication Data

Names: Mestern, Pat Mattaini, author.

Title: Rachael's legacy / Pat Mestern.

Description:
[Second edition.]. | Sonoita, AZ : Canterbury House, [2022] | First published in print in 1988.

Identifiers:
ISBN: 9781945401374 (print) | 9780988889713 (Ebook) | LCCN: 2022932712

Subjects:
LCSH: Nineteen twenties—New York (State)—New York—Fiction. | Upper class—New
York (State)—New York—Fiction. | Mennonites—Ontario—Wellington County—Fiction.
| Nineteen twenties—Ontario—Wellington County—Fiction. | Adoptees—Fiction.
| Culture conflict—Fiction. | Life change events—Fiction. | Families—Fiction. |
Self-realization—Fiction. | Mothers and daughters—Fiction. | Time travel—Fiction. |
Wellington (Ont. : County)—History—Fiction. | Canadian fiction. | LCGFT: Historical
fiction. | Romance fiction. | Detective and mystery fiction. | BISAC: LITERARY
COLLECTIONS / Canadian. | FICTION / Historical. | FICTION / Small Town & Rural.

Classification: LCC: PR9199.3.M446 R33 2022 | DDC: 813/.54—dc23

Canterbury House Publishing is committed to publishing works of quality
and integrity. We are proud to offer this book to our readers. The story,
the experiences, opinions and words are the author's alone.
www.CanterburyHousePublishing.com

Dedicated to Joseph Francis (Jimmy) Mattaini who always marched to the tune of a different drummer.

If a man doesn't keep pace with his companions, perhaps he hears a different drummer. Let him step to the music he hears, however distant or far away.

—HENRY DAVID THOREAU

APRIL 1905

CHAPTER ONE

MARYBOROUGH

PEOPLE PASSING THE VALLEY lately looked closely at the white house, watching for a glimpse of Rachael, for there had been talk that Rachael Gingerich was not well. Stranger yet, the lady from Pennsylvania, Anna Carliss, had just arrived and was staying at Lilac Hill. This morning Margaret Smith hurried through the backfields to Rachael's. And, according to Old Man Martin, the coffin maker, the blue moon had risen the night before in the April sky and he'd seen a raven circle the white house three times before noon—both bad omens. No one particularly wanted to believe Old Man Martin, but he had been right on too many occasions to be dismissed completely.

"Just as the sun was rising," he said, "Salome Gingerich arrived at her son's house, and she hasn't left yet." Old Man Martin had never seen a time when two full moons rose in a month where the second, the blue moon, hadn't heralded a death, or two. He took some time from his work to look up the valley at sundown, his eyes catching Rachael's house just as a shaft of sunlight caught the dwelling, turning its windows to gold. "The Hand of the Lord is on Jacob Gingerich's house," Old Man Martin murmured. "I was right."

Standing by the window near the kitchen stove, Anna Carliss glanced up the valley and across the Conestoga River to the crossroads. All was dark except for the soft glow of oil lamps in the Martin Woodworking Shop. Anna shivered and, turning away from the window, quietly walked back to her chair by the fire, where she turned her full attention to the cradle Jacob Gingerich had painstakingly fashioned for his first-born child. Touching the cradle gently, Anna set it to rocking. Four hours earlier, she had helped Mary Gingerich bathe Abraham, the second newborn, and placed him with his brother, Adam, toe-to-toe, in the cradle. Anna bent and lovingly touched a pink cheek, then glanced up at Caleb standing by the table.

"They are beautiful babies, Caleb. They are fair of face, blue of eye and healthy baby boys."

Caleb glanced quickly at the cradle, then came to Anna's side. Squatting near her, he asked quietly, "There is something wrong?" He glanced quickly at his brother Jacob, standing across the room by a window, his back to Anna and the cradle. "All is not right, is it?"

Anna nodded. "It's not good, Caleb." She spoke in a whisper. "Mother Gingerich doesn't know what the matter is. Rachael is not responding to the herbs. She should have a doctor, Caleb, and quickly."

Caleb rose and walked over to Jacob. "Brother Jacob," he said, "we should tend the cattle. The womenfolk will call you quickly if you are needed. You will feel much better doing a man's work tonight while the women tend Rachael."

Jacob shook his head violently. "You go tend the cattle, Caleb. Father will help. I will stay near Rachael."

"Should father not go for the doctor?" Caleb asked.

"It is not necessary," answered Jacob. "Mother Gingerich knows what she is doing. She has birthed every Mennonite child in this community and some that are not of our faith too."

Caleb shrugged and walked toward the door leading to the woodshed and summer kitchen.

"I'll bring in some wood," he said. "You should build up the fire."

Anna paid little attention to the conversation between the brothers. She let her eyes wander around Rachael's kitchen instead, seeking out the little touches of colour her dear friend had managed to add to the rather austere room. Bright pillow covers were on chair and daybed. Colourful pictures hung from the walls. Brightly embroidered splash cloths hung behind the wash bench and dry sink. Cheerful braided rugs adorned bare wooden floors, scrubbed pale from lye water. Gay hand-painted designs bordered window and door openings.

"Jacob," she asked quietly, "you love Rachael very much, don't you?"

Jacob, used to Anna's straightforward manner of questioning, didn't answer immediately but turned from his window to look directly at Rachael's friend.

"I mean," Anna said, blushing slightly under his steady glance, "that you must love Rachael to allow her such freedoms as pictures on her walls and decorations around her doors. It's not your father's way, is it?"

Jacob lowered his gaze to the floor. "It is not my father's

way, and it should not be my way. But I could not say no to Rachael."

One of the babies began to fuss and Anna turned her attention to the cradle, rocking it gently, knowing Jacob would not continue to converse with her, and that she could not continue her conversation with him.

Caleb appeared at the door, his arms full of wood. "Sun's going down quickly," he said. "We will need to get to the cattle soon, or we will need lanterns in the barn."

Anna looked quickly from Caleb to Jacob. "Has Patrick arrived yet?" she asked. "Margaret sent him down the valley for some more herbs. Please, Jacob, would you look down the valley to see if he's coming along the path from Lilac Hill?"

Jacob walked over to the window again and looked out over the valley. Before he could give an answer Mother Salome Gingerich burst into the kitchen.

"Hot water, Caleb! Quickly. We need hot water. There is a third child on its way."

"Another child?" Anna asked incredulously.

"Yah," Mother Gingerich replied briskly.

Margaret Smith appeared in the doorway. "Come quickly, Mother Gingerich."

Salome rushed past Margaret, calling over her shoulder, "Please. Hot water, Caleb."

Both Anna and Jacob ran in the direction of the hall and birthing room, but Margaret stood firmly in the doorway.

"No Jacob," she commanded, her voice halting him halfway across the kitchen. "You stay with Caleb." Margaret gave Caleb a stern look. "Keep Jacob in the kitchen, Caleb. Anna, come with me."

Caleb shook his head and stood in front of Jacob. Anna

followed Margaret as she turned on her heel and disappeared down the back hall.

"It isn't good, Anna. Mother Gingerich didn't know there was another child. She applied hot compresses to assist with the afterbirth, and I fear she's caused massive bleeding."

"Who was to know?" asked Anna. "Who was to know there were even two?"

"Jacob should have allowed Rachael a doctor." Margaret replied. "You know Rachael has not been well for the past four months."

"Mother of God!" exclaimed Anna. "What are we going to do with three?"

"And no mother to tend them," muttered Margaret. "Rachael is bleeding to death. She hasn't the strength to bear this child."

A scream rent the air. "My God," Margaret said. "She's been delivered." Taking Anna's arm, Margaret ran down the hall and into the dimly lit room, where Mother Gingerich and Mary were bent over a quivering form lying on the bed.

"Someone . . . Margaret!" called Salome. "Help me!"

Margaret quickly joined Salome at bedside.

"Ahlmehchdich" prayed Salome.

Margaret took charge of the situation. "Tend Rachael. Give me the child."

"It's not breathing," Salome said.

Margaret, breaking away from the women by the bed, held the small, withered bit of flesh up in the air. "Anna, run for towels . . . cloths. Bring anything you can find. Make sure the cloths are warm. Get them from behind the stove. Run, woman. I'm behind you with the child."

Out of the room and down the hall both women ran.

Anna, racing through the door, snatched towels from the rack behind the stove. Margaret swore softly behind her, and faintly, very faintly, a choking sound accompanied both.

"Lord Almighty!" Margaret said when in the light of the oil lamp she saw what she was carrying. "Good Lord Almighty!" Grabbing towels from Anna, she began to wrap the baby. The choking sounds continued for a few seconds and then stopped. Margaret gently slapped the bundle of dish towels and the noise began again. Parting some of the bloodied towels, she worked quickly to clean the child's mouth and throat of mucus. "Look, Anna."

Anna obediently looked into the bundle of towels, as did Jacob and Caleb, who had come quickly to their side.

"What is it?" Caleb asked in amazement.

"Such a question!" Anna answered.

"It's a babe," said Margaret. "The smallest wee bit of a thing I have ever seen, and I've seen a good many born in my lifetime." Parting the towels a little more, tenderly, as though the child might fall apart at any moment, Margaret continued, "And, notably it's the smallest baby I have ever seen. It's a girl and she's got everything she needs to survive—arms, legs, all her fingers and all her toes."

"Ahlmehchdich," whispered Caleb. "She is nothing. She is minute."

"She is alive and breathing," scolded Anna.

"Jacob!" Mary Gingerich was at the door. "Mother Gingerich says you must come quickly now."

Jacob, paying no further attention to the baby, ran after Mary while Margaret turned her full attention to the bundle she was holding.

"Well, at least she is breathing, Anna. But she's so tiny she might not live. She has not got much of a chance."

"Is there nothing we can do?" asked Anna.

"There is no one can care for her properly," Margaret replied. "She can't be raised here. There are two already, and this one is not healthy." Margaret looked directly at Anna. "She maybe was not meant to live. She is so small."

"Give her to me," Anna demanded.

Margaret carefully handed the bundle to Anna. "Keep her eyes covered," she said firmly. "They're not developed yet. And don't hold her too hard. She is three pounds of butter at most. There is not a doctor who would give this one a chance. He would just put her in a shoe box and let her die."

"There is one doctor who would try," Anna stated. "Groves. He would not let this baby die."

"Don't be considering it," Margaret responded. "It's a thirty-mile drive."

"Why not?" Anna asked impatiently. "Margaret, I am not going to let this baby die. Jacob is with Rachael. The child she gave birth to is not going to die!"

Margaret gave Anna a curious look. "You are the limit, Anna Carliss. Groves might be able to help, but we've got to get the child to him immediately."

"I'll take her." Anna held the bundle close to her bosom.

"Why not, Mrs. Smith?" asked Caleb, who had stood silently by the two women. "I can drive to Fergus. I've got Mrs. Carliss's fastest team at Jacob's barn now just in case Jacob decided a doctor was needed."

"We'll do it then!" Margaret exclaimed. "We might lose her on the way. But we are sure to lose her here. Caleb, get the team. Gather all the blankets and robes you can find and don't waste a moment. If you see Patrick coming from Lilac Hill, tell him to come quickly. He should stay with Jacob. Bring one of Rachael's shawls for Anna when you come back in."

"What do I do?" asked Anna.

"Give me the child," commanded Margaret. "Unbutton your waist."

Anna looked startled and glanced quickly around the room.

"The men have all gone," Margaret said. "Do as I say. Unbutton your waist. You have to keep the baby as warm as possible, and the warmest place is on your breast and close to your heart. It will do this wee one the world of good to hear a heartbeat."

Anna hesitantly unbuttoned her waist, and when she had finished, Margaret placed the baby against her breast. "Now we'll tuck her in with whatever we can find to keep her warm." She removed one blanket from the babies in the cradle.

"She's moving," Anna whispered. "I can feel her moving against my breast."

"She is a spunky wee thing," replied Margaret, busy tucking the baby close to Anna, "but it's a wonder she wasn't born dead. Mother Gingerich shouldn't have applied hot compresses."

"Did you notice the hair?" Anna asked. "What there was of it."

"Black, black as coal."

"And her skin?" Anna said.

"Well, you can't tell with a baby this small, and she's not been cleaned up, but I would guess it is not exactly pure white."

"Oh, Margaret," Anna exclaimed. "She will look just like Rachael."

"That she might," replied Margaret. "Or she might look like her Grandpa Joseph Erie. But, if we don't stop talking, and if Caleb doesn't come soon, we won't have to worry about her looks."

Caleb, as though he heard his name, came from the woodshed, a black shawl in his hands. Close on his heels was Patrick Smith.

"It is that bad, is it?" Patrick asked when he saw Margaret.

Margaret nodded. "She's small. Her breathing is irregular. She's bluish in colour. Stay close, Patrick. I'm thinking Jacob is going to need you."

Margaret adjusted Anna's waist so it wasn't too unlady-like and wrapped her tightly in Rachael's shawl.

"And what if I don't feel her move on the way down to Fergus?" Anna asked.

"Don't dare look. Caleb, you wrap this woman and child in blankets and robes and don't spare those horses. Get to Fergus quickly."

Patrick placed his hand on Caleb's shoulder. "You can do it Caleb. You are the best man I know with horses. Give them their head. They are the fastest team in Wellington. Good luck. Godspeed."

"Margaret," Anna said quietly. "What about Rachael?"

Margaret gently kissed Anna on the cheek. "Save the child. "Don't worry about Rachael."

Turning to Caleb, she said. "Take Anna. Go, Caleb. Pray that the baby will live. That is the only thing we can do now."

Yes, thought Anna as the baby moved against her breast, this child is Rachael's legacy. She must live.

"A moment." Salome appeared at the door. "Erie wants to speak with Anna. She wants to see the child. Come quickly, life's breath is leaving her."

Anna, with the babe tucked against her bosom went to say her last goodbyes to Rachael Gingerich.

The glow of several oil lamps in the kitchen silhouetted the figures of Patrick Smith and Jacob on Rachael's porch. While Jacob paced bank and forth from one end to the other, Patrick lounged against one of the support posts, studying the darkened valley. Not one to believe in the total finality of death, Patrick watched the valley and night sky for some sign that would tell him that Rachael's spirit still lived even though her body lay in death. By reason of Irish birth, Patrick felt he had a right to superstitions regarding death. At the exact moment his mother died ten years before, a lone Canada goose had flown over their Belwood home. Patrick knew his mother loved the sound of geese high overhead during their autumnal flights south, so it wasn't difficult for his Irish mind to see his mother's spirit flying free like the beautiful, winged goose. Way down Rachael's valley, the lights burned late at Old Man Martin's where Father Abraham Gingerich had been sent for a coffin. Overhead, the blue moon of April cast its eerie glow.

Patrick inhaled the cool night breezes, trying to dispel the death air of the house from his lungs. Searching the northwest sky, his sharp eyes saw a shooting star carving a brilliant arch toward earth. Patrick smiled and shifted his weight against the support.

"Thank you, Lord," he said. Forever, now, he would

associate shooting stars with Rachael, an appropriate sign for such a gentle, sincere woman.

His grief somewhat appeased, Patrick's mind turned to Jacob. It wouldn't be easy for Jacob to overcome his despair. He was a deeply religious man and he loved Rachael.

"Grief shows in many different ways," Margaret had cautioned. "Stay near Jacob. His emotions run deep."

"Ahlmehchdich," Jacob was saying over and over again. "Why, Patrick? Why? Inside I have two bhubey boys . . . Aynlich. But no Rachael, why?"

"You have three children, Jacob." Patrick turned away from the valley to look at Jacob. "You must not forget your daughter."

"Vah sich tsvelt dehs drit sich," said Jacob.

"Don't give me that old wives' tale," Patrick replied. "There is no bad luck in a third child. Rachael died because . . . because of other complications."

"She died because of the girl's birth." Jacob stopped pacing "This third child is . . . Oongvinst . . . Oomglicklich."

Patrick stood tall and walked over to Jacob. "This girl is neither unwanted or unlucky. You are distraught and you are saying things you don't mean, Brother Jacob." Patrick placed his hand on Jacob's shoulder. "Do not blame the child for your wife's death."

Jacob pulled away from Patrick's protective hand. "Fahdah says I must not question the Ahlmehchdich. I must accept what He gives. But I have lost Rachael." Jacob's voice broke.

Patrick placed his hand on Jacob's shoulder again. This time Jacob didn't pull away.

"Had Fahdah had his way I would not have married Rachael. He wished me to marry Miriam. Rachael was not one of our kind and he did not approve. Moodah made him bless our union."

"I wasn't aware of any problem between you and Abraham," Patrick said, frowning. He knew Abraham Gingerich to be a very reasonable man and couldn't think of him ever denying his son the right to marry whomever he pleased.

"It was because she was not born of our faith," Jacob hung his head. "And, because she was not . . ." He didn't finish but began pacing the porch. "I married Rachael because I loved her. I was willing to spend my life with her. I was willing to change my way of life for her. I would have left the church for her."

Patrick Smith realized the full extent of Jacob's love for Rachael. Rarely did a Mennonite ever leave the faith, and this was one of Bishop Gingerich's children.

"How am I to raise two newborn sons with no wife?" Jacob asked.

"And a daughter," Patrick interjected. "Jacob, don't forget your daughter."

"I do not know this daughter, Patrick. I saw her for a moment before I was called to Rachael's side and never when Anna came to the room. It is as thought the child has disappeared. When I returned to the kitchen she was gone, taken from me as Rachael was taken from me."

"Anna left quickly for Fergus to try to save your child. She did not remove the wee thing from you on purpose."

"If the child was meant to die, it should die here."

"And, if it was meant to live?" asked Patrick.

Jacob ignored Patrick's question and said instead, "Rachael's last words were for Anna, requesting she care for the girl and asking the child be called Erie. She had no time to say goodbye to me. Would you not think her last words would be for me, her husband, and not for the child that killed her?"

"The child didn't kill her!" Patrick Smith stood squarely in front of Jacob and put his hand on the man's shoulders. "You must listen, Jacob. You must never blame your daughter for Rachael's death."

Patrick looked closely at Jacob to see if his words were making any impact. At least Jacob hadn't removed his hands.

Continuing, Patrick appealed directly to Jacob's love for Rachael. "Why the wee bairn is the spitting image of Rachael. Margaret says she has black hair and dusky skin and . . ."

"And that's why Fahdah did not wish me to marry Rachael, "Jacob interrupted. "He warned . . ." Jacob hesitated mid-sentence, then said quickly, "It is wrong to speak against Fahdah." He changed the subject quickly. "The boys are fair-haired, blue-eyed and healthy. They look Gingerich."

"Regardless of their looks," Patrick said, "you are going to raise all three. If Caleb and Anna reach Fergus in time, Erie Gingerich will live. If anyone can save her, Groves will. Your family will raise your children for you. Margaret is close by too. You will make do, Jacob. After the hurt is gone, you will be alright. Your father always said you were a born leader. Caleb calls you 'the chosen one.' Look beyond your time with Rachael. You have years to live yet, Jacob, and much good to do."

Patrick glanced past Jacob. Removing his hands from his friend's shoulders, he said, "Prepare yourself. I see lanterns coming down the valley path from your father's farm and buggies are coming up your lane."

"One buggy will be Fahdah and Martin with the coffin. The lights are carried by people come to sit the body." Jacob sighed heavily and turned toward the kitchen door. "I always had strength, Patrick Smith. Whenever our kind needed assistance or comfort, Fahdah or I was there. They will expect I will have strength now."

"You are like your father, Jacob. Your religion will see you through trial and tribulation."

The crying of a baby and Abraham's voice from the yard interrupted the conversation.

"Jacob," Abraham Gingerich called. "Come. I have brought Miriam to care for the children."

"Before you go in, Jacob, look at the sky. See the meteorite shower? Always think of Rachael when you see a shooting star. She's watching over you."

"Foolish man," Jacob said, "to think a star would be watching me."

Patrick held Margaret by the arm and the lantern high as they crossed the footbridge leading to Lilac Hill. Margaret Smith could barely contain her anger.

"Patrick," she said, eyes flashing. "How dare Abraham bring that woman into the house so soon after Rachael's death. Ant, at the bedside, he told Mother Gingerich his union with Rachael had been a 'marriage of the flesh.' I just couldn't believe what I was hearing."

"The beggar!" Smitty swore.

"And Jacob didn't say anything. He just stood there and accepted Miriam into his house."

"Figures," Smitty said. "Wait until I tell you what Jacob revealed to me tonight."

"The sad part about this whole thing is that the wee girl

is being blamed for Rachael's death, and it was really Mother Gingerich who should accept the blame."

"No one should accept the blame," said Smitty. "These things do happen."

Patrick and Margaret reached the porch at Lilac Hill. "Can we rest here awhile?"

Margaret sat heavily on the steps. "Promise me, Patrick, I will be near a doctor when your child is due."

Patrick put his arm around Margaret. "I promise," he said.

"When you pick William up at the train station tomorrow, you'd better tell him the whole story. Turn William right around and send him down to Fergus to be with Anna. She'll want her husband with her. Whatever he does, don't let him bring that wee baby back here to be raised by Jacob. He doesn't want her. Mark my word, Patrick, Abraham will have Jacob married to Miriam as soon as the mourning period is over."

"I feel sorry for Jacob," said Patrick. "He is caught between the old and the new, his father and his love for Rachael."

"I feel sorry for the wee girl," replied Margaret. "If she lives, she will be Rachael all over again."

"Two beautiful, healthy boys," Old Man Martin told everyone after he left Jacob Gingerich's "And the mother, Rachael, dead."

Thereafter, up and down Maryborough, word spread that Jacob Gingerich was a widower with twin boys to raise. Through circumstances, no one except the Gingerich, Smith and Carliss families knew about Caleb Gingerich and Anna Carliss's race to Fergus to try to save a small baby girl. And it remained that way for twenty years.

MAY 1925

CHAPTER TWO

NEW YORK

WILLIAM'S DAKOTA APARTMENT had fifteen rooms including a reception room, a library, a morning room, a parlour, several bedrooms, and a private ballroom. William's father had brought painters from Italy to decorate the ballroom's twenty-four-foot ceilings. The library was lined with leather panels purchased from an estate in England. William had inherited the apartment from his mother. He, in turn, would leave it to Erie. Such was tradition.

William scrutinized the dining table. He had instructed Francis to set it up in the morning room by a window which afforded the best view of Central Park. The soft glow of candles reflected in the crystal and silver on the white damask cloth. Francis had remembered the centerpiece of yellow roses and white daisies. William left a gaily wrapped package at Anna's place then rang for Amy. She appeared, starched white cap perched on grey hair and curtsied.

"Is everything ready in the kitchen, Amy?"

"It is, Sir."

"I'll go get Anna."

When William reappeared in the morning room his arm was linked through Anna's. She was radiant in a blue silk dress. Francis held the chair for her.

"We'll have champagne, Francis. Anna, dearest, open your gift."

Anna carefully undid the wrappings, opened the box, and removed an exquisite antique music box; two porcelain birds on a jeweled branch in a golden cage.

"It is exceptional, William. It must be one of a kind."

"It appears to be French. When I found it in a shop in Atlanta, I knew you must have it for your collection."

Francis had served champagne and now stood at a respectable distance awaiting further orders.

"To the twenty-first anniversary of our meeting," William said, holding his glass up to salute Anna.

"To my dearest husband."

Has it been twenty-one years since I met this beautiful woman, thought William, reaching across the table to hold Anna's hand. *My Anna has not changed. Her hair is still the colour of honey. She never appears to age. How could I be so fortunate. I don't deserve a woman so rare as Anna.*

Anna smiled at William. She could spend hours with him, content to hold his hand. *Such a patient, caring husband,* she thought, sipping her champagne. *But he looks tired tonight, poor dear.*

"Shall we begin?" asked William.

"I'm so hungry," replied Anna. "Erie and I went shopping after we left your office this morning. That young woman has so much energy. I simply can't keep up with her." As Francis served a fruit soup, Anna smiled at him then said, "How long have you worked for us?"

"Twenty years, ma'am and you have celebrated this special anniversary in many places. I particularly liked Rome, ma'am."

William laughed. "Remember our tenth anniversary when both Erie and I had the measles."

Anna's laugh was infectious and beautiful. "We must be the only couple that celebrate the anniversary of our meeting."

"Are you happy, Anna?"

"Deliriously, to use a favorite expression of Erie's."

"And you, William?"

"Yes. Look, Anna dearest. The lights are shining on the pond in the park." From their vantage point, seven floors up, Central Park lay before them . . . The Green . . . North Meadow . . . West Drive.

If I concentrate on the park, Anna thought, *I can almost believe I'm in Maine. I can forget the buildings around us and believe the trees are at Seawind.*

"Thank God for Central Park," said William. Then he grimaced at a sharp pain in his back. "It is the only thing that keeps me sane in New York City. I would much rather be in Pennsylvania at the main house. Would you be happy, Anna, if I told you I'm planning to spend the entire summer in Maine with you? I've decided not to join Bill in the bush this year."

"William, you love the bush! You've been spending July with Bill for the past five years. It's the only opportunity you take to go rock-hounding and to spend some time with my half-brother."

"Bill can do without me this year. I am spending the summer with you in Maine."

"Remember the autumn we spent in Panama?"

Both laughed. "Never again," said William. "Would you mind my being underfoot for the entire summer? I have made no commitments that would take me away."

"That is the best present you can give me," replied Anna. "I shall spoil you terribly."

When Francis removed the soup plates and served a lobster salad, William motioned to him to refill their champagne glasses. He smiled at Anna. *In our twenty-one years we have disagreed on only one issue*, he reflected. *We had differing views on when Erie should be told about her lineage.* Anna was right. With Erie's marriage to Arthur Moore pending, she should have been told sooner. William changed position to try to ease the pain which persisted in his back.

"Are you uncomfortable, William? There are softer chairs in the apartment."

"It's nothing, Anna . . . a muscle spasm in my back . . . nothing."

"Where shall we be for our twenty-first anniversary?" Anna asked.

"We always wanted to spend some time in Greece. Let's plan a trip to Greece, a small hotel by the sea," William said.

"That would be delightful! Yes, Greece. But first we must have Erie's wedding planned, if there is to be a wedding."

William turned serious. "We weren't very bright, were we, Anna? We never thought through the consequences of raising Erie in these circumstances. She will be trapped now, not one of her people, not one of ours."

"She is her father's child, her mother's legacy, your protégé and my very special daughter."

"Erie is an intelligent woman," William observed. "When the time comes, she will make the right decision. When dinner is over let's adjourn to the ballroom? We have the entire room to ourselves. He was cut short by a coughing fit.

"That," Anna observed, "is a heart cough! Rather than dance, let's take a ride through Central Park. We can embarrass the driver by bundling in the back of the landau."

William took his wife's hands and held them to his chest. "Anna, promise me that if anything happens, if there's any problem you might have, if I'm not around, listen to Ian Oliver's advice."

"Of course," Anna said. "But, William, why are you telling me this now? Are you not feeling well? Is there a problem?"

"No, my dearest. It's just that Ian Oliver has been my personal financial adviser, and friend for years. I . . . he can assist with any questions you or Erie might have, should a situation arise if I'm . . . away."

JUNE 1925

CHAPTER THREE

MARYBOROUGH

SMITTY STOOD IN THE TUNNEL examining a wooden sub-floor by the light of Caleb's lantern. Both men were dressed in dark clothing.

"No one has tampered with the floor," whispered Smitty.

"Then let's get to work."

Caleb hung the lantern on a hook in a beam overhead. Smitty carefully removed a section of sub-floor and passed it to Caleb, who stacked it against the dirt wall. The only sound other than the scraping of wood was water dripping in the damp underground tunnel behind them. Neither of them spoke. Both worked quickly to remove the wood separating them from the trapdoor. When the last board was stacked, Caleb placed the lantern twenty feet back down the tunnel while Smitty eased several large bolts, muffling the sound with a heavy piece of canvas.

"My turn tonight," he whispered. "We've got to move fifteen barrels and I'm stronger than you are."

The comment brought a grunt from Caleb, who had carried twenty barrels the length of the warehouse the night before. Both were close in age and build: tall, muscular men in their mid-forties.

Smitty raised the trapdoor six inches and peered into the warehouse. He saw no one. He opened the door another foot and listened intently. Hearing nothing unusual, he pulled himself through the opening and secured the door against a stack of barrels.

The two men usually moved twenty barrels at a time. That was all the water wagon would hold. Because this particular warehouse had been tapped on a number of recent nights, the remaining barrels of uncut whiskey were now quite a distance from the trapdoor. They had agreed that fifteen barrels were all they could manage in the time they had.

Smitty slipped thick felt slippers over his huge boots and walked silently to a long rack two aisles to the left of the door. He ran his fingers round the lips of the first six barrels in the rack. The absence of two small nicks in their rims told him these barrels contained pure, uncut whiskey. He set to work. Removing one from the rack, he shouldered it, walked catlike to the trapdoor, and handed it down to Caleb. Caleb took the container and disappeared, but returned several minutes later with a similar barrel, which he handed up to Smitty. The return trip to the rack always seemed easier for Smitty, although he knew that water weighed just as much as whiskey.

By the time Smitty had exchanged the fifth barrel he had worked up a good sweat. He stopped to wipe his forehead, then froze where he stood. Voices came from the direction of Jake's makeshift office. Motioning that Caleb should remain in the tunnel, Smitty sneaked between the long racks to a position where he could see Jake. One glance told him everything.

"Damn!" he muttered. He retraced his steps and bent down to confer with Caleb. "The snoopers are here."

"What are they doing?"

"Gabbing with Jake. They have got their feet up on his table and he's serving them coffee, cool as a cucumber. He's playing our game."

"Obviously they're in no rush to leave," Caleb said. "As long as they aren't looking around, we may as well carry on."

"They must be on to something," Smitty said, "otherwise they wouldn't bother to come to the warehouse at night. They are the same two fellows that have been asking questions in Drayton."

"Let's just get on with the job," Caleb said. "If you're afraid of getting caught, I'll change places with you."

"I don't mind stealing cheese right off the dining room table," Smitty retorted, rising from his haunches. "Just get yourself out if there's trouble."

"Like hell I will!" replied Caleb.

Smitty continued, taking extra precautions now to prevent any noise. He listened intently after lifting each barrel from the rack and again when filling the empty spot with one that Caleb handed him. While replacing the eleventh barrel something fell on his head. Smitty reached up and removed the offending object. He looked up into the rafters, where several raccoons stared back at him. The animals began to shuffle slowly along a wooden beam.

"Darn raccoons have lined the rafters with bread," muttered Smitty. "Jake's been feeding them again."

Shuffling . . . a squeal . . . and more bread rained down, this time on a rack of barrels.

"The devil! They're coming down!" Smitty watched as the fat, saucy raccoons waddled to the nearest crossbeam and began to climb down, in his direction, probably expecting to be given more bread crusts. At the same time, he became aware of Jake's deep voice wafting throughout the warehouse.

"It's only raccoons," said Jake loudly.

Smitty quickly crept to the edge of the nearest barrel rack. Jake and the snoopers stood outside the office. The snoopers were looking around, their eyes trying to penetrate the black interior of the building.

"Didn't sound like raccoons to me," said one snooper.

"You wouldn't know what a raccoon sounds like," replied the other.

"Look." Jake shone his flashlight up into the rafters. "It's raccoons. The place is lousy with them."

The flashlight moved down the crossbeam from a top rafter.

Smitty turned and wasted no time reaching the trapdoor. "Darn fool is leading them right to us," he hissed at Caleb.

"What's that?" asked one of the snoopers. "It sounded like someone talking."

"Look, I told you it was raccoons." Jake swung his light to the other end of the warehouse. "They're over here too."

"Quick Caleb," Smitty said, "find me a small stone."

Presently a hand passed a good-sized pebble through the door.

"About time," growled Smitty.

"You try to find a stone in the dark," Caleb said.

"It is voices," said the snooper. "Over here."

Smitty threw the stone. It arched high, hit a rafter, and landed with a sharp thud thirty feet away on a rack of barrels.

"Shine your light over here again," one snooper told Jake. "Go get the car," he told his partner. "Bring it in the shipping door. Leave the lights on so we can see who's in here."

Smitty heard the snooper heading in his direction.

"Good throw," said Caleb sarcastically. "You may as well have stood up and waved your arms. Now what?"

Smitty crouched and whispered, "We can't let them find the trapdoor or we've lost this warehouse and Jake will be in a lot of trouble."

"Shine your light here," the snooper shouted at Jake and pointed toward Smitty's corner.

"It don't work anymore," Jake answered, hitting the light hard with his hand. The back fell off. The batteries fell out and Jake kicked then behind him.

Smitty heard the shipping door open.

"I wouldn't bring the car in here," cautioned Jake.

"Why not?" asked the snooper.

"I wouldn't drive a car onto this old floor."

Smitty looked closely at the nearest rack of barrels. "Caleb, come up here," he whispered.

Caleb popped through the door and crouched beside Smitty.

"Look," Smitty said. "There are wedges holding the racks at this end, and at the other end too, to compensate for the uneven floor."

Caleb quickly moved to the first rack of barrels. Peering down the row, he rejoined Smitty and said, "Looks like an interesting situation."

"What would happen," Smitty pondered, "if we removed the wedges at this end?"

"Barrels all over the place," chuckled Caleb.

"And the weight of the car at the other end might help too," said Smitty.

"Don't move!" the snooper commanded. "Nobody move in there. You can't get out past us. Show yourselves."

"We need wire," said Caleb.

"There is a small roll in the tunnel," Smitty said. He disappeared through the trapdoor, ran and reappeared a moment later with a roll of strong picture wire.

"What's your plan?"

"You stay in the tunnel. I'll wire the wedges. If I'm caught, I don't have a wife at home to worry about me."

Caleb worked quickly. He wrapped one end of the wire around one wedge and the other around another. He then handed the mid-section down to Smitty.

The Ford appeared in the opening, lights shining on the opposite wall, away from Smitty and Caleb.

"Swing the car, you fool," shouted the snooper. "Shine the lights over here."

Caleb slipped through the trapdoor, lowering it after him, leaving a two-inch gap to monitor the situation.

"You're making a mistake," said Jake "It's raccoons."

"Raccoons be damned!" the snooper spat.

Smitty removed the felt slippers and gave one to Caleb. "Protect your hand with this." He slid one slipper onto his hand. Caleb did likewise.

"As soon as the lights hit the rack," Caleb said, "and on the count of three, pull hard, and duck when you hear the barrels coming at us."

As the snooper maneuvered the car round, Jake danced back and forth in the headlights.

"Get out of the way, you fool!" the snooper commanded.

"The floor's moving," Jake cautioned as the Ford's lights hit the rack.

"One . . . two . . . three," counted Caleb. He and Smitty pulled together, leaning back with the effort.

Nothing happened.

"Harder," Smitty said. "Pull harder." The pair strained against the picture wire. Caleb felt it cut through the felt slipper.

"Look out!" yelled Jake. "Run! The racks are breaking away!"

Caleb and Smitty fell on their backs in the tunnel, the trapdoor slamming above them. A thunderous roar ensued.

"Quick!" Caleb was on his feet. "I'll bolt the door. Hand me the boards." The two threw the sub-floor together and raced through the tunnel.

In the warehouse, one snooper was trying to extricate himself from the car which was surrounded by barrels. Jake leaned against an outside wall, smiling to himself. The smell of whiskey was everywhere. Some of the barrels had broken when they crashed against the car. The second snooper sat on the hood of the Ford, staring at the chaos. "Boss isn't going to like this," he said. He looked into the rafters where the raccoons had scurried to safety. "Don't tell me this was raccoons."

"Wasn't raccoons," Jake answered. "The weight of the Ford on the floor shifted a board or two and a couple of wedges let loose, that's all. That's what your boss gets for storing whiskey in an old warehouse. I'll have some men pile the barrels back up again tomorrow. I won't say anything about the broken ones."

"What's that?" asked the snooper, looking out a back window.

"It's the city water wagon," replied Jake. "They work at night when they can get around the streets easily."

"Struck out again. The company's still losing whiskey," said the snooper who was seated on the Ford. "We think we know who, but we don't know how."

"Well, let's not let this good whiskey go to waste," said Jake, dipping a finger into one of the broken barrels and tasting it to make sure it was uncut whiskey and not water. "Let's drink to the raccoons' health."

CHAPTER FOUR
New York City

THE SLEEK CADILLAC PULLED UP near the corner of Lennox and 147th Street, behind Mayor Jimmy Walker's Duesenberg, causing a minor traffic jam, but no policeman moved to interfere. The chauffeur, after opening the door for Arthur Moore IV, walked round the car to open the curbside door for Erie Carliss. With the chauffeur standing at attention, Arthur gave an assisting hand to Erie, who exited gracefully despite the clinging, décolleté green silk gown she was wearing. Casually draping a silk shawl over one shoulder, she took Arthur's arm.

As they climbed the colonnade to the entrance of the Cotton Club, Arthur whispered, "You are causing quite a sensation, my dear. Even the mayor's wife can't outshine you tonight."

"I thought perhaps the crowds were staring at you," Erie laughed.

"You wouldn't believe who I had to bribe for an invitation to this evening's little affair," Arthur said.

The Cotton Club, located over the Globe Theatre, had the best booze, the best music, and the richest clientele in New York City. Drink was supplied by the "Phoenix Cereal and Beverage Company" or from the private contraband stock of Lucky Luciano, a frequent patron.

The door, zealously guarded by a giant of a man, opened immediately for Arthur, who slipped him a five-dollar bill for his efforts.

Charles, the maître d', led the way through the crowded, smoky room to a private booth at the rear of the lounge. Erie acknowledged greetings from various tables, including one from boxer Jack Dempsey.

"We are in honourable company tonight," she said, smiling when the mayor tipped his hand in her direction.

"Charles," Arthur said. "We are trying for a little privacy tonight. Could you discourage people from joining us? If they ask at the door, please decline bringing them to our booth. I'm expecting a messenger, and Roosie will be joining us in the booth."

Charles signaled a waiter for service and several responded immediately. Arthur's booth allowed them to see everyone in the large room, but also gave some privacy through a series of moveable screens.

Removing a jeweled holder from her evening bag, Erie crossed her long, slender legs and sat back against the plush velvet. With slow, deliberate movements she selected a cigarette from her case, placed it in the holder and leaned toward Arthur for a light. Her shimmering black hair, held loosely in an upsweep by gold clips, framed an exquisite face dominated by large, brown, expressive eyes.

Arthur lit her cigarette and raised his hand to run several

fingers along her delicate chin. "You're beautiful," he said, "the most beautiful woman in New York City."

"How can I marry such a liar!" Erie laughed.

"Because you love me," replied Arthur, kissing her. "To you," he saluted, tipping his glass in Erie's direction.

Erie responded by raising her glass.

Arthur glanced at his watch, then toward the entrance. "Will you excuse me, dear? I won't be long. I promised to meet this messenger outside at ten. He is bringing some papers I need for a transaction."

Erie dismissed Arthur with a smile and an admonishment, "Always business, isn't it, Arthur. You never completely relax." *Interesting*, she thought as she watched him move through the room. *I only began to appreciate Arthur two years ago though our families moved in the same social circle for years.*

After the Long Island Yacht Club regatta Arthur Moore had become a frequent guest in the Carliss home. When he visited Seawind the previous summer his friendship had blossomed into romance. When Arthur formally asked for Erie's hand in marriage in December, William requested the engagement not be publicized or celebrated until after her twenty-first birthday, to make business matters less complicated for Erie. Both Arthur and she agreed to William's request. Erie was in no rush to marry. She did find that Arthur's intense nature made him a difficult man to understand on occasion.

Arthur slid back into the booth beside her. Retrieving a cigarette, he said. "I was slightly annoyed with you tonight. Tables for the Duke are hard to come by, and you almost cancelled. Why?"

"I was waiting for William's call. When I spoke with him

last evening he wasn't feeling well. He promised he would ring tonight by nine and he hasn't. It isn't like him not to call when he promises. I've asked Ian to take the call when it comes."

"You are a big girl, Erie. You don't need to hear from Daddy every night."

"It is business, Arthur. And don't call William, Daddy."

Arthur poured another drink for himself. "Sorry. How is William making out in San Francisco? He was selling some land on the coast, wasn't he?"

"With stocks the way they are, William wanted to be on top of any potentially disastrous situation. Carliss Enterprises is unloading as much land as they can in California to have cash on hand for some deal underway in Cuba. You know how it is, Arthur. Moore Holdings are in the middle of it too. Everyone's looking for a safe place to invest. They are either buying in or selling out."

"You shouldn't be so involved in Carliss Enterprises. You should be a 'kept' woman, Erie. Let me keep you."

Arthur slipped his arm around Erie's bare back. "I'm ready to marry you. Set the date. Stay home. Have my children. Tend to my needs."

"Arthur Moore, remember your promise to William. We aren't even officially engaged. I'm enjoying my introduction to the business world and find working with William fascinating. He's teaching me so much. I just asked your opinion of the market and financial situation, and you pretend you didn't want to hear me. William takes me seriously."

Arthur removed his hand from Erie's back and began playing with his shot glass. "My opinion of the present situation is that ultimately the whole damn works is going to blow. The market's going to fall and we'll lose everything if we're not careful." Arthur took a drink and continued, "If I lost the mansion on Long Island, how would you feel about sharing a log cabin with me and our ten children?"

"I'd hope this scenario wouldn't occur, Arthur. If it did, I could adjust. The question is, could you? By the way, I'm not about to have ten children either. I wouldn't make a good mother."

"You don't know until you've tried it." Arthur said. "Marry me and join the Horticultural Club. Flowers can be as exciting as business. You can have tea with the ladies every afternoon, play bridge with the Vanderbilts, winter in Florida . . ."

"Afternoon teas bore me," Erie retorted. "And, you haven't answered my question. Could you live in a log cabin?"

Arthur changed the subject. "Look who Roosie is escorting tonight."

"Roosie looks great, doesn't he?" Erie said, her eyes on the couple Charles was leading toward their booth. "But does his wife ever accompany him?"

"When you have Rivona," Arthur said rising to meet Roosie, "who needs a wife?"

"I'll remember you said that. Roosie," Erie offered her hand. "How is your wife?"

"The last time I saw her, she was fine," Roosie said seating himself beside Erie just a little too close for comfort. "She's in Europe spending my fortunes on clothing. You are stunning as usual." His eyes took in Erie's daring neckline.

Erie smiled, touched Roosie's cheek, and said, "You're sweet but I definitely wouldn't want to be your wife."

Arthur assisted Rivona to her chair, then seated himself at the table. Drinks were poured for all, and another bottle was ordered from the ever-attentive waiter. One of the rules of the Cotton Club was that you ordered whiskey by the bottle, but opened and poured it yourself. If the house was raided, the person holding the open bottle was charged.

"Rivona," Erie's gaze fell on the woman seated opposite her, "you are ravishing tonight. It's kind of you to keep Roosie company."

Rivona acknowledged the compliment by raising her glass of whiskey just as the house lights dimmed and the rasping voice of The Duke came through the microphone. "Surprising how some of these black people succeed," she said.

With The Duke's rendition of "The Saints" reverberating through the room, Arthur allowed himself a good look at Rivona. Why had he ever found her attractive? Her blonde, bobbed hair and Teutonic features were in sharp contrast to Erie's jet black locks and Mediterranean complexion. Intellectually, there was no comparison. Erie Rachael Carliss was a clever woman, almost too intelligent for Arthur's tastes. He found her obsession with business unacceptable. Rivona was Erie's exact opposite in many ways.

Arthur took a drink and thought, *Rivona had proposed they bed the second evening of their fling.* But try as he might, he still could not persuade Erie to sleep with him. Still, in many ways, he was pleased. Erie had strong morals. That made her all the more attractive to him as a wife. Or was it his fascination with the mysterious side of her. There were many questions that went unanswered by Erie Carliss. Applause interrupted Arthur's thoughts. The Duke broke into "Primitive Primadonna."

When Rivona turned to look at Arthur he said, "Finding the show interesting?"

"I get tired of the sound these blacks play," Rivona complained.

"I like the music," Erie countered.

"Does Erie have a little darky blood in her?" quipped Rivona.

Arthur interjected. "Anyone for another drink?"

Roosie passed his glass across the table. "I need another shot," he said. "Did you follow the market today?"

"Couldn't help but," responded Arthur. "I was at the Exchange all day."

"And how are you defending your investments?" Roosie asked.

"Diversify," Arthur advised. "Don't put all your money in one basket."

"Diversify into what?" asked Erie. "Everything's crazy. Best thing now is to simply stash some case in a safe place."

"Bank it?" asked Roosie.

"No," Erie replied, refusing another glass of whiskey. "William says the banks are under pressure. Put the cash in your wall safe, in a mattress, anywhere but in a bank."

"William Carliss is crazy," Roosie snorted. "The banks are solid."

"He's not so crazy," mused Arthur. "Carliss is on the right track. But the money is in booze. Look around you. At one hundred and fifty dollars a bottle. There's money being spent here tonight. It comes from private safes across the country . . . mattresses . . . basements . . . cookie jars. Booze is the second largest profit-making business today. The bootleggers, rum runners, gangsters, spotters, boaters, and proprietors of the blind pigs are making the money."

Erie shivered and pulled her shawl around her shoulders.

"I agree," she said. "There's a lot of money in booze, but there's also danger. Yesterday some poor shopkeeper was shot to death because he wouldn't co-operate with the mob."

"Not so loud," said Roosie, looking around nervously.

Arthur laughed. "Easy, Roosie. You're surrounded by friends here."

"Who wants to associate with people like Al Capone, Bugs Moran, Johnny Torrio?" Erie asked. "Do you, Arthur?"

Arthur shrugged. "Four fifths of the supply of liquor in the United States comes from Canada. It's smuggled across the river at Detroit. This bottle here probably came from a distillery in Ontario."

"You seem to know a lot about bootlegging." Erie glanced shrewdly at Arthur.

"I am just stating," Arthur continued, "that we should all take a lesson from Lucky Luciano. He'll have the money to move when the market fails. Look who has just come in . . . over there."

"Frank Costello entertaining, among others, the police commissioner for the City of New York," Erie observed.

"Costello's another one who will prosper," Arthur said.

"No wonder this club hasn't been raided," said Roosie.

The Costello party made its way slowly toward the Moore table.

"Look at the jewels the woman is wearing!" exclaimed Rivona.

Roosie and Arthur rose as the party arrived. Frank Costello, in his brisk, businesslike way, made the introductions.

"Arthur Moore, this is Rocco Perri and Bessi Starkman, down from Canada for a visit."

"We've met," Arthur said as he dutifully shook hands with the couple.

"Arthur's fiancée, Erie Carliss."

Rocco Perri's eyes took in every detail of Erie's face and figure. Erie unconsciously drew her shawl around her shoulder, feeling naked in his glance.

"Pleased to meet you," Erie said, not feeling the least bit pleased or comfortable in the presence of Costello and company.

Roosie and Rivona were introduced, giving Erie an opportunity to take a close look at Bessi Starkman. *A tough woman*, she thought. *Not a nice person to know.*

"I was saying, Miss Carliss . . . your party will join us for drinks?"

"Sorry," said Erie, "I was admiring your wife's jewelry. It is lovely. It suits you . . . Ms. Star . . . Mrs. Perri."

Bessi managed a smile. "It's Mrs. Perri now," she said.

Rocco countered with a compliment for Erie. "A beautiful woman needs adornments. You should be draped in diamonds."

Arthur, sensing some hostility from Rivona and Bessi Starkmanto at Rocco's remark, said, "We'll join you later."

With that, Costello moved the party away from the table. Roosie whistled softly and sat down. Arthur was already seated and lighting up a cigarette. "Interesting," he said. "The Big One from Canada."

CHAPTER FIVE

MARYBOROUGH

SALOME GINGERICH PICKED through the basket of small cloth squares she always kept beside her. Her eyes scanned the bright colours. Once, she glanced up at the people in the room. Their mouths moved but she understood little that was said. *It must be an important day*, she thought, *so many people were in the house*. The men were eating and the women serving. Was it a wedding? When the men finished, someone would lead her to the table and she would eat too.

Her hand moved through the basket. Over and over she turned the bits of cloth until she suddenly grasped a bright blue square which she recognized as a part of Abraham's old shirt. Satisfied with her find, Salome retrieved needle and thread from the bib of her apron. She reached into a large pocket and removed a yellow quilt square.

As she slowly basted the blue patch onto the yellow one, she concentrated on Abraham, silently speaking to the image of him she held in her mind. *When you wore this shirt, Abraham, you were angry yet. Jacob and Rachael were out in the buggy inviting relatives to their wedding and you had angry words with Caleb. You were a good husband, but you saw the left and right without remembering there was a middle too. You forgot, husband, that you upset your father too. Why did you forbid Jacob to marry Rachael? He disobeyed you, and you said no more but turned on Caleb.*

A strange noise in Jacob's yard, brought the men to their feet and Salome out of her daydream. Through the window, Salome could see the man Patrick Smith. She did not recognize the machine that was making the noise. Salome went back to her sewing.

"Sit, Ehsah," Jacob addressed the people in the room. He met Patrick at the door, barring his entry to the kitchen with his arm.

"Is there a problem?" he asked. "You have disturbed our Sabbath meal."

"I am sorry to bother you, Jacob. I saw the buggies and realize I am intruding. I know it's Sunday, but could I speak with you a moment privately?"

"Come. We will talk on the porch. Is it about Caleb?"

"It's not Caleb. I saw him . . . last night. He was in fine fettle then."

Jacob followed Patrick along the porch. Salome, stitching carefully paid no attention to the low murmuring outside the window until she heard the name William Carliss.

"You heard me, Jacob. William Carliss died yesterday. His family had a history of heart disease, but this was totally unexpected."

"You did not need to disturb my Sabbath to tell me this."

"I thought you might want to know," replied Patrick. "We received the telegram today. No one else would have told you. No one else would know."

"William Carliss," Salome said aloud, trying desperately to form a picture of the man in her mind.

"Hush, grohs-moodah." Miriam was standing by Salome's chair. "Doo sin hoong-ahrich. Coom. Ehsah. Put the square in the pocket, yet."

WABABIMIGA LAKE

Wababimiga Lake was difficult to reach. Situated north and east of Geraldton, it was accessible by water and portage or by bush plane. Like any northern lake, pine and birch grew to the water's edge in some places, while huge granite outcroppings rose above its waters in others. Traces of gold had been found near Wababimiga Lake, and Industrial Mining had established a prospector's camp, manned by Bill O'Grady.

Bill stood on the company dock scanning the southern sky. Fifteen minutes before he had discerned the faint sound of a bush plane motor. *This must be important*, he thought. *The company doesn't send a plane for a social visit, and the monthly supplies arrived last week.* As the tiny dot on the horizon grew, Bill recognized the large-bodied Norseman, usually flown by Frank.

The plane made one pass over Bill, dipping its wings in salute, before circling to land. Bill waved both arms then bent and effortlessly lifted his canoe up onto the dock. The Norseman landed on the glassy surface of the bay and taxied toward shore. Sixty feet out, the pilot cut the motor, stepped out onto a pontoon, and waved. As the left pontoon gently bumped against the wood, he threw a rope to Bill.

"Perfect landing," Bill yelled, catching the rope. In seconds the plane was secured.

"Frank, it is good to see you."

The small fellow stepped off the pontoon and shook Bill's hand.

"You might not think so when I tell you why I flew in."

Bill threw his arm around Frank's shoulder. "Out with it, man. There's no sense in keeping news to yourself. Tell me I'm fired and I can leave this God-forsaken lake."

Frank laughed. "I'll get my bag." He climbed back into the Norseman, did some tidying up in the cockpit, and stepped out again with a knapsack in hand.

"Before I forget, I brought your mail." Frank handed Bill several envelopes.

"What you have to tell me isn't written here," said Bill, slapping the envelopes.

Frank shook his head. "I received word yesterday," he said. "That William Carliss is dead. My news is as simple and painful as that."

"When?" asked Bill incredulously.

"Day before yesterday. The company dispatched me as soon as they received the telegram from Anna. Orders are you are to pack up. The funeral is in New York City. William's body has to be transported from Maine, so you have time to get to New York to attend. I'll fly you to Buffalo. The company has taken care of the arrangements for you from there."

"What happened?" Bill found it difficult to believe William was dead.

"A heart attack," said Frank. "His death was mentioned in yesterday's Toronto paper. It apparently was sudden. The newspaper listed the surviving relatives as Anna, his wife, and his daughter, Erie Carliss."

"You sure of that?"

"That's the way it was read to me over the telephone. How soon do you think we can leave?"

Bill looked west, then north over Wababimiga Lake. "The wind's changing from the west to the north. I think we can leave as soon as the fog lifts in the morning. If we leave it any longer than that we might have a storm to fly through."

"I'll make supper," Frank said. "You begin to pack."

"The ore bags are labelled. The canoe can be lashed to a pontoon and the tent can be stashed in the bush until next year."

Bill took stock of his situation, then went to work taking down his camp. In the meantime, Frank found several cans of vegetables, tin plates and cups, potatoes, and tinned bully beef. Opening the cans of vegetables, he placed them in the coals to let the contents boil. He tucked the potatoes under the coals and sliced the bully beef onto plates. The coffee was already brewed.

"Come eat," Frank called.

Bill sat with his back against a large tree truck, his feet to the fire.

"I can't say I'm sorry to be leaving this lake," he said. "The black flies are deadly and the loneliness catches up with me."

"Where are you going next?" asked Frank, helping himself to a mug of coffee and pouring one for Bill.

"Company tells me I'm headed for New Liskeard again. I found traces of garnets north of there last year. Where there are garnets, there might be diamonds."

"Speaking of diamonds," said Frank, "one of those letters I brought is from Erie."

"I haven't answered any of her letters since she wrote that she was unofficially engaged to Arthur Moore. She is so young, Frank. She shouldn't be engaged to anyone yet."

"You're jealous, old fellow!"

"I'll not deny that," answered Bill. "Did you bring smokes?"

Frank reached into a jacket pocket and threw a packet at Bill who relaxed against the trunk, enjoying the first cigarette he'd had in a week. When had he seen Erie last? Two and a half years ago at Christmas. She was seventeen and just beginning to realize the effect she had on men. He was twenty-four and absolutely charmed by her. After Christmas she had gone back to college, and he had returned to Canada. Although he was in constant touch with Anna and William, he kept his letters to Erie infrequent and informal.

"The sooner we get your gear packed, the sooner we can get some sleep. It's going to be a long day for both of us tomorrow." Frank interrupted Bill's thoughts.

"I wouldn't be here if it hadn't been for William Carliss," said Bill, looking at Frank. "And you wouldn't be a big-shot bush pilot if it hadn't been for him either."

"We've both lost a friend," replied Frank.

"I feel I've lost a father. I spent the first good years of my life with Anna and William."

Frank took a cigarette from the packet and sat down beside Bill. For the next hour they reminisced about their early lives in Fergus and Maryborough Township. And long after Frank had turned in for the night, Bill lay awake, thinking about Erie Carliss.

THE AUTUMN
OF 1925

CHAPTER SIX

CAMDEN, MAINE

IT WAS EASY TO SEE WHY William chose Camden, Maine for Anna's summer home. The highway from the north hugged the coastline until it rounded Mount Battie and descended into the village. From the south, two tall church steeples dominated the horizon. Chestnut Street lead to the center of the village, which wrapped itself around the harbour. Lobster boats lay at anchor with masted schooners, rum runners, and, more recently, the sleek sailing yachts of the summer folk. Estates lined the length of the Old Carriage Way between Camden and Rockport, and further south to Portland.

Seawind sat on a prominence of land one half mile down the Carriage Way. The main house of weathered grey shingle could not be missed if approached by sea. Yet, if approached by land, one had to look sharply for the entrance gates. William wished it that way. He wanted privacy for his family.

Built as a wedding gift, Seawind was an architectural masterpiece. Its central staircase was open to the third floor and illuminated by natural light through a thirty-foot stained-glass window. The house appeared to be anchored to the coast by massive stone chimneys on its north and south sides. All fireplaces were constructed of rocks William had collected around the world. From glassed-in porches which encircled the house, Anna could see Camden, the bay, and the steeple of the white church in Rockport.

Seated in the south porch, Anna watched two figures on the beach braving a southeast wind off the bay. "Amy," she called.

"Yes, ma'am."

"Would you tell Francis to go bring Erie and Ian off the beach. Erie will catch her death of cold. Ask Jennie to make up a tea tray. Ian will demand hot cocoa."

"Yes, ma'am." Amy disappeared through beaded glass curtains.

How lonely it is here, thought Anna. She glanced to the north to Mount Battee where William requested to be buried. *I am a fool, William. For the past three months I have secluded myself at Seawind. I thought I didn't need the world. I've travelled no further than your grave. I have been miserable to Ian and snappy with Erie.* Anna sighed then whispered, "William, she has asked permission to marry in December, before her twenty-first birthday. You and I know she must not marry Arthur until she learns of her past. We were going to do this together. You were the one that wished to wait. I argued that she should be told on her sixteenth birthday."

"Anna, what's wrong?" Erie kissed Anna's damp cheek. "You mustn't cry. Ian and I are here."

"I was thinking of William," said Anna. "I find myself doing that often. Sit down. I've ordered tea."

Amy brought a tray laden with cakes and Jeannie followed

with the tea and china. Erie curled up in a large wicker chair beside Anna. Ian chose a rocker opposite them.

"May I ask a serious question?" Anna asked Erie.

Erie nodded.

"You know you are our chosen child, Erie. Have you ever wondered who your parents might be?"

Erie was taken by surprise by Anna's directness, but answered, "As a matter of fact, I used to think a lot about who I might belong to, but when I decided to learn the business of running Carliss Enterprises, I put the issue out of my mind. I must say, no. No. I don't think about it."

Anna wasn't prepared for such a negative response, but that answer did tell her Erie should have been told about her parents at an earlier age. "Don't you wish to know?"

"Why should I? It was obvious to me when I thought about it in a mature way, that my parents didn't want me. You and William did. Remember, too, I am not the first child you raised."

"What do you mean?" said Anna.

"Take Bill O'Grady as an example . . . and the children of your friends in Ontario, Margaret and Patrick Smith, raised with your financial assistance."

"Bill O'Grady is my half-brother," said Anna.

Ian who had been listening to the conversation spoke up. "If you are marrying Arthur Moore, wouldn't you want to know your background? His family is so society conscious. It is a wonder they haven't hired a detective to verify your pedigree."

Erie leaned forward to reach a tea cake. "They have asked a lot of questions. I've told them I'm a Carliss from Pennsylvania on one side and a Graham from Montreal on the other."

"That is not true," Anna said.

"It's explanation enough for Arthur." Erie glanced from Anna to Ian. "This little chat is contrived, isn't it? When I asked you, Ian Oliver, if I could break my promise to William without complicating legalities at Carliss Enterprises, you said, 'Ask Anna.' When I asked Anna, she said, 'Ask Ian.' Now both of you are pushing me to familiarize myself with my ancestry. I really don't wish to know. The past three months have been extremely difficult for me. I don't need to be burdened with any more." Erie rose from her chair and stood at the window, her back to Ian and Anna.

Anna glanced to Ian for direction. Ian poured himself another cup of cocoa and addressed Erie.

"Have you heard the name Caleb Gingerich?" he asked.

"Yes," Erie answered, not turning around. "William has had some . . . dealings with him recently. Occasionally his name was mentioned, especially when we were discussing grain shipments. He seems to be a grain dealer."

"Caleb Gingerich was not only a business associate of William's; he is your uncle. Does that not interest you?"

"A little," Erie said, still looking out the window to the bay.

"Caleb Gingerich is a brother to Jacob Gingerich . . . your father," Ian said.

Erie's back stiffened. She whirled around to face Ian. "You've managed to tell me who my father is. Are you satisfied? Should I care? What will you say next, my mother was a prostitute? Anna, wasn't that the occupation of the mother of those children up north that your friend raised?"

"Is that what you were afraid to hear?" said Ian.

Anna was on her feet. "Erie Carliss! Don't you dare speak

of your mother in those terms. Sit down and listen to what I have to say."

"If I choose not to?" Erie glared at Anna.

"Sit down, Erie." Ian Oliver spoke quietly, but firmly. "You're acting like the child I knew ten years ago. What Anna has to say will have a profound effect on your marriage to Arthur and on your future plans."

"It's that bad, is it?"

"It depends on how you look at the situation," replied Ian. "Please sit down."

Erie sat down. "Go ahead. I may as well hear it from you as from one of Mrs. Moore's snippy, gossipy acquaintances."

"This is as difficult for me as for you," Anna said. "The past three months have been the worst in my life. But I accepted you as part of my life twenty years ago, and I must assume some responsibility now." Anna's hand trembled as she tucked a stray hair into her chignon. "I should begin with your birth, for I raised you from birth. You were born to Jacob and Rachael Gingerich, an Old Order Mennonite couple who lived in Maryborough Township, Wellington County, Ontario."

"A Mennonite?" asked Erie.

"You were the third child born of Rachael."

"If I am the third child, I obviously have brothers and sisters."

"You have twin brothers, Abraham and Adam."

"Are they younger or older than me?"

"They're the same age. You were born four hours after Adam. There is a medical explanation . . . details . . . technical things . . ." Anna's cheeks coloured. She wasn't about to discuss intimate medical details in front of Ian Oliver. "Your mother died shortly after your birth. You were so tiny, so delicate . . ." Anna smiled. "Caleb Gingerich and I took you to Fergus, where Dr. Groves attended you. I can remember the drive yet. Margaret wrapped you in towels and placed you against my breast. The horses ran full out. The gravel flew. We nearly tipped twice. When we arrived you were barely breathing."

"I obviously lived," said Erie.

"It took six months of care to bring you around," replied Anna. "By the time you could join your brothers, your father had remarried and didn't want you."

"Didn't want me?"

Anna came to Jacob's defense. "You must understand the situation he was in . . . It . . . he . . ."

She glanced from floor to ceiling, then looked directly at Erie. "By the time you were healthy enough to travel it was also apparent to William and me that we couldn't give you up. We couldn't have children of our own. William suffered a serious accident just after we were married and he was . . ." Anna glanced shyly at Ian. "He was . . . we simply couldn't have children."

Erie said nothing. She watched Anna, who was trembling now quite visibly.

"William and I lavished all our love and attention on you. Our lives revolved around you. But we realized one day we would have to tell you about your parents."

"Why?" asked Erie. "If you love me so, why tell me now about my ancestry. Does it matter that much?"

"Oh yes," Anna said. "It matters very much, especially if you are marrying a man like Arthur Moore."

"Has father seen me?" asked Erie. "Have you sent photographs?"

"No," replied Anna. "He saw you for a brief moment after you were born, but not since. When you were six years old we went to Fergus. William travelled to Maryborough to reason with Jacob, but Jacob refused to see him. I sent photographs, but they were returned, envelopes unopened."

"Why would he refuse to see his daughter?"

"That I can't answer," Anna said. "As for the photographs, the Old Order Mennonites do not allow pictures to be taken of themselves. I suspect Miriam sent everything back and Jacob doesn't know the envelopes existed."

"Who is Miriam?"

"Your father's second wife." Anna left her chair and walked to the window that faced inland to Mount Battee. "I want you to come with me to Maryborough, Erie. I'll be leaving next week to visit Patrick and Margaret Smith. I would appreciate your company. I want you to ask your father why he wouldn't accept you. I want you to fully understand your ancestry. I have told you your father's ancestry. Your mother . . . oh Ian, I can't continue."

Ian assisted Anna back to her chair. Erie knelt before Anna and took her trembling hands.

"I'm sorry I was a little short with you, Anna. I'm glad you told me."

"Will you come with me?" asked Anna. "Please I do want you to be with me."

Ian glanced at both women through his thick glasses. Erie was as pale as Anna.

"I'll make the arrangements," he said. "Shall we say you'll leave next Monday? Carliss Enterprises can do without Erie for a while. When you're in Ontario, Erie, you can check your uncle's business interests. William and he were discussing a lucrative proposition just before William died. It was all done by phone, so I have little information on the situation."

Erie kissed Anna's cheek. "I'll go," she said. "Anna, I am going to ring for Amy to come put you to bed. Again, I'm sorry I was harsh with you."

"It's I who should apologize," Anna said. "You have been under a great deal of pressure since William passed away."

"Hush," Erie said. "I'll call Amy."

Anna lay facing Mount Battee, a picture of William in her hands. *I didn't do it properly, William. Erie was so angry. Yet she had to know. I'm so tired. I can't fight with Erie. I've lost you. I must never lose Erie.*

CHAPTER SEVEN

New York City

ARTHUR MOORE WHEELED his Stutz onto Fiftieth Street and into the garage at the Waldorf Tower. He waved his hand at the attendant, one of several that insured security at the Tower twenty-four hours a day.

"Arthur, you are mad!" Erie shouted over the roar of the engine.

"They're used to me," laughed Arthur. "I rarely get the opportunity to drive myself around these days. When I do, I drive."

"Does 'drive' give you the right to graze an old man on Park Avenue?" Erie removed her head scarf, letting her hair cascade down her back. "And you didn't even stop to see if he was alright."

"I looked in the rear-view mirror," replied Arthur. "You exaggerate. I didn't hit him. He was a little shaken up but still standing."

Arthur swung his long legs over the door of the low-slung roadster and walked around to open Erie's door.

"I'll take the taxi back to the Dakota if you insist on driving like a fool."

Arthur silenced Erie by kissing her.

A private elevator whisked the couple quickly to the ninth floor where a maid opened the door at Arthur's signal. He was taken aback by a strange face. "Where's Garth?" he demanded "Who are you and why are you in my apartment?"

"Mabel, sir." The black maid curtsied. "Mister Moore Senior sent me from the big house. Garth's been fighting again."

"You can't trust these people," Arthur fumed. "Garth's always getting himself beat up." He swung around to confront Mabel. "I've never laid eyes on you before. Do you really work for my family? How did you get in here?"

"Three years in the big house, sir. All that time I worked in the kitchen or the laundry. Mister Moore Senior, sir, he gave me a note for the fellows at the door."

"Well, I never frequent the kitchen or the laundry," Arthur said. "I suppose you can cook. Father wouldn't have sent you if you weren't handy."

"Yes, sir." Mabel curtsied again.

"There'll be two for dinner. We'll have lamb chops." Arthur waved his hand to dismiss Mabel and lead the way to his lounge. "Drink?"

"Just one, Arthur." Erie sank into the plush sofa, took off her shoes and made herself comfortable.

"Damn Garth!" Arthur swore. "He's helped himself to the liquor too. He has good taste. He took the most expensive bottle. How did he get past the boys?"

"Why so much security in this building?" Erie asked.

"Lucky Luciano lives on the top floor," replied Arthur.

Erie raised her eyebrows in surprise. "Really, Arthur. You should choose your neighbours more carefully."

"I should choose my household staff more carefully too," responded Arthur. "Garth has helped himself to my liquor, probably gotten himself beaten up in a whorehouse in Harlem. You pick them off the streets, give them work and they repay you by stealing and fighting."

"We've not had trouble with our servants," countered Erie. "They have all been faithful to us, but they're all Irish."

"That explains it," said Arthur, handing Erie a whiskey. He sat beside her and reached to stroke her hair. "Don't ever have your hair cut. I love it long. These modern bobs bore me."

"You're marrying me for my hair?"

"I'm marrying you because I have this insane notion I love you," Arthur replied, "And, for other reason too. I'll be honest. We have a lot in common. We have wealth. We have pedigree."

"A pedigree! Arthur, tell me exactly how far back you can trace the Moore family?"

"Well," Arthur mused. "I'm Arthur the Fourth. But before the fourth there were numbers one, two, and three. And before that there were three Henrys. That's seven generations, the last five on American soil. The Moore line goes back to fourteenth century England. Our money came from spices, slaves, and cotton. Father likes to tell people that our money was ballast on the Mayflower. Mother always quips that her people met the Mayflower. One of her ancestors, to the disgrace of the family, married a native Indian."

"Do you want to hear my pedigree, Arthur?"

"You're a gypsy from France, the result of a love tryst."

"Be serious, Arthur."

"Go ahead. Bore me with details." Arthur leaned to place a kiss on Erie's cheek.

"My pedigree goes no further than Maryborough Township, Ontario, 1905—both parents. Your exotic creature is a Mennonite, adopted by William and Anna Carliss. That's not something your parents would accept."

Arthur had stretched himself beside Erie on the sofa. *She's right*, he thought. His parents would fuss when they found out that Erie was both Mennonite and adopted. They wouldn't easily accept the fact Erie had no Carliss blood in her veins. But, as long as she had access to the Carliss fortune . . .

"Adopted . . . a Mennonite? Buggies . . . black clothing . . . lots of children?"

"I am no such person!" Erie said. "My parents were."

"Touchy."

"Would you expect me to be otherwise?" asked Erie. "I just found out myself. How would you react to the news that your parents were Eskimos?"

Arthur held Erie's chin in his slender fingers. "You don't look German to me. With your dark hair and dusky complexion, I'd have sworn you had some Italian blood running through your veins. How did you find out you were Mennonite? Who told you?"

"One question at a time," replied Erie. "I have known I was adopted for a number of years. Anna told me about my parents because she's concerned about how you and your family would react. After all they're all for 'keeping the pedigree.' I don't wish to embarrass any of you. As for my colouring, there are dark-haired Mennonites too. Some Germans are very dark complexioned. The Romans did leave their mark in Europe if you remember your history lessons."

"If you knew you were adopted, why didn't you tell me before?"

"When we were just friends, it didn't seem to matter. I wanted to see you to tell you that I'm leaving for Ontario to meet my father. My mother is dead."

"This is not a good time to leave New York City, Erie. Or have you given up your business career. Even as an adopted daughter, you're the heir apparent to Carliss Enterprises, aren't you?"

"I haven't given up, Arthur. I'll be back within the month. Ian feels it won't hurt if I accompany Anna to Maryborough and meet my father."

"Maybe you should leave Carliss Enterprises, Erie." Arthur left the sofa and walked to the window overlooking the Vanderbilt mansion.

"Why doesn't Carliss Enterprises and my firm merge?" Arthur continued. "They will after we're married. Let's start the process now."

"Don't pressure me, Arthur. I have no intentions of amalgamating with your firm after our marriage. I feel I can carry on with Carliss Enterprises."

"Ian Oliver might think differently," Arthur said, coming to sit down beside Erie again. "Look, I'll be fifty before you decide to have children. Think of me for a change."

Erie reached for Arthur's hands. "I am thinking of you. That is why I'm going to Maryborough. I love you. I will marry you, Arthur. But, please let me see my father. Let me ask a few questions."

"Go to Ontario," Arthur said. "See your relatives. But set a date for our wedding, now—today."

"No. I won't set a date until I have met my father. Arthur,

listen. What if there are problems? What if there is mental instability in the family—anything unusual? I promise to marry you, but only after I know all about my parents."

"Set a date," Arthur demanded. "If we set a date and make it public, my parents would think twice about fussing if they don't like . . ."

"No, I promise you, Arthur, when we marry you won't have to wait ten years for an heir. But you have to promise me I can run Carliss Enterprises after our marriage, if I choose to do so."

"You don't have to work, Erie. I have money. I'll inherit money. I've an estate on the Vineyard, a camp in New Hampshire, a home on Long Island, this apartment . . ."

"I can match you home for home, dollar for dollar, and brain for brain."

"You are a vixen, Erie Carliss."

Arthur reached over to give Erie a passionate embrace but was interrupted by Mabel.

"Sir," she said, "you didn't say what time you expected dinner. There are no lamb chops, sir."

"Seven o'clock," snapped Arthur, furious at being disturbed. "And, for heaven's sake, go get some lamb chops if you have to. If say lamb chops, I mean lamb chops."

Mabel stood her ground.

"Well, go damn it!"

"I would sir, but I believe you need to give me some money for the lamb chops."

"Garth runs an account at the butcher," Arthur fumed. "Oh, damn," he swore again. "Never mind the lamb chops. We'll go out for dinner."

Mabel scurried from the room.

"You don't need to snap at her, Arthur," said Erie. "She is a kitchen maid who is helping out because Garth is laid up. Don't chide her so. If Mabel had the opportunities we were given, she would be living as affluently as we are, and she would not be getting yelled at."

"You can't tell me that sort of person is equal to me!"

"Arthur Moore!" Erie's eyes flashed. "Your intolerance of Africans truly astonishes and infuriates me."

Arthur tactfully changed the subject. "When did you say you were leaving?"

"Within the week. We'll be in Fergus for one day before we reach Drayton."

"I'll phone you every night."

"That will be impossible," Erie laughed. "I understand the Smiths don't have a phone. It is best you write. I'll be at Lilac Hill, care of Patrick Smith, General Delivery, Drayton, Ontario."

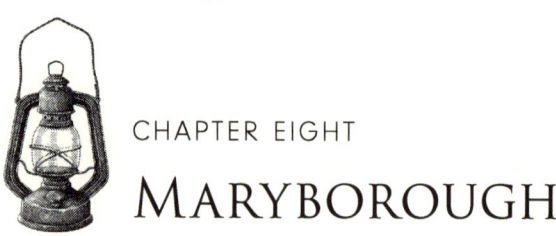

CHAPTER EIGHT

MARYBOROUGH

THE BLACK STARLESS NIGHT did nothing to raise Patrick Smith's spirits as he drove his team along the line fence. Caleb was supposed to have met him at the house at ten o'clock. When he hadn't appeared by eleven o'clock, Smitty had harnessed the team and set out himself. Margaret had said she would send Caleb back to the cottage when he arrived.

"Don't forget to show him the telegram," Smitty had reminded his wife.

Smitty tied the team above Lilac Hill and walked down a well-defined path to the cottage. He didn't dare light a lantern. That would arouse Jacob Gingerich's curiosity. He picked his way carefully around the south side of the cottage and disappeared behind a large clump of lilac bushes, where he worked for twenty minutes dismantling an elaborate system of stove pipes. Occasionally he stopped to listen for Caleb, then went back to work. Several of the pipe systems ran up through the lilac bushes. One ran parallel to the cottage and emerged behind Leta's maple tree. The ingeniously devised system allowed smoke to dissipate swiftly, and in many directions, thus not drawing attention to the cottage. All pipes originated at one point, a window into the cottage.

After piling the pipe lengths, Smitty walked round to the porch and climbed the steps. He stopped to listen again and looked across the valley to Jacob Gingerich's farmhouse where the light still shone in the kitchen window.

Despite the darkness of the cottage, Smitty walked directly to a tin lantern in a corner of the main room. He picked it up and wove his way around cloth-shrouded pieces of furniture. Entering a small room off the main area, he swore when he accidentally kicked an old tin can. Piled against one wall was a bedstead, washstand, bonnet chest, and chair. Smitty reached into his pocket and retrieved a candle stump which he lit and placed in the lantern. Putting the light on the floor, he shut the bedroom door.

"There you are," he said, talking to a gleaming apparatus set squarely in the center of the room. He touched it carefully. "You're cool enough." Smitty worked quickly, removing the stovepipe which ran to the bedroom window from the boiler. The window had been covered with wood to shut out all light.

With his back to the bedroom door, he began to dismantle the delicate network of copper tubing . . .

Can't break anything, he thought. *Can't replace it without someone asking questions.*

Smitty suddenly froze, listened, turned swiftly and readied himself for a fight. "You'd better be friend," he warned. "Or you'd better be ready for a good licking."

Caleb chuckled. "I was almost on you," he said. "You're slipping, Smitty."

Smitty relaxed. "I can smell government men a mile away," he retorted. "And you, two miles away. Shut the door so your brother can't see the light and help me dismantle the still. Did you read the telegram?"

"I got one like it this afternoon. I'm surprised Anna is bringing Erie home."

"Did you know," Smitty said as he worked, "I haven't seen Anna Carliss in ten years. I almost proposed to her once, a long time ago. But we weren't made for each other. She was a lady. She had breeding. She deserved William Carliss."

"I liked her too," said Caleb. "You should have seen the way she took care of Erie in the first weeks of that baby's life. I never thought I would covet another man's wife."

"I thought you told me you didn't know her too well."

"Well, I lied," replied Caleb. "Watched her every minute she was around here. But I only touched her once. When she fell off a ladder and I caught her."

"The best man won. William Carliss understood Anna." Patrick lowered the distilling unit to the floor. "I couldn't believe he was dead. When the first telegram came, I just felt sick. Margaret and I couldn't afford to attend the funeral. Then we heard nothing until Ian Oliver sent this telegram telling us Anna was coming with Erie for a visit and wants to stay at Lilac Hill. And, of more importance, Erie wants to talk to Jacob."

"Well," Caleb said, "talking to Jacob isn't going to be easy. I'm late because I went over there to test the waters, so to speak, to tell him she was coming."

"And what did he say?"

"Nothing doing. He says he won't meet Anna. He won't

meet Erie either. I told him I was going to talk to Salome afore they arrived, and I did too."

"You fox!" Smitty snorted. "Now you've stirred the pot."

"You better believe it," replied Caleb. "Salome went right to her basket and began muttering 'Rachael . . . Rachael . . . Rachael.'"

"Where was Miriam?"

"Upstairs. She didn't come down. I also told him I was going to make sure Erie sees Adam and Abraham."

"What did Bishop Gingerich say about that?"

"He ordered me off his property. He just about took a poker to me. I never saw him lose his temper before and I've driven him pretty hard. It's a wonder you didn't hear him over here."

Smitty whistled softly. "Jacob has a lot to think about in the next several weeks. His past is finally catching up with him."

"It's about time," Caleb said. "Lift this tank, will you? Jacob's an honest and good man, but he has to be realistic." Caleb changed the subject. "I know why we're moving the still. It is sitting in the middle of Anna's bedroom. She wouldn't appreciate a still at Lilac Hill."

"Not when it is a federal offence to own one."

Smitty stood up and stretch his arms. "All we've got to do is get this up to the wagon without too much noise. The stove pipes are all out back. We'll have to wash in the cattle trough when we're done this move."

"Where are you going with the still? You are one of my biggest suppliers. You've got to set up again."

"If farming paid, I wouldn't be hauling this apparatus

around," said Smitty. "I don't know where I'm going to put it. I hear the government boys have been snooping around here lately."

Caleb thought a moment. "There are certain people they don't touch. Tell me, who is the most respected man in this community?"

"Sure as shooting, it's Bishop Gingerich," Smitty answered.

"Right," said Caleb. "Now tell me, who hasn't the government searched up here?"

"The Old Order Mennonites. Government knows they are too religious to break the liquor laws. And they don't own fast cars or telephones. What are you thinking?"

A sly grin crossed Caleb's face. "You set up in Bishop Jacob's old sugar shanty. There's been no one there since April. It is in the back of nowhere. There's plenty of wood chopped. And he won't need the shanty until early next spring."

"Be damned!" Smitty swore. "There is no end to your tricks, is there?"

"Nope," said Caleb. "I've had years of practice and I've had good teachers. Margaret says I lie awake nights thinking up schemes, just like you."

"She does, does she?" Smitty rubbed his filthy hands against his pant legs. "There's one thing that bothers me, Caleb. I know you were dealing with William Carliss. Margaret tells me Erie has been working with William in the business. William told me a year ago she had a real business mind. But I don't want her to get involved in this dirty bit."

"I suspect she knows what she is getting into."

"I don't like this whole set-up, Caleb. I'm going along with you only because poor farmers all over Waterloo, Huron, and Wellington are counting on you to put bread on their tables.

But, if the deal falls through, one of them might get himself miffed enough to blow the whistle on everyone."

"That's why so few people know who 'everyone is,'" Caleb said. "I'm riding herd on them." He stooped to lift the tank. "I just draw the line at moving their stills."

"You're getting old, Caleb. You're puffing like an old man."

"If you don't stop talking and lead the way, I'll drop this on your bloody head, Smitty."

"Honest, I'd only ask a friend to help. I'll take the tank off your hands at the porch."

"When is Anna coming?" Caleb walked carefully behind Smitty, who held the light at knee level.

"Telegram didn't say exactly, but I'm going into Drayton tomorrow. There'll be a letter for sure telling us the time and day to pick them up." Smitty blew the candle and set the lantern down inside the porch door.

"I wonder what she'll think of Maryborough now."

"I wonder what she'll think of us," Smitty countered. "We're not exactly in the twentieth century up this way yet. She used to life in New York City."

"Whatever her thoughts," Caleb said, "she'll be lady enough to keep them to herself. Your turn to carry the tank."

CHAPTER NINE

FERGUS

GROVEHURST DOMINATED QUEEN STREET, its east side facing the Royal Alexandria Hospital, its north side the Grand River. The location of the red brick house suited the old doctor perfectly. From its front verandah and side gardens he had a clear view over the river to the old Electric Light Company and St. David Street. If he stepped out of the side entrance, crossed the lawn and the gravel road, he was at his hospital. Standing on the verandah, Groves checked his watch for the sixth time, then looked down Queen Street.

"They're late," he muttered. "The train was on time. I heard the whistle. They must have driven the long way down from the station."

"Did you wish something, sir?" a maid passing inside the front door addressed Groves.

"Is the tea table set up in the garden, Lily?"

"It is, sir. Everything is ready for your company."

Finally! A cloud a dust! Groves's car rounded the corner of St. David Street. The doctor straightened his tie, polished his right shoe against the back of his left trouser leg and slowly descended the steps. *Don't appear too anxious*, he cautioned himself, watching the car pull up beside the walk-way. The rear door opened. Erie Carliss stepped out, turned, and helped Anna from the vehicle while the driver, Archie, opened the trunk to remove the luggage.

"It is Rachael Gingerich come alive again!" exclaimed Groves.

"Abraham Groves." Anna waved a gloved hand and quickly walked the few steps from the car to the old doctor.

"It's been years, my good friend." Anna extended her hand, which Groves, in an old-fashioned gesture, kissed gallantly.

"My dear Anna, you haven't changed one bit." Groves scrutinized every inch of Anna's face. He finally turned to look at Erie.

"This is our Erie," Anna said.

Erie's reaction to the tiny, precise old man with the snow-white shock of hair was instantaneous and vocal. "You're not at all what I expected." She laughed. "From my mother's rav-ings I was prepared to meet a dashing, handsome man who stood seven feet tall."

Groves's old eyes twinkled. "You are exactly what I expected Erie Carliss. You are Rachael Gingerich and Moses Erie all wrapped in one delightful bundle."

"She is," Anna answered hesitantly, glancing at Groves.

Quick to perceive Anna's discomfort, the old doctor sug-gested, "It's such a lovely day for September. Let's have tea in the garden." Groves led Anna and Erie through to the rose garden and lowered himself carefully into a wooden lawn chair beside a large bird cage suspended on a stand. Inside the cage was a motley green parrot.

"I see you still have your friend," Anna said. "How old is she now?"

"Nineteen years old," Groves said, tapping the bird's cage.

A maid, obviously in the family way, approached carrying a tea tray laden with cookies, teapot, and cups.

Groves waited until Lily was out of earshot before explaining. "Lily's from Toronto. The father of her child won't marry her, so she's with us until the baby's born. Her parents don't want her at home. Nice young girl. Wants to keep the baby."

"You still have a soft heart." Anna said.

Groves indicated several wicker chairs with a wave of a delicate hand. "You must excuse an old man for forgetting his manners. Sit down. Please sit down."

Anna and Erie sat opposite Groves, facing the river. Erie removed her hat and made herself comfortable in her chair. "Shall I pour the tea?" asked Anna.

"Please do," Groves replied, his attention more on Erie than Anna.

"Why do I have the feeling I am being examined," Erie asked, accepting a cup from Anna. "It isn't polite to stare, Doctor Groves."

"You are being examined." Groves leaned over to take a cup from Anna. "You would be the pride of Moses Erie if he were alive now. You are the culmination of the mating of the races. I have always thought it to be the perfect solution."

"I am the what?!" Erie exclaimed.

"Abraham!" Anna interrupted. "I haven't told her!"

"Shame," Groves chided.

"Told me what?" Erie said.

Groves and Anna glanced at each other over their teacups. "You begin," the old gentleman said.

"Please do," Erie demanded. "I . . ."

"Before Anna begins . . ." Groves raised his hand to silence Erie, "let me say you are an astute young woman. If you have your mother's sensibility, you'll have no problem accepting the truth."

"What truth?" Erie said.

Anna lowered her eyes to avoid Groves's penetrating gaze. "I tried to tell her but had difficulty enough letting Erie know about her Mennonite heritage," she apologized.

"Is it too difficult for you? Would you like me to begin?"

"Someone begin," Erie said, "or I'll go find a stiff drink."

Groves laughed. "You'll not find a bootlegger in this village, not if the Beatty Brothers have anything to do about it. Well, Anna, is it you or I?"

"I'll tell her," Anna said. "I should have at Seawind." Anna sat on the edge of her chair, closed her eyes, composed herself, and began, "You've heard of the United Empire Loyalists, haven't you, Erie?"

"Of course."

"Well, your great grandfather, Israel Moses Erie, was a United Empire Loyalist who settled in Nova Scotia after the American Revolution . . . in 1782, I believe."

"That bit of information should placate Arthur Moore's family. Where did the Erie family originate? England? When did they arrive in the colonies?"

Anna answered in a subdued voice. "Israel Moses Erie arrived in Maryland in 1752. He was born in Senegal, Africa."

"Senegal? Was he in some sort of colonial service?"

"In a sense," Anna said.

"In what capacity did he serve?"

"Slave," Anna whispered.

Erie leaned forward in her chair. "I beg your pardon?"

"Slave," Anna repeated louder. "Israel Moses Erie was a slave."

Groves took over. "Israel Erie came to the colonies as a slave and was purchased by James Showcroft. He later belonged to James's son, Luke, a British Officer. He was given his freedom after the American Revolution and came to Canada with his wife and some of his fourteen children. His youngest child, Moses Erie, your grandfather was born in Lower Canada."

"You're all crazy," Erie said. "You expect me to believe my grandfather was African; therefore, my mother was African?"

"Your mother, Rachael, was half-African," Anna corrected.

"Your grandmother was from Scotland . . . white . . . Presbyterian."

"I don't believe you," Erie replied hoarsely. "I don't believe one word you have just said." Erie left her chair and walked to the edge of Groves's rose garden. Opening her purse she found a cigarette, lit it, and stood with her back to Groves and Anna. Moments passed before she moved. She found another cigarette and lit it.

"There is no peace of mind for a worldly woman," Groves observed.

Erie whirled around to answer Groves. "There is no peace in heart for a deceived woman," she snapped. "Why didn't you tell me I was black, Anna? Why have you deceived me so?"

"I haven't deceived you," Anna answered. "I protected you."

"From what?" asked Erie, returning to her chair. "From my background? Do you realize the consequences had I married

Arthur Moore and had children . . . black children? Do you know how I feel now?"

Anna shook her head.

"Unclean!"

"Why so?" Groves asked, his hands drawn to his lips in a pensive gesture.

"I attended the best schools, moved in the richest circles, dated the most eligible men in the United States—white men who'll be shocked when they hear I am black—or half black—or whatever the mix is!" Erie exclaimed. "If they suspected . . . Do you know what Arthur Moore will do when I tell him my father was black?" Erie laughed bitterly. "Do you know what a sensation this information will cause among the people I associate with? I can hear Rivona now."

"If Arthur loves you, it shouldn't matter," Anna said. "You haven't changed your personality, nor your looks, nor your devotion to him. It's time people stopped fussing about race and began to accept people for what they are, and what they can achieve."

"Erie, if such news matters so much to these folks," Groves interjected, "are they people you really want to know?"

"It won't matter? Are you serious? Won't matter . . . don't worry . . ."

"Erie," Groves's voice was firm, "you are not black. You are a mixture of some of the finest races on earth."

"You are splitting hairs, dear doctor. Look at me! What will my children inherit from me? Will one be white, one black, one in-between?"

"You need not have children if you feel so strongly about their colour," Groves said, "Or you can lead the way for many women just like you; hold your head high, achieve much."

"Erie," Anna said, "are you concerned you have African blood in you? Or are you concerned about people's reaction to you if they know your background? You have lived happily for twenty years without the knowledge. You can't change the way you feel about yourself so quickly."

"I can't think properly. I can't answer your questions at the moment," Erie said.

"Erie." Anna rose and sat on the arm of Erie's chair. Clasping one of Erie's hands in both hers, Anna implored, "Look at me. Look at the one responsible for the predicament you're in. Tell me you would have wished to have died in Maryborough. Tell me I made a mistake in bringing you to Groves, in keeping you alive, in loving you, cherishing you as a daughter."

"I can't do that!" Erie cried.

"Of course, you can't. I knew what I was doing. Had you been as black as coal I would have done the same thing and loved you just as much. The circumstances under which I was born were almost as tragic as yours. But the woman who raised me had the philosophy that every child is born for a purpose. The harder the baby has to fight to survive, the more important the purpose. When I felt you against my breast, I knew you were destined for great things. I raised you . . . loved you. William loved you." Anna bent to kiss Erie's forehead. "You are my daughter and a very special woman."

Erie threw her arms around Anna. "You have been through so much," she whispered. "William's death and now me. And yet, you talk such wisdom. I am so confused at the moment."

"You have a right to be."

"May I have some time to myself?" Erie looked from Groves to Anna.

"Do you want me to call Archie, my driver?" Groves asked. "Would you like a quiet drive?"

"I'd like that," Erie said. "Yes, I would appreciate a long drive, if I can do the driving. May I freshen up?"

Groves laughed. "I'm not sure Archie will like that arrangement, but what you ask for you get. Just go to the back door and call Lily. She will show you the facilities. I'll call Archie." Groves rose slowly from his chair. "I'll tell him to let you drive as far and as quickly as you wish, as long as you don't head for the American border."

After Erie disappeared into the house with Lily, Groves returned to the garden and turned his attention to Anna. "Will she be alright?" he asked.

"She'll be fine," replied Anna. "She is a level-headed woman. We raised her to respect all races . . . colours."

"And, what about you? Are you well?"

"No," Anna whispered. "I feel that I am about to fall apart. I'm weary and heartbroken."

"My poor, dear Anna." Groves patted her hand. "Just one more day until you have Margaret Smith for company. For now, you have to put up with me. Shall we go for a little walk? I will show you my kingdom."

Anna smiled. "We've been through a lot before, haven't we? I was just so unprepared for William's death. I loved him so. My whole life revolved around him and Erie."

"You still have Erie."

"Do I? Did you notice that I have never encouraged her to call me mother, but 'Anna?' I always wanted her to know and understand her true mother's story. I'm afraid of what will happen in Maryborough. I don't want to share Erie with

Jacob Gingerich, but she must choose her own destiny. She's all I have left and I might lose her."

"You're doing the right thing, Anna. You realize that. Had you brought her to Maryborough ten years ago, she would have been at a very impressionable age. You might have definitely lost her then. She's completely devoted to you now." Groves took Anna's cold, trembling hands in his. "Just don't play on her sympathies. Be as analytical as she is about the situation."

Anna and Erie sat on the brow of Vinegar Hill, sweaters buttoned against the night wind. As it grew darker, lights came on until the entire village twinkled below them. Sounds of automobiles mingled with the occasional rumble of a farm wagon, harness jingling, climbing Tower Street Hill.

"You seem to know a lot about Fergus," said Erie, as Anna pointed out a number of prominent buildings.

"I haven't told you much about my life," Anna replied. "But I can say that the months I spent in Fergus were some of the happiest in my life. It was also a time of anguish and frustration, and I was only twenty, like yourself. This is where I met William."

Waltz music drifted up the valley. Anna smiled. "There must be entertainment at the Town Hall. Perhaps a dance. William and I so loved to dance. After we drove around Central Park, we danced in the ballroom at the Dakota. Francis tended the Victrola and served champagne until the small hours of the morning."

"You know," said Erie, "I did a lot of thinking while driving around with Archie. At first, I decided I wouldn't tell

Arthur. I'd marry him and handle the consequences as they came along. Then I remembered how he felt about his black servants and realized that if I didn't tell him, I wasn't being fair to him or myself. I've decided to write Arthur. I'll be honest with him and spare him the embarrassment of breaking the engagement. I will break it off first."

"Don't do anything rash," Anna cautioned. "If he loves you . . ."

"If he loves me," Erie repeated. "I'm having some doubts about his intentions too, and Bill's visit in July didn't help matters." Erie ground the butt of her cigarette into the ground and pulled her sweater more tightly around her. *Arthur will never marry me*, she thought. *No one will marry me. Who wants to take the chance? I'll carry on with Carliss Enterprises. There are a few contracts we might lose because of my colour, but they won't matter. There are more we can pick up.*

"You're not considering leaving William's firm, are you?" Anna asked.

"Not unless you wish to have the responsibility, Mother."

"I want nothing to do with the business," Anna said. "I have my own interests. Ian is my financial advisor, as well as yours. You do realize that no one in the United States but Ian Oliver knows of your ancestry. If anyone finds out, it will be through Arthur Moore—if you tell him."

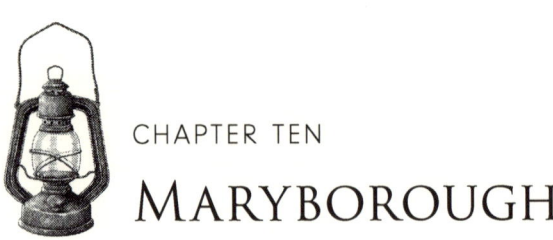

CHAPTER TEN

MARYBOROUGH

AFTER THE TRAIN STEAMED OUT of the Fergus Station, it swung north and west, crossed the Irvine River, and settled into a long haul over the clay plain of North Wellington. A shallow valley or low moraine occasionally broke the monotony, but for the most part, the train had an easy pull to Drayton. Wagons stopped as the engine whistled through rural crossings, the horses stomping nervously. Once Erie saw a car waiting at a crossing. Children waved, kicking up the dust of the roadbed with their shoeless feet. Farmers worked their fields, tractors or teams of horses methodically pulling machinery.

Erie was unprepared for Drayton. As the train pulled out of a long cut, Drayton lay to the left. It was an oasis of yellow brick buildings and green trees on the far side of a wide valley—the track and station being on one side, the village proper on the other. A river, almost dry, separated the two.

"Drayton," the conductor called walking through their car. "All off for Drayton."

Erie assisted Anna in gathering her hat and purse. Anna eagerly scanned the figures standing on the platform. "Patrick Smith won't recognize me after all these years, Erie. Look for a tall, well-built man."

"He sounds like a formidable person." Erie, with the assistance of the conductor, stepped lightly to the platform.

"He is," answered Anna following closely behind. "He . . ." A roar issued from the small crowd on the platform then Anna was caught up in the embrace of a huge man dressed in plaid shirt and coveralls.

"Anna!" Anna's feet were off the ground, her hat on the platform. Erie retrieved the hat while Anna tried to extricate herself from the man's embrace."

"P . . . P . . . Patrick. You haven't changed one bit!" Anna stammered. "Let me go!"

I'll admit, Erie thought watching Patrick Smith, *Anna's description of the man was correct. The plaid shirt covered the body of a boxer. He was a man who can hold his own in any fight.*

Smitty released Anna, but only to arm's length.

"I'd know you anywhere, girl," he said.

The trio began to attract an unusual amount of attention because of Smitty's loud voice. "Where's Erie? Where is she?" Smitty looked around, let go of Anna, and crushed Erie to his chest. Erie, grabbing her hat, was smothered in his flannel shirt, which smelled faintly of whiskey. "Let me take a good look at you." He held Erie away from him as he had Anna. "Good Lord, it is Rachael, isn't it?"

Smitty looked approvingly at both women. "Wait until Margaret sees the pair of you! I'll get your luggage. You stand over there by the sign." Smitty led them round the west side of the station.

"There are six pieces. All have our names on them," Erie called after Smitty. She then turned to Anna. "What a fellow! He's the best male specimen I've seen in a long time!"

Anna laughed. "He certainly is. But don't tell him that. He gets such a swelled head. I wonder which vehicle is his?" Erie looked around the station yard for a car.

"I don't see the car." Anna looked too.

Smitty strode around the corner, two valises in each hand, and one under each arm. "Have I got the right ones?" he asked.

Erie giggled and nodded.

"This way, then. I brought the larger wagon. I didn't know how much luggage you'd bring." Smitty stopped beside a team of greys. "I even polished the harness in your honour."

"Beautiful," said Anna, who appreciated good horseflesh. "I'll bet they're fast."

Erie gasped when she surveyed their conveyance. "You aren't serious. This is a farm wagon, Anna!"

Anna laughed, leaning against the vehicle for support.

"He's serious," she laughed again. "Smitty, don't you have a car?"

Erie smiled. Since William's death, Anna rarely laughed. It was good to hear her now.

"Well, I do and I don't," Smitty answered evasively. "Today, I don't. Who wants to sit beside me? Speak it! Not many women get that privilege."

"I will," said Anna. "I believe Erie would prefer to walk."

"Walk! It's three miles," Smitty said to Erie. "You never thought about me bringing a wagon, did you?" He laughed so heartily a black horse snorted nervously nearby. Smitty's team stood perfectly still.

"This isn't the city. You would not believe what we haven't got yet."

"I'm afraid to ask," Erie replied shrewdly, eyeing Smitty.

Smitty lifted Anna into the wagon first, then Erie. Lifting each woman was effortless on his part. It was as easy for him as lifting a sack of grain. Climbing into the driver's seat, he maneuvered the team around other wagons in the lot and reined right onto the county road. The team trotted down a hill, over a narrow bridge and through the main street of the village.

"Other than a new Town Hall," Smitty said proudly, "Drayton hasn't changed much in twenty years. A few more cars on the road, that's all."

Every bone in Erie's body was shaken by the ride. She concentrated on staying on top of a number of gunny sacks filled with straw. One big bump, she feared, and she would bounce right out onto the road. Smitty let the horses set their own pace. Maryborough Township rolled by as the team headed for home. At Martin's Corner, Smitty reined right onto the concession line and Anna directed Erie's attention to a valley ahead of them.

"The Conestoga River valley," she shouted.

Down into the valley, across a concrete bridge, and up the other side the team paced. Along a tree-lined road Smitty slowed them down. "There it is, Anna . . . Lilac Hill."

"Just as I remember it," Anna said.

Smitty turned the team right into a short laneway. A large, brown mongrel barked excitedly.

"Margaret," Smitty bellowed. "Margaret!" He pulled up beside a solid looking yellow brick house and leapt from the wagon just as Margaret, untying her apron, rushed from the porch. Smitty commanded the dog to be quiet and lifted Anna, then Erie from the box.

Margaret Smith was every inch an Irish Woman, Erie mused, watching her walk toward the wagon. Tall, big-boned, red-headed, and a perfect match for Patrick Smith.

"Margaret!" Anna embraced the woman. "It has been a long time." The two embraced with such emotion that an embarrassed Smitty shuffled from foot to foot. "Come on," Smitty said finally. "It's time they remembered we're here."

"Let them be," Erie said.

"Those two can talk for days," Smitty said. He took Erie by the elbow. "Margaret, you are forgetting someone."

Breaking away from Anna, Margaret wiped her eyes on her apron and looked at Erie. Wrapping her ample arms around the young woman, she said, "I am so pleased you came to Maryborough." Margaret Smith smelled of fresh baked bread, warm biscuits, kitchen spices, and jam. Erie understood instantly why she was Anna's best friend.

Margaret stood back from Erie to have a better look. "Child, I knew you would be a beauty the moment I first laid eyes on you."

"At least you haven't told me yet that I'm the reincarnation of Rachael."

"That was a foregone conclusion." Margaret smiled.

"Anna told me that I was ugly . . . scrawny . . . red . . . tiny."

"You were all those things, and beautiful too." Margaret put one arm around Erie and drew Anna to her with the other.

"I didn't get to do that," teased Smitty.

"Tie the team, Patrick. We ladies will be in the parlour."

"The parlour," groaned Smitty. "Best teacups too, the ones I get my fingers caught in . . ."

Erie giggled. "Is he always like this?"

"Never dull around here," Margaret retorted, giving Smitty a loving look.

Inside, Margaret led the way down a dark hall to the parlour.

"Could I use your facilities before I sit down?" asked Erie. "I had my kidneys bounced a bit much on the ride."

"Sure can," Margaret answered. "I'll show you the way. Sit down, Anna. I'll be right back. How is she?" Margaret led Erie past the stairway and through the back hall.

"She's been quiet all the way north on the train, but was quite good at Groves's yesterday. She isn't sleeping well at night and she misses William terribly." Erie gave her progress report quickly. "I know she's looking forward to her stay here. Of course, that is somewhat complicated by the fact that I am here too. Have we passed the washroom?"

"No," replied Margaret grinning. She opened the back door. "See that small grey building down by the pear tree, set in amongst the orange blossom bushes? That's it. I put a new Eaton's catalogue in there this morning. Always check before you close the door. Grab a burdock leaf or two just in case. Latch the door from the inside so you won't be surprised . . ."

"I can't . . ." Erie protested. "You don't expect me . . ."

"Course you can," Margaret said. "You'll have to get used to an outhouse. That's all we have out here. You should see the one at Lilac Hill. Papered it myself, just for you."

"Oh Lord," Erie swore. "What next?"

"Wash up over here," Margaret pointed to a graniteware

jug and basin on a high wooden table by the back door. "Away you go. I know what you're used to in the city, but you'll survive the outhouse and the Eaton's catalogue. I put out a clean towel. I'll go join Anna. She looks so pale, poor thing."

Who's the poor thing when it comes to washrooms, thought Erie. She looked at Margaret retreating inside, then walked along a well-trodden path to the building. Holding her nose, she let herself in and locked the door. As for grabbing a few burdock leaves, she didn't have a clue as to what they looked like.

Anna, Margaret, and Smitty were in earnest conversation when Erie returned from her little excursion. Anna was semi-reclined on an old-fashioned horsehair lounge. Margaret was fussing around her like a mother hen.

"There she is," Smitty said, his eyes twinkling. "She didn't fall in after all."

"Before I ask any more foolish questions," said Erie dryly, "what else are you lacking?"

"Electricity, hot running water, telephone." Margaret counted each off on her fingers. "We're as backward as you can get, except for the Old Order, and they live as they do by choice. As soon as the lines come through, and we can afford the service, we'll have lights and telephone. Tea, Erie?"

Margaret had the teapot poised over a cup.

"No, thank you," answered Erie, looking slyly at Smitty. "I am quite tired of tea. A drink of whiskey would be more appreciated."

"A young lady like yourself doesn't drink whiskey," Smitty admonished.

"Doesn't one?"

"There's none of that around here. It's prohibition. We're as dry as a bone."

Reaching into a pocket, Erie removed a small bottle. "I just happen to have some," she said. "I was sitting out there in your facility contemplating the interior decorations . . . reading the Eaton's catalogue, when I spied what appeared to be mickey under the eaves."

Margaret and Smitty exchanged quick glances.

"Sure enough," Erie continued watching for Smitty's reaction. "When I did investigate, I found one mickey full and another half full of good-smelling brew. It does pay to use an outhouse after all." She smiled sweetly at Smitty.

"Must belong to one of the threshers," Smitty said.

"Finders keepers," laughed Erie. "Shall we share it? Or would you prefer me to hide it again, Patrick Smith?"

Smitty's laugh filled the room. "You are one foxy devil, you are," he said. "We'll drink up the evidence. It's just mickey I bought from the bootlegger for my . . . arthritis."

"I'll have tea," Anna glanced warily at Erie.

"So will I," added Margaret.

"I'll have one small glass of this potent drew, with a little ice, please."

"Ice?" It was Margaret's turn to laugh. "Where do you expect to find clean ice in Maryborough at this time of the year?"

Tea and drinks served, three talked while one listened. Erie perceived from the conversation that Patrick and Margaret had two children, both away from home. Patrick farmed for a living but made little at it. The land was heavy clay. The old furniture in the sparsely furnished parlour told

Erie that Margaret had little money. Something bothered her about Patrick Smith. By his very temperament he was no farmer. He wasn't the type to stay put on the land for long. Margaret, on the other hand, radiated calmness among chaos.

"Enjoying your nip?" Smitty interrupted her observations.

"Pardon?"

"Your nip? You act as though you have tasted a good cut whiskey before."

"That I have," replied Erie. "And this taste is a rare commodity these days. You've got a good supplier."

"The best," Smitty winked. He recognized a compliment when one was given.

"I gather you and Caleb Gingerich are friends?" Erie caught Smitty off guard. "Business associates?"

"We're like brothers, you see," answered Smitty cautiously. "I have been keeping him out of trouble for over twenty years. I believe you want to talk to him?"

"I do. What exactly is Caleb's occupation?"

"He . . . deals in . . . grain, among other things," replied Smitty evasively. "He's a good horse trader."

Erie changed the subject, once again catching Smitty off-guard.

"What about my father, Jacob Gingerich? Have you spoken with him? Does he know I am here?"

Anna and Margaret stopped talking.

"Jacob says he won't meet you under any circumstances," Smitty said. "I am sorry."

"Impossible," Anna said.

"I suspect Jacob is afraid to meet Erie because he'd have to acknowledge her as his child before his congregation. I mean, how can a bishop suddenly produce a twenty-year-old daughter when he has never acknowledged that she was ever born?"

"Hasn't he?" asked Anna. "Has he never mentioned Erie?"

"Not that I know about. My Charlie was born four and a half months after Jacob's three. When Smitty went to register the birth, he made a point of looking to see how Jacob registered his children. There wasn't anything in the book. Jacob didn't register any of his children."

"That answers one question we had, doesn't it, Mother?"

Anna shook her head.

"How can the births not be registered?"

"Half the births in Wellington aren't registered. And the Old Order don't believe in anything having to do with government."

Anna closed her eyes. "If you are not registered in Maryborough and William didn't register you in Fergus, where might your birth be noted?"

"Why is it so important Erie be registered?" Margaret asked.

"Legalities concerning Carliss Enterprises. If Erie is registered as a Gingerich, it will cause problems for Carliss Enterprises. And worse, Margaret, I don't know if Erie was at some point officially adopted by William. I can't find any papers to indicate she was. We discussed an adoption. William was to take care of everything, given the circumstances."

Smitty whistled long and low.

"That's a pretty kettle of fish, isn't it? If she wasn't adopted by William, Jacob could lay claim to her. The running of Carliss Enterprises would fall on your shoulders and there'd be big trouble with the shareholders and probate."

"You've stated the facts," agreed Erie.

Smitty whistled again, then said to Erie, "What are you going to do, girl?"

"I'm going to carry on as though I was adopted by William. And I'm going to meet my father as soon as possible. If necessary, I'll walk right up to him and introduce myself."

"No," Anna said quickly. "You mustn't do anything like that. For all Jacob Gingerich has not acknowledged you, he does hold a position of great authority among his people. You must respect that position and not embarrass him in any way in public."

"Anna's right," Margaret cautioned. "It won't do to wave a banner in front of Bishop Gingerich. He is a man of principles. But, for the life of me, I can't understand his reasoning for not acknowledging you twenty years ago."

"What kind of man is my father?"

"Deeply religious, fair-minded, a leader, a man of quick temper but reasonable," Margaret said. "Dreadfully strict with Adam and Abraham though. He has no other children. Miriam didn't produce children for him."

"And Miriam? What is she like? Does she look like Rachael?" Anna asked.

"Completely opposite Rachael," Margaret explained, filling Anna's cup with tea. "She's blonde, plain as sticks and was the youngest daughter of a bishop in the Old Order from Pennsylvania. She's rarely seen outside Jacob's house. She is always at Adam and Abraham to marry."

"Jacob won't allow it," Patrick carried on with the story. "He is afraid of black grandchildren, I would suspect. Can you imagine the stir that would cause?"

"That bit of information tells me one thing," Erie sat up in her chair. "If Miriam is always at Adam and Abraham to marry and have children, she doesn't know about Rachael's background—or she is much more liberal in her thinking than Jacob. How would Jacob have handled the situation if Rachael had lived?"

Margaret shrugged. "Adam and Abraham don't know why their father won't allow a marriage. They have been raised like normal Mennonite children, but they don't go to church 'sings' and 'times' like other people their own age. They aren't given the opportunity to meet girls of their own religion."

"What are they like?"

"Abraham's quiet," Smitty said. "Adam is more outgoing. He will be around for the barn dance at the Wilsons, just like a shadow. His father won't know about him attending though."

Erie shivered. Was she ready for a confrontation with her father . . . a meeting with her brothers? *My life is moving too quickly for my liking*, she thought.

"There is Salome," Smitty was saying, his words trailing off as if he'd said something wrong.

"Salome lives in the doddy haus at Jacob's," explained Margaret. "She moved there after her husband died."

Erie, finished her drink, rose, placed the glass on the table, and walked slowly around Margaret's parlour, looking out one window and then another. Several black buggies passed slowly on the road. Were they Mennonites? Were they related to her? How could one tell?

"Why don't you drive Erie down the back lane with the luggage. See she gets comfortable at Lilac Hill. I'll keep Anna here with me until after dinner. We need a chance to catch up on old times. Don't forget to show Erie how to use the lamp and light the stove."

"Lamp and stove?" Erie echoed Margaret's words.

Margaret began clearing the teacups. Anna rose to help but was ordered to lie down again.

"I'm going to get some mending for us to do. We may as well keep our hands busy along with our tongues."

"See you in the yard," Smitty said to Erie as he left the room.

Erie, with a handful of dirty cups, followed Margaret to the kitchen.

"Don't you worry about Anna," Margaret said. "Fresh air and Margaret Smith will do her a world of good." She kissed Erie on the cheek. "I'm a little worried about you. And don't you take anything from Patrick Smith. You just give back what he gives you. That's the way I handle him."

Late at night, after Anna had gone to bed, Erie sat at a table on the porch at Lilac Hill. By the light of a lamp, she began a letter to Arthur Moore.

My dearest Arthur . . . she began. She stared at the paper, crumpled it, and began with a new sheet.

Arthur, we have reached our ultimate destination . . . She eventually crumpled that sheet too.

Do you remember a conversation we had in your apartment about blacks having equal opportunities?

Erie gathered all her pages together and carried them into the cottage with her and threw them in the stove. "A letter is not the way to do this," she muttered. "I must tell him personally."

All the while she sat outside unaware that someone was watching her from Jacob Gingerich's sleeping porch.

CHAPTER ELEVEN

KITCHENER

"EASY," CALEB CAUTIONED. The trap door opened into the warehouse and Caleb's head popped up. "Coast is clear." He emerged, boots encased in felt slippers. Jake had conveniently restacked the barrels close to the trap door. Tonight's quota of twenty barrels was going to be easy. Caleb checked the rim and was about to lift his first keg when he saw the shirt and noticed a shadow pass a window on the street side of the warehouse. He sneaked to the end of the rack and peeked at Jake's office. He retraced his steps and dropped through the trapdoor, pulling it shut behind him. "Give me the subfloor."

Smitty wasted no time complying with Caleb's order.

"There's a red shirt hanging on the rack," Caleb explained. "Snoopers are here somewhere. I saw one patrolling outside the building."

Both ran down the tunnel and out the opening at the other end. They moved a heavy jam cupboard in front of the gaping hole in the wall. "You stay in the house," Caleb commanded. "If anyone's going to be questioned, it'll be me. You've got an excuse for staying here."

Smitty nodded agreement.

"Take care. You are not carrying anything, but we don't want them to get suspicious of the wagon. We have one more load to get from the other end of town."

Caleb sneaked out the side door of the house, looked around, crossed the street, and disappeared behind a garage. Moments later a city water wagon emerged from behind the garage pulled by a team of grey horses. At the first street the wagon turned left, away from the warehouse. Halfway down the street, Caleb saw two figures, one on either side of the road. As he approached, they stepped into the middle of the street. As it was a cloudy night, he just might go undetected if he was cunning enough. Caleb pulled his hat low over his forehead and hunched himself down in the seat. He reined the team in and immediately recognized the snoopers.

"You there, halt."

"Goo—dahn Ohvahd."

"What'd he say?"

"I dunno."

Caleb smiled and held the reins in his left hand, keeping his right free for any emergencies.

"Where're you going so late at night?"

"Doo Kalmshd gay voo dah fruhsh vahksd."

"Watch him. I'll look at the wagon."

Caleb, high up on his perch, suddenly realized he was still wearing the felt slippers. He eased one foot, then the other off the footrest.

"Find anything?"

The snooper walking around the wagon turned a valve.

"No water," he said. He banged the side of the huge wooden barrel. "Sounds empty." He climbed the ladder at the side of the wagon and opened the lid. Putting his arm inside the tank he yelled, "Dry. Doesn't smell like whiskey either."

The snooper standing below Caleb poked him in the leg with his hand. "Whiskey, we're looking for whiskey."

"Doo gayd ahm ay awah nie oon ahm ahnah awash nows."

"Mennonite," the snooper explained to his friend. "Can't speak English."

"They all understand English."

The snooper on top of the wagon reached across the tank and tapped Caleb on the shoulder. Caleb didn't turn around but pulled the reins through the fingers on his left hand a little tighter. He had been working the reins undetected ever since he'd been stopped. One of the greys snorted and stepped backward.

"Hold that team."

Caleb tightened the reins just a little more. The second grey moved.

"Can you understand English?" The snooper lying across the tank asked.

Caleb shrugged and pointed at his right ear, shaking his head. "Ah blindey sie find ah airbs."

"I think he's trying to tell us he's deaf." The snooper behind Caleb clapped his hands together. Caleb tightened the reins a little more. Both horses stepped backwards.

"We're wasting our time," said the snooper, quickly climbing off the wagon. "This one's clean. Get going."

Caleb almost moved the greys on command but thought better. If he was playing deaf . . . *Nearly caught me*, he thought. *I'm slipping.*

"I could have sworn he said water wagon," one snooper said to the other," but it isn't this one."

So, someone's talking. It's time to get out. Caleb listened, but no more was said.

"Go on, get moving."

Caleb still sat. Until there was a hand motion, he wasn't going anywhere.

"Go on." The snooper motioned Caleb on.

Caleb nodded and left.

"Did you see his odd-looking boots? They were big felt slippers and they had mud on them."

"Maybe they wear them in the barn?"

"Nah, prayer slippers. They gotta be prayer slippers."

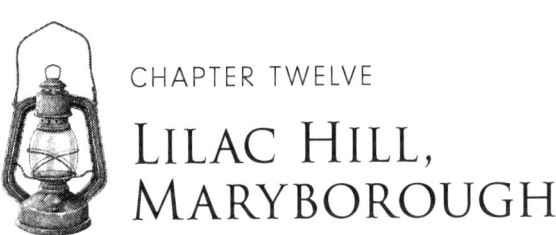

CHAPTER TWELVE

LILAC HILL, MARYBOROUGH

A MIST DRAPED RACHAEL'S VALLEY, appearing purple, then pink, then gold as a September sunrise swept the eastern horizon. An occasional bright shaft of light broke through the white mantle and lit portions of the valley with the brilliance of a jewel. Ones haft, as though on purpose, struck Erie's bedroom window. Another lit the kitchen windows at Jacob Gingerich's farmhouse where an unusual amount of activity was taking place.

Erie groaned and rolled over to avoid the bright light. She groped for her watch. Eyes bleary with sleep, she focused on its hands. "Five thirty," she moaned. "What an unearthly hour to be wakened."

It didn't take her long to realize she wouldn't go back to sleep. Nature called and she faced a walk to the little building behind the lilac bushes. Groaning again, she slipped out of the warm bed. A thick braid of hair fell over her right shoulder. She pulled her feet back quickly when they touched the cold floor. Accustomed to a maid delivering coffee and toast

to her bedside, then running a hot bath for her, Erie felt definitely out of her element at Lilac Hill.

She tied a silk robe around her trim figure and slipped her
feet into a pair of shoes. Tiptoeing to the front door, she let
herself out and returned moments later soaked to her knees
from the tall, damp grass. Erie had rarely seen a September
dew, let alone walked through one to an outhouse. Inside, she
sniffed. There was a faint but distinct odour of alcohol about
Lilac Hill.

Leaving wet footprints in her wake, Erie walked to Anna's
room. She opened the door slightly and was again assaulted
by the strong aroma of alcohol. Anna lay sleeping, one delicate hand to her throat. Whatever concoction Margaret had
given her the evening before worked. There hadn't been a
sound from Anna's room all night. Erie retraced her steps to
the porch and took a tin pitcher off a hook by the door.

"Water for washing is in the barrel at the edge of the
porch," Smitty had said. Looking into the barrel, Erie grimaced at the sight of water beetles.

"I didn't want to wash anyway," she muttered, putting the
pitcher on the porch floor. What next? She looked at her feet.
Obviously, she had to get out of her wet clothing.

Back in the cottage Erie changed into cotton blouse and
sport trousers. Undoing her hair, she brushed it and tied it at
the nape of her neck with a red ribbon.

"Now for something to eat," she said.

Margaret had packed a large tin-lined box with "necessi-
ties" just in case anyone got hungry between meals. Giving the
stove a wicked look, Erie decided she wasn't about to learn its
eccentricities for a cup of hot coffee, although Margaret had
packed ground coffee, canned milk, and sugar. There was a

coffee pot on the shelf. She reached into the box for a loaf of homemade bread, a small crock of butter, and a jar of raspberry jam. *What else do I need? A maid, a nice hot tub of water, and Arthur.* At the thought of Arthur, Erie frowned. *What to do about Arthur? What will he think? What will he say?*

Erie searched the box for a bread knife and hacked at the loaf.

"What a turn of events!" she said aloud. Religious prejudice she could handle. Being of Mennonite parentage didn't bother her much. She was actually curious about their religion and customs. She could definitely live with the knowledge she was born Mennonite. Colour prejudice was different. And to be black! That was an absolute crime in the "society" she kept. No one she knew associated with coloured people. But then, why not?

Erie buttered her bread, slathered jam on the thick slices, and picked them up. Retreating to the porch, she lowered herself carefully into one of the rustic twig chairs by the railing. Contentedly eating her bread and jam, Erie glanced across the mist shrouded valley. The sun, a little higher now, silhouetted the Gingerich house against a pink and yellow sky. *So beautiful*, Erie thought. *So Monet.*

Erie's musings were interrupted by a rustling in the bushes at the side of the cottage. "Who's there?" Erie called softly. "Ah, probably only an animal."

Erie looked over at her father's house again. Light shone from the windows on the lower floor, and someone stood on the porch. The snap of a dry twig down the path brought Erie to her feet. Looking over the porch railing she called, "Is someone there? Answer me!" She listened but heard nothing more.

Fool, she chided herself. *You're hearing things. Sit down and enjoy the morning.* Leaning back in the chair, Erie closed her eyes and massaged the back of her neck with her long slender fingers, thus missing the boney, withered hand reaching through the wooden railing on the porch. Only when the claw-like fingers tightened around Erie's slender ankle did she look down in terror. Her eyes focused on the hand, then through the spindles onto the face of an old woman. The woman's eyes burned like black coals and her mouth twisted grotesquely as she wailed, "Rachael . . . Rachael . . ."

Erie screamed and leapt from the chair, wrenching the hand from her ankle. Her screams echoed up and down Rachael's Valley. She ran toward the door of the cottage, right into the arms of Anna. She clung to Anna and pointed in the general direction of the apparition.

Anna, holding Erie close to her, looked past her. She stroked the dark hair. "It's Ouma Gingerich, your grandmother." Anna let go of Erie and, taking her hand, led her toward the dark clad figure who never stopped wailing, "Rachael . . . Rachael . . . Rachael."

"Ouma . . . Ouma," Anna called. "Ouma, hush. It's me, Anna."

Before Anna could say more, a large woman, black shawl over her shoulders, stepped up to the wizened figure, followed closely by two young, blonde-haired men. "Haym," she commanded.

The young men complied by gently lifting the old lady to her feet and leading her away from the porch. As they left, one looked back. His eyes met Erie's.

"Haym, yet!" The woman pointed in the direction of Jacob's farm.

"Wait," Anna called. "Salome. Come back."

The two men hesitated and Ouma Salome turned to look at Anna.

"Go home," the woman spoke to Anna and Erie. "Go back to your home. Leave Jacob alone."

"Who are you?" Erie demanded placing her arm protectively around Anna.

"It is no matter who I am. Go home. Leave before you do harm to Jacob." Turning abruptly on her heel, the woman drew her shawl over her head and walked into the mist which still clung to the valley floor.

"Who was that?"

"It had to be Miriam," Anna said, watching the retreating figures. "And, the two young men must be Adam and Abraham, your brothers."

Erie led Anna to a chair and sat down herself.

A shaft of light breaking free of its misty boundaries suddenly shone on three figures wending their way up the valley path to Jacob's house. The men were carrying Salome.

"Erie," Anna spoke slowly. "Perhaps we shouldn't have come. We are an intrusion on their lives."

"An intrusion on their lives? Mother!" Erie turned flashing eyes on Anna. "They're an intrusion on my life."

"They're part of your life, Erie. They're your brothers, your grandmother. But you're not of their life. We should have left well enough alone."

Erie was exasperated. "Twenty years ago I was removed from that life and I can't say I'm sorry. But I can't deny now that I don't have brothers. I can't deny the fact one of my grandparents was African. I can't deny the fact that woman, Salome, is crazy."

"Crazy because she thinks she killed Rachael," Anna's voice had a bitter ring to it.

"I beg your pardon?"

"Salome was the midwife at your birth. She didn't treat Rachael in the proper way for the condition she was in. It wasn't her fault. It was Abraham's fault . . . your grandfather. He should have had a doctor present. At any rate, Salome had never attended a birthing before where twins, then one other child, was born. She applied hot compresses to Rachael's abdomen when she shouldn't have. She assumed the birthing was over, but complications set in. Instead, she contributed to Rachael's bleeding to death and blames herself. She lost her mind shortly after Rachael's death. The bishop kept her locked away in his house. After the old bishop died, Jacob assumed responsibility for Salome. She saw you and decided you were Rachael come back to life."

"Oh, Mother. What next?"

"I don't know. I honestly cannot say. How did Salome know you were here?" Both women sat looking across Rachael's Valley, pondering that question.

"It had to be Smitty or Caleb," Anna finally surmised. "Those two men!"

CHAPTER THIRTEEN

GINGERICH FARM

SALOME ROCKED BACK AND FORTH, her eyes closed. Voices and faces tumbled round in her mind. One of them sat beside her, humming a tune and snipping at a piece of cloth. If it wasn't this one, it was the other. They never went away. Rachael was there again, down the valley but he stopped her this time and made her sit in the rocking chair.

"Woman's work, broodah?" Abraham looked over the porch rail, "Who are you adding to grohs moodah's basket today?"

Adam positioned a small cardboard template on the cloth and cut out a square.

"This is Margaret Smith. She gave me her pink apron."

"Mrs. Smith is not dead."

"You do not have to die to go in grohs moodah's basket."

"How does she know?" Abraham nodded toward Salome.

"When I showed her the apron and told her it was from Mrs. Smith, she nodded. She remembers."

"A woman's work is what you get for telling fahdah you were going to the dance tonight."

"At least I told him the truth. You're not going to the 'sing.' You're heading for Alma. He'll find you out and you'll do woman's work too."

"He forbid you to go tonight?"

"Yes, but I've broken no rule, yet. I don't dance. I watch. He can't stop me."

Salome opened her eyes and stared at Abraham.

"Does she know what we say, Adam?"

"It makes no matter. Look Ouma, Margaret Smith." Adam dropped several cloth squares in her basket.

Salome picked one out and looked at it. Adam patted her hand and cut another square.

"I saw the woman that upset her. She was at the swamp in the back field with a lady and Mrs. Smith. They were picking elderberries. Did fahdah say who she was?"

"Fahdah told Miriam they were from New York City."

"She is pretty. Maybe you will dance after all tonight."

"Abraham, I will not dance."

Salome, who had closed her eyes again, caught fragments of the conversation. She remembered dancing. But she did not dance. Caleb danced and he stayed with a woman. Was it the one from far away? Margaret Smith was the one that took the child. Where did she put it? Was it with Rachael? She must see. Salome opened her eyes and tried to get out of her chair.

"That is clever, Adam. You've tied Ouma to the chair round the middle."

"She will go if I don't. I chased her twice before I thought of her apron strings. Maybe she'll stay now. She can't see the women in the swamp."

"When I saw them, the dark-haired one was not happy looking."

"Maybe they don't have elderberries in the city."

Humbug! Erie thought as she trudged along the edge of the swamp behind Margaret and Anna. Her blouse was torn, her trousers stained, and her back sore. *What were those hellish berries called? Elderberries . . .* Takes years off a person's life to get to them, but they make a good pie, Smitty had said. Pie indeed. To add spice to her day, Margaret had announced at some point in the middle of the swamp that she had invited Bill O'Grady down from New Liskeard for a stay. He would be arriving just in time for the barn dance at Wilson's. The last time Anna and Erie had seen Bill was at William's funeral.

Erie wiped her brow with her sleeve. *All I need is Bill O'Grady.* At Anna's insistence he had spent a month at Seawind after the funeral. Erie spent the entire month either arguing with him or wishing he'd stay for the entire summer—and she longed constantly for him to kiss her! Mr. O'Grady had a very disturbing effect on Erie Carliss. She smiled as she recalled Arthur's posturing when Bill was around: "Cock on a rock," was how Bill described Arthur's behaviour, and quite accurately. At least a barn dance would be less hazardous to one's health than berry picking. Bill was just another problem she'd have to deal with.

CHAPTER FOURTEEN

Long Island Sound

THE LAWN AT THE BREAKERS stretched to the shore, a manicured sea of green. From the Portico, the tennis courts were to the right behind a boxwood hedge. The formal gardens, surrounded by yews, were to the left. Moore's private yacht lay at anchor in the bay, dwarfing sleek racing sloops which rocked in the gentle swell close to the private dock. Liveried servants waited attentively on Dane Moore's weekend guests. Arthur, in tennis white, crossed the lawn and threw himself into a chair on the Portico. Dane Moore looked up from her book, Rivona from her drink.

"It is too beastly hot to play tennis today." Arthur snapped his fingers. A servant stepped forward. "A tall one over ice, with lemon."

"What a ghastly way to drink beer," Rivona said.

"I learned the custom in South Africa where they have ghastly beer. Where are the others?"

"I assume your friends are still bashing the ball around the courts. Father and his cohorts are in the billiard room.

I've sent the car for several of the ladies who insisted on having their hair done." Dane Moore went back to her reading.

When his drink arrived, Arthur nursed it and surveyed his kingdom. The house would be shut up on the first of October when his mother moved her household back to the city, which was a pity. Arthur loved the Sound. This was as far from civilization as he wished to get. He tolerated his forays further afield to please his mother and Erie. He thought Anna Carliss's Seawind an absurdity. But he had heard last week that Sir Harry Oakes was building a summer home in Bar Harbour. Perhaps purchasing a bit of land in Maine wouldn't be a bad investment.

"A sandwich, sir?" Mabel stood beside Arthur.

"So, you've been promoted from the laundry, have you?" Arthur chose a cheese and watercress concoction.

"It's a pity your friend . . . Erie couldn't join us this weekend. Where did you say she was visiting?" asked Dane.

Arthur noticed that his mother always pretended to forget Erie's name.

"Erie is visiting relatives near a village called Drayton, close to Kitchener in Ontario, Canada."

"How do you know so much about that God-forsaken country?" asked Rivona.

How indeed, thought Arthur. It all began with a phone call from Frank Costello. That call led to an invitation to go to Toronto. Arthur never asked many questions of Costello. It didn't pay to be too knowledgeable about the mob's activities. As long as Costello paid him well for services rendered, Arthur was happy. This Costello business involved a large amount of whiskey coming in from Canada. In the course of the conversation, Costello mentioned it was unusual that Erie was in Ontario.

Assured by Arthur that she was visiting relatives and not on business for Carliss Enterprises, Costello hedged on any further information, other than to say Arthur should go to Toronto as soon as possible. He should book into the Queen's Hotel and not draw too much attention to himself.

After thinking about Erie's sudden decision to visit Ontario, Arthur had approached Ian Oliver. How long was she staying? Where exactly was Drayton? He received an answer to only one question. Drayton was near Kitchener. So, what was Erie really doing in Ontario?

Arthur summoned the servant and ordered up another drink. Was she actually visiting relatives as she said? Her Mennonite story did seem far-fetched when he thought about it. Or was she there on business for Carliss Enterprises? If the deal was as large as Costello hinted, the Carliss firm might be involved, too, if they knew about it.

"Isn't that correct, Arthur?" Rivona was speaking. Whenever Erie was unavailable Dane Moore managed to include Rivona as a weekend guest.

"Say what?"

"It's Erie's loss, isn't it? She chose to go away knowing you had tickets for 'No, No Nanette.' So I'm going to accompany you instead."

"Mother will have to accompany you. I'm leaving for Toronto. I won't be in the city on September 20th."

"Running to your dolly, are you?"

"You can be obnoxious, Rivona!" Maybe he did welcome the opportunity to go to Toronto. He would find time to see Erie. He had written to let her know he was coming.

CHAPTER FIFTEEN

MARYBOROUGH, WILSON'S BARN

WITH CHORES FINISHED, people converged on Wilson's farm. Cars and buggies filled the pasture and yard. Wilson had removed the machinery from the threshing floor in the barn and swept the area clean, then set up wooden benches and kitchen chairs. Two fiddlers and an accordionist warmed up in a corner. People stood chatting in groups awaiting the call for the dance to begin.

Smitty was as proud as a peacock escorting his three beautiful women, as he described them, down his lane, across the road, and up Wilson's drive. He carried a large basket full of Margaret's chocolate cake and elderberry pies. He had cautioned Erie not to smoke in the barn and not to break too many young men's hearts.

Margaret led the way to the drive shed where the food was laid out on long harvest tables. When she introduced Anna and Erie, eyebrows went up, but few questions were asked. Smitty did the introductions at the barn, but left after several minutes to talk with three men in a dark corner by the granary. Margaret explained that if the ladies wanted a drink, they should help themselves at a table where a huge washtub had been filled with cider. They were heading back to the drive shed to help make sandwiches when Margaret spied Bill striding up the drive.

"Lordy, lordy. Bill's arrived."

Bill O'Grady dropped his valise and broke into a run. He embraced Margaret and then Anna.

He's still as handsome as ever, Erie thought. *And probably just as aggravating. He's more tanned than he was in July and he's lost some weight. I believe I'm actually glad to see him.*

Detaching himself from Margaret and Anna, Bill turned to Erie. "And look at you, my charmer. How are you?"

Erie didn't shy away from his embrace. His arms felt quite natural around her.

Bill let go and said, "I just got off the train and hitched a ride out with the Henderson's. I need a shave and change."

"Go on over to the farm," Margaret said. "The door isn't locked."

Bill retrieved his valise and left, while Margaret led the way to Wilson's front porch where she and Anna immediately began talking about mutual friends. Erie sat on the steps, her arms around one of the supports, paying no attention to the conversation. Her thoughts were far away, in New York City.

I wonder what Arthur's doing tonight. He's probably at the Club. And he won't be alone. Rivona will attach herself to him. She never lets up. It doesn't matter now, does it? Erie bent her head. *Is it easy to stop loving a man? Was it love? Arthur and his so important pedigree. My news will be akin to introducing the plague to England again.*

"A penny for your thoughts?" a voice interrupted.

"They're worth more than a penny," Erie said.

Smitty sat on the step beside her. "You were so deep in thought I didn't want to disturb you. But then maybe you want a bit of a diversion. Do you want to dance? I'm not much of a dancer, but I won't trip over your feet. Mine are always fair game."

"I'd love to dance."

Smitty walked with Erie across the lawn. "You're not going to have a spare moment once I get you on the dance floor. The fellows around here haven't seen such a beautiful woman in a long time."

On the dance floor he admitted he understated his prowess. Smitty was an excellent dancer and guided Erie through several waltzes. When one of the fiddlers called "Square up," Erie begged off and stood with the ladies. Smitty found her there for the next set of waltzes.

"I didn't think you'd be a wallflower?"

"I was asked, but I can't square dance."

It was during a waltz that Erie looked up and saw Adam sitting on a beam in the hay mow.

"That's my brother, isn't it?"

Smitty glanced up and waved. "It's Adam."

"Why's he sitting up there?"

"There's no sense in him being down here. He won't dance. He hasn't risked his father's wrath doing that yet. He gets into enough trouble *just* coming to the dances."

"He's attended dances before?"

"Sure. Whenever there's a barn dance in the community. He has been so often we've made him the firewalker.

"Firewalker?"

"Yeh. He watches for smokers, like he's doing now. When he sees one he . . ."

"May I interrupt?" One of the Wilson boys tapped Smitty on the shoulder and whispered in his ear. Smitty graciously gave Erie over to the lad to complete the dance and left.

"I had a message for Mr. Smith. If you don't wish to dance . . ."

"I'd like to dance, thank you. You have quite a crowd here tonight."

"It's near the end of harvest and maybe the last time for a barn dance so everyone's here. Some are out from Drayton. The bridge crew just came in. They are over by the tub of cider."

Erie noticed a half dozen flannel-shirted men standing round the table.

"They're a rough and tumble bunch, aren't they?"

"Bridge building is hard work."

"Your name is?"

"John, ma'am, and it sure is a pleasure dancing with you!"

The waltz was followed by a polka. Erie was breathless by the end of the number. "I could use a drink of cider," she said, declining John's request for another dance.

John led her to a bench and brought her a glass. He then danced off with one of the pretty local girls.

"May I have this dance?" One of the bridge builders stood beside her.

"I should like to finish my drink first. Too bad it's only cider."

"Under the circumstances, that's all it can be." The fellow laughed. "We had a jug on the wagon when we arrived, but Smitty took it from us. I guess he doesn't want trouble tonight."

"I should know your name before I dance with you." Erie rose.

"Name is Charlie. I'm lead hand at the bridge."

The dance with Charlie led to one with every member of the crew. Charlie introduced them one at a time. They were all polite enough, didn't ask too many questions and all danced well. Erie was finally rescued by Bill who'd come looking for her.

"It took longer than I thought to clean up. I met Smitty down the lane. Darn fools that bring booze . . ." Bill whirled Erie round the floor.

"Adam's here." Erie pointed up at the beam.

"How do you feel about that?"

"As long as he's up there and I'm down here, I can handle the situation. He is a good looking fellow, isn't he?"

"It runs in the family. You look gorgeous tonight." Bill kissed Erie's forehead. "Let's pick up where we left off at Seawind. Let's pretend I didn't go back to the bush."

"Bill, please. I told you that Arthur and I plan to get married. Don't you ever give up?"

"Never, because you didn't exactly repulse my advances. I think you enjoyed them."

"I put up with you because of Anna."

"Kibosh!" said Bill swinging Erie off her feet. "Anna didn't demand you return my kisses, which you did."

"You caught me in a weak moment. Arthur wasn't there."

"Have you thought about my proposal?"

"I didn't even take it seriously. You were half drunk the night you made it."

"You'd like to think so, wouldn't you? Uh, oh, trouble!" He nodded toward the barn doors.

Two men stood in the entrance, one smoking.

"Who are they?"

"I don't know, but people are staying clear of them."

Bill danced in the center of the floor, keeping other couples between him and the two men who walked around the dance floor, surveying everyone. No one spoke to them. Most ignored their presence. When they returned to the entrance, they stood alone.

"Look. John Wilson is approaching them. He's asked the one to butt his cigarette."

"Did he?" Erie's back was to the men.

"No. He blew smoke in John's face. Don't argue, John. That's a good fellow. Just walk away from them."

"Bill, Adam's coming down from the beam. Dance me into a corner. I don't want to meet him."

Bill led Erie to the cider table, where they stood behind Charlie and the bridge crew.

Adam picked a bucket off the floor and walked toward the door.

"What is he doing?"

"He's going to ask the fellow to butt the cigarette," said a bridge builder.

"Brave lad," Bill said. "I wish him luck."

Adam, bucket in hand, stood in front of the fellow who was smoking. "Please put the cigarette in," he asked. The man nudged his companion, then blew smoke in Adam's face.

"Put the cigarette in," repeated Adam calmly.

"Are you going to make me?"

"Just put the cigarette in the pail."

"He needs some help, boys." Charlie walked toward the door. His cohorts followed and took up positions behind Adam.

The musicians stopped playing as everyone in the barn watched the scene at the door.

"Ask the man again," said Charlie.

"Put the cigarette in the pail," Adam said.

"You heard the lad." Charlie stepped forward. "Do as he says or I'll measure you for concrete boots."

The cigarette landed in the pail.

"Now give me the packet."

The packet was handed over and landed in the pail too.

"Mr. Wilson," Charlie called. "Did you invite these men to come tonight?"

"I didn't," a voice said.

"Will you leave, or shall we escort you?"

"Let's take them out," one of the bridge builders said.

"No, we'll be polite enough to give them the choice," Charlie answered.

"We're leaving." The two men turned and left the barn.

"You forgot your cigarettes." Charlie retrieved a sopping wet packet from Adam's pail and threw it out the door. "Good lad," he said, putting his arm around Adam's shoulder and leading him toward the cider table.

"Can we leave the barn, Bill? I can't face Adam now. He's coming this way."

Bill took Erie's elbow and walked quickly past the crew, out of the barn and over to one of the rail fences enclosing the orchard.

"Stay here. I'll be right back."

Erie saw Adam standing in the doorway. Bill spoke to him briefly and entered the barn.

Spunky kid, Erie thought. *I wonder what he would have done if the bridge crew hadn't interfered? My brother! We were in the same building together and he doesn't know I'm his sister.* All the frustrations of the past week finally caught up with Erie. She began to cry.

Bill stood beside her, glasses of cider in hand. He set them down by a fence post and took Erie by the arm. He led her through a gate and into the orchard. Leaning against the trunk of a tree, he drew a cigarette case and lighter from his pants pocket, lit one cigarette, and handed it to Erie; then he lit another for himself.

"The firewalker won't find us here. Do you want to talk about it?"

"Not really."

Bill drew pensively on his cigarette then dropped it in the damp grass. He spread his arms to Erie.

"Come here."

Erie dropped her cigarette and went willingly into his arms. He held her close, but gently, as she cried on his shoulder.

"I know what you're going through. I was the bastard child of a casual relationship, raised by a prostitute, rescued by Anna, educated by William Carliss, and have no family to speak of except Anna. I spend my life chipping away at rocks in the bush and I am perfectly happy with my existence, except for one small problem I've encountered." Bill tightened his arms around Erie a little. "I love you and you haven't said you will marry me yet."

CHAPTER SIXTEEN

LILAC HILL

FOR A SECOND Erie thought she was back in New York. The aroma of coffee wafted through the cottage. She drew herself further under the quilt, then thought she detected the aroma of frying eggs. Opening her eyes, she saw the painted walls of her small room and surmised she'd been dreaming. No one made coffee for her at Lilac Hill.

The aroma persisted. Erie heard thumping in the main room. Furthermore, her bedroom door was open and the entire cottage felt toasty warm. She got up, wrapped herself in robe and slippers, tidied her braid, and peeked through the door.

Bill, his back to her, was busy at the sideboard. The table was set for two in a haphazard way. The coffee pot bubbled on the back of the stove. Hearing footsteps, Bill turned around.

"Ah, awake at last. I'll give you five minutes to make yourself presentable. Off with you."

"What are you doing here?"

"No questions until after toilette. But don't take long. The eggs will be cooked beyond recognition."

Erie scurried past him to the front door. With a promise of a hot cup of coffee, it didn't take her long to finish her ablutions. Then she sat at the table eyeing Bill suspiciously. "Let me get this correct," she said. "Anna stayed at Margaret's after the dance because Smitty was going to be away. You walked me down the back lane, but I remember you leaving as soon as you had lit my lamp."

Bill deftly sliced a loaf of bread and placed the pieces on a stove lid to toast. "I started back to Smitty's, but I kept thinking about what you told me Miriam had said. So I turned around and came back. I took a blanket from Anna's room and slept on the porch for the night. I thought Miriam might confront you again, especially if Adam caused problems when he went home. I walked across the valley this morning to purchase eggs for our breakfast. Jacob was civil enough, didn't say much. Miriam left the room when I entered. Adam got the eggs. When I offered to pay, Jacob said, "Frohgah Kihshd Kaygehid.""

"Meaning?"

"With my limited knowledge of their dialect, I believe it translates loosely into 'asking doesn't cost any money.' He wouldn't accept payment for the eggs, but he called Adam back when the lad started to accompany me down the hill."

"Does Jacob know you?"

"Of course. I spent enough time with him when I was younger that he can't help but know me."

Bill buttered the toast, dished up the eggs, poured hot coffee then sat down.

"I don't believe you stayed here because you thought Miriam would come," Erie said. "I think you stayed because of those two men that showed up at the barn dance. What was that all about?"

"The less you know about those two, the better off you'll be."

"I'm not a child," Erie responded slightly annoyed that Bill wouldn't confide in her.

"I'm fully aware of that." Bill changed the subject rather abruptly. "Your father isn't going to meet you. You realize that. He pushed you away years ago and he'll never relent."

"I've never truly thought of him as a father in the sense that William was a father."

"Well, like it or not, Jacob is rightfully your father. His blood runs in your veins."

Erie sipped her coffee. "I want to meet him." She picked at her eggs, then asked, "Can I confide in you?"

"You know you can."

"I'm in a predicament. No one knows if my birth was registered. No one knows if I've been formally adopted. My involvement with Carliss Enterprises hinges on the answers we might find. We do know I'm not in the Gingerich bible. I'm not registered in Maryborough or Fergus. Groves can't find an adoption record in Toronto."

"Now, that is an interesting predicament, I must say, especially with Caleb's . . ."

"Do continue . . ."

Bill got up and began clearing the table. "Did we resolve anything last night?"

"No, I'm just as confused. I haven't stopped loving Arthur."

Bill filled the dishpan with hot water. "I'm used to chipping away at rocks without getting instant results. Sooner or later I'll strike the vein."

"I'm not a rock."

"I might be referring to Arthur."

It was Erie's turn to change the subject. Whenever she and Bill discussed Arthur, the scene always turned ugly. "Bill, did you ever meet my mother, Rachael?"

"Yes." Bill left the dishes and sat down beside Erie. "I came to stay with Smitty and Margaret while Anna and William went off on their honeymoon. I spent my time between Rachael and Margaret. I was young, seven, but I remember Rachael very well. She looked exotic. During the day she wore her hair up under the prayer cap. But at night she would let it down. She laughed a lot. She was tall, but perhaps only because I was small. She sat beside the fire with Jacob in the evening, holding his hand, talking to him. I was always disappointed that I couldn't sit on her knee, but she was expecting. She would place a small stool beside her and would keep one hand on me while she held Jacob's with the other. She would sing such beautiful songs."

Bill stopped talking. He looked earnestly at Erie. "She was a gem. You are not unlike her in looks. Sehl cahn mahyoh saynah mit ay awy."

"I beg your pardon."

"An old Deutsche saying, Erie 'that can be seen with one eye . . . Havah, Kehsahl shvahts,' Jacob used to say as he stroked Rachael's hair . . . kettle black hair. I can remember that phrase as though it was spoken yesterday."

"You paint a lovely picture of my mother."

"She was an exceptional woman." Bill leaned forward to kiss Erie on the forehead.

"Don't do that."

"Why not? Come on, eat up. You've got to be sharp for your Uncle Caleb. We'll do the dishes and go see if he's arrived at Smitty's."

"I'd no idea I would see him today. Smitty wouldn't say when he was coming."

"Smitty probably didn't know. I saw him at the station in Kitchener when I arrived. He assured me he'd be here this afternoon." Bill laughed. "He told me he was mailing a box of slippers to me in Toronto. He said when I got back I should throw them out. Funny man! He did have a box with him. Has anyone told you about Caleb?"

"I've heard stories. I gather he's a character."

"That's putting it mildly! He's a man to be reckoned with. Don't underestimate him, and don't let him deceive you, Erie. He's a clever fellow."

Erie finished her breakfast and helped dry the dishes, paying little attention to Bill's patter.

So, she thought, *I get to talk with Caleb Gingerich today. If he is as clever as Ian Oliver says, I'd better be careful. If he's dealing in grain, he is probably dealing in whiskey. That's the cover they all use, unless he's actually an honest man.*

"I've lost you," said Bill removing the tea towel from Erie's hands. "Why don't you go change? I'll finish the dishes."

"How did you learn such womanly arts?"

"The bush is a great equalizer."

CHAPTER SEVENTEEN
KITCHENER

CALEB'S STUTTGARD 200 roared down the dusty concession road in Woolwich Township scattering dogs and chickens in all directions. Trees and fence posts flashed past. Erie hung onto her hat for fear of losing it out a window. Uncle Caleb, handling the wheel of the big machine obviously liked speed.

Erie sneaked a look at Caleb. He was over six feet tall, blonde-haired, blue-eyed, and much too muscular to look comfortable in the business suit he was wearing. He was lightning quick, alert to unusual sounds and strange people. Erie liked him instantly.

"Like what you see?"

Erie averted her eyes, embarrassed that she had been caught looking at him.

"Take your hat off. Enjoy the wind."

"Speed, I'm used to. Dirt roads I'm not." But she did remove her hat to let her hair blow freely round her face. It was a great feeling.

Caleb laughed. "Just like your mother. She liked speed."

"Which one?" asked Erie. "I seem to have two mothers these days."

Caleb laughed. "Anna. Rachael was horse and buggy Mennonite. She couldn't ride in a car, although I think if there'd been cars around when she lived, she would have loved to take a ride." Slowing to enter a main road, Caleb frowned. "I don't like it at all," he muttered looking in his rear-view mirror.

Erie glanced in her side mirror. The two men that were at the barn dance were in a Ford that pulled up behind Caleb's Stuttgard.

"We'll take it easy for a while. We could outrun them, but I don't want to draw attention to you."

Caleb eased the Stuttgard onto the main road and drove very slowly gesturing that the Ford should go first. "I like to keep those fellows in front of me."

"Who are they?"

"Let's just say they're not friends," Caleb responded dryly. "Don't worry about them. Just lean back and enjoy the ride."

Erie did as she was told. *Pretty part of Ontario*, she thought. *I could live here.*

"We'll be in Waterloo soon. The road's getting busier. Ford's left us behind. They know we'll be easy to spot with this car."

The final five miles were busy with motor cars, buggies, and farm wagons. Caleb drove slowly and eventually turned onto a small street off King Street in Waterloo.

"See that building over there?" He didn't point but gave a nod of his head. "That's the 'headquarters' for our business."

"Baeker Vinegar Company." Erie read the sign across the brickwork.

"Do you mind if we don't talk business in the car or if I don't take you to the comfort of a good hotel for a chat. I'd prefer we be somewhere no one can overhear what we're going to discuss."

"You lead, I follow."

Caleb wheeled the Stuttgard back onto King Street and ten minutes later off again onto a small side street.

"Another of our branch offices." He nodded to a non-descriptive story-frame building which carried signage indicated it was a Felt Factory. Several side streets later, Caleb parked the car at Victoria Park. There, sitting on an ornate bench near the pond, while children played around them and mothers pushed wicker prams along the pathway Caleb tried to outline the business arrangements he had been negotiating with William Carliss. "Ian Oliver tells me you can be trusted and that you have an astute business mind. I usually don't deal with women in regards to . . . business matters. But I do trust Ian."

"If you don't trust me," Erie said, "we may as well not hold this conversation."

"I do trust you," Caleb said, "but this deal could turn ugly."

"I think I already know part of your 'business' and I'm not concerned about the consequences should something go wrong. I'm sure you can handle the situation if business turns sour."

Caleb instinctively looked around the park before beginning. "It's simple," he said, loosening his tie and stretching his long legs out onto the grass. "Both you and I know prohibition is almost over. It can't last. But, at the moment, alcohol in any quantity is a very saleable commodity. We are in the business of whiskey, my dear."

"Who are 'we'?" Erie knew she wouldn't get a straight answer but nevertheless asked.

"Partners . . . small businessmen . . . dirt farmers. You know that it is quite legal to manufacture alcohol or spirits in Canada as long as it's sold for medicinal purposes by prescription. We also know it can only be manufactured under license and that it can be sold to the United States . . . if a buyer can be found."

"And, you don't have a license," interrupted Erie before Caleb could finish his sentence.

"Who says we're manufacturing," asked Caleb.

"I know you are," countered Erie. "The fact you're being followed by those fellows in the Ford tells me a lot."

Caleb gave Erie a shrewd look and continued, "There's a small distillery, licensed to manufacture that we . . ."

Again, Erie interrupted. "The large distilling companies have already made overtures to the small distilleries. If they won't sell their product, the big fellows simply buy the distillery. You would only draw attention to yourself by trying to purchase a distillery to cover your tracks."

"You're clever, aren't you?"

"Clever enough to know that you and your cohorts are manufacturing alcohol right under the noses of the law. You're storing it in your 'businesses.' When prohibition ends, good, aged whiskey will be in short supply. I'll bet you have hundreds of gallons stored away and stills all over the countryside."

Caleb started to interrupt. "Only part . . ."

"William didn't write down anything about your deal and he didn't speak to me about it, but I assume you need money to pay off your 'employees' and a few others involved."

Caleb shrugged. *May as well go along for now,* he thought. "As long as our employees can supply us and we can pay them, the system will work. If we don't get caught, we stand to make a fortune. We have had some product stored for four years."

"You have been at this for four years and no one's been caught?"

"It's not for want of them trying. We've come pretty close," Caleb admitted.

"The business is controlled by some nasty individuals," warned Erie. "I've met a few of them."

"Don't worry. We've been extremely careful."

Caleb had to turn his head from Erie to suppress a laugh. This conversation wasn't turning out the way he wished it, but perhaps it was best she didn't know the entire situation . . . yet.

"Poor Smitty," said Erie. "He shouldn't be involved."

That statement was too much for Caleb. He laughed heartily. "Smitty is not poor, nor is he innocent. He is in this up to here." He indicated an imaginary line on his neck.

"I assumed he was, but only because you got him involved. Lilac Hill was used—had a still in it, wasn't it?"

Caleb nodded an affirmative.

"I should have said 'poor Margaret.' "

"You can feel sorry for Margaret," admitted Caleb. "Never feel sorry for Smitty."

Erie steered the conversation back to business. "How much money was William going to invest?"

"We're not asking for Carliss Enterprises to invest any money. We need their name only."

Erie glanced across the pond. "Hush, Uncle Caleb."

"Is there anything wrong?"

Erie looked at the women passing by the bench and across the pond again. "Can we walk?"

"Certainly." Caleb rose and took Erie's arm.

"If I'm interested in your deal, we'd better conclude the business while I can still use the Carliss name; and there'll be a price for the use of that name."

"We can move quickly, this week. Margaret tells me you're asking about your registration. I can tell you that you're not registered at all, nor are you formally adopted. I was with William when he approached Jacob."

"I thought so," Erie said.

"My brother was a stupid man," declared Caleb "He didn't want to see you. But he wouldn't give you up for adoption. The only thing William could get from Jacob was a paper stating that he could raise you until you were twenty-one years of age."

"Therefore, I'm in the position of being either a Gingerich or a Carliss?"

"Correct. All you need are three affidavits from citizens of Canada stating that you were born on a certain date, of certain parents, in a certain year. You could obtain these affidavits from myself, Patrick Smith, and Dr. Groves. But do you wish to be a Gingerich or a Carliss?"

"To choose Gingerich would be the truth. To choose Carliss is to ask people to lie for me."

"Not so! Anna Carliss saved your life. She raised you as though she had born you herself. I drove her to Fergus. I heard her prayers. I saw her tears of joy when Groves said you would live. You are her child. The only thing she didn't experience were your birth pains."

"I was born Gingerich," countered Erie.

"You were raised a Carliss. I'm your uncle and I say you are a Carliss."

"Only because you need the name."

"Erie Carliss!" Caleb stopped walking.

"Keep walking, Uncle Caleb. Look around you."

Caleb casually glanced behind him and began walking again.

"Anna, Ian Oliver and you are the only people associated with Carliss Enterprises that know you were not born a Carliss. If you choose 'Carliss,' Ian Oliver wouldn't question your decision. He's dedicated to Anna. He'll accept the affidavits at face value and will present them to probate as evidence you were born a Carliss. Groves would back him up. He would explain your registration, or lack of it, was simply an oversight on the part of your parents who were in Ontario when you were born."

"If you have all the answers, tell me why my father refused to let William adopt me when I was a child?"

"Jacob listened to his father after Rachael's death instead of listening to his heart. Jacob needs you, Erie. You alone can put your father out of his misery."

"Out of his misery?" said Erie. "I don't understand you, Caleb."

"Sometimes I don't understand myself. Let's change the subject. What is New York like these days? I haven't been there since 1919. You must find Maryborough boring."

"I haven't had a chance to get bored."

"I always said country living was good for the constitution. Are they still following us?"

Erie bent to straighten a stocking. "They're standing by a light fixture watching us."

"Shall we leave this fair city for Maryborough?"

"An excellent idea."

Should I or should I not tell him that I thought I saw Bessi Starkman watching us from across the pond? Erie thought. Was it really Bessi? Does she have anything to do with the men in the Ford? Perhaps it was just a mom who looked like Bessi pushing a carriage.

"Do you know Bessi Starkman?"

Caleb stopped walking again. "Woman of the biggest gangster in Ontario. Some say the brains behind him. Why do you ask?"

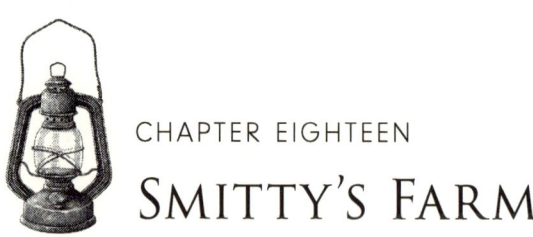

CHAPTER EIGHTEEN

SMITTY'S FARM

BILL HAD DRIVEN Anna and Margaret to the Village of Arthur to meet friends, leaving Erie to make Smitty an early supper, or a late lunch, depending on when he showed up. He appeared around four o'clock giving no explanation as to where he'd been. Margaret had prepared food, so the only thing Erie had to do was make tea, which she accomplished after Smitty stoked the stove. After eating, Smitty suggested they sit on the back porch where he could whittle without getting wood chips all over Margaret's kitchen floor.

Smitty teetered back and forth on a chair and examined a piece of wood. Erie reclined in an old wooden rocker. She looked intently at the horizon. Although it was not yet five o'clock, there seemed to be a haze over a huge stand of maples on the Gingerich farm. She bent to pick up a kitten that rubbed itself against her leg and stroked its soft fur. Now seemed as good a time as any to ask Smitty about Caleb.

"You've lived among the Mennonites for years, Smitty.

Why did Caleb leave the faith? What will happen to Adam if he leaves?"

"You are full of questions, aren't you?" Smitty whittled slowly, turning the wood with each stroke of his knife.

"I need answers and I trust you'll be honest with me. I've heard more stories about Patrick Smith than I can repeat, and some I can't, if they're true."

"People are joshing you. Don't believe anything you hear."

"Or see," replied Erie. She looked again at the Gingerich bush and frowned.

"Smitty, I'm having a difficult time distinguishing Mennonites from everybody else around here. Everyone drives a horse and buggy."

"There's little that distinguished 'them' from 'us' now. There'll come a time when the division will be more pronounced because some won't drive cars, nor will they accept electricity or the telephone. They don't like to use the telegraph and some frown on riding the train, except in emergencies. There are a number of different groups within their own community. Each lives within their own interpretation of the faith. Jacob is from the Old Order. He'll never have electricity and phone. Nor will he drive a car."

The kitten settled in Erie's lap.

"The main difference is their religion, their dress, and their method of raising their children. They are good people. They live to a very strict code of conduct. Their children are raised to obey and to work. Their customs might seem strange to you and me. But what is unacceptable for one group, works for another. Who are we to criticize?"

"I'm not criticizing, Smitty."

"Take Caleb, for instance." Smitty was warming to the subject. "I knew Caleb would be a rebel the first day I laid eyes on him. He left the faith and went to Toronto. He came back one year later—stood up in front of the congregation and said he was sorry he'd become 'worldly.' Six months later he was back in Toronto. Old Bishop Gingerich didn't give him breathing room, said his ways were against the church . . . shunned the fellow . . . course, that was after the ruckus in Owen Sound . . ."

"What happened in Owen Sound?"

"That's not for young ladies to know. Take my word for it. Bishop Gingerich was not pleased."

"To be shunned?"

"That means 'put away.' Family don't speak or eat with the person. The community turns its back on the person . . ."

"I've been shunned?"

"No, no. Jacob hasn't shunned you. He didn't know you in the first place. You did nothing wrong." Smitty shifted his weight and hunched over his whittling.

"What will happen to Adam?" Erie questioned.

"I don't know. Caleb still comes back. He can never break completely. He still needs to hear the wheat growing in the fields. Jacob talks to him. Blood is thicker than water."

"He needs to see the wheat growing because he has a vested interest in the crop," laughed Erie. "He must have nerves of steel and eyes like this kitten. I never met a man that was so aware of what's going on around him—other than yourself."

"He does admit to being able to see in the dark on occasions." Smitty smiled at the compliment Erie had paid Caleb and himself.

"Those two men at the barn dance?"

"Snoopers. They've been around far too much recently. They're looking for . . . booze."

"Aren't you taking unnecessary risks associating with Caleb?"

"I am always careful, Erie." Smitty rubbed his thumb along the piece of wood. "Don't you worry your pretty little head about me. What are your plans?"

"I can't spend much time here. I'm going to confront Jacob if he won't meet me. If he doesn't come to me, I'll simply go to him."

Smitty snapped his knife shut and again rubbed his hand carefully over his wooden creation.

"Fair enough. Two days ago I counselled you not to approach Jacob. I'm going to change my counsel." Smitty handed Erie a small wooden spoon with her initials carved in the bowl. "It might not hurt to stir the pot."

"Thank you, Smitty. Could something be on fire over there? Is that smoke coming from the bush?"

"Yep, it's smoke," Smitty said. "It's my still. I must have stoked it a bit much."

"Your still!"

"Not so loud," Smitty leaned back in his chair, a wide grin on his face. "I'm some upset with what I see, but I'm not going near the place. I think I'll just sit here awhile and see what Jacob's going to do."

"Patrick Smith. You scoundrel!"

"Jacob's the one that will have to deal with the situation. He'll be racing across the fields now. He won't let anyone near the shanty when he sees what's burning. People will say 'shame on Bishop Gingerich for breaking the law.'" Smitty chuckled. "I can hear Jacob now. He'll be furious."

"You devil, Patrick Smith. You absolute devil. You set the fire?"

"I wouldn't normally do a thing like that, but the devil always has fingers in the details."

Smitty retrieved his knife from a pocket. Selecting another small piece of wood from the pile by the back door, he settled himself comfortably, glancing to the sugar bush once in a while to check on the situation. If he read Jacob right, he had nothing to worry about. No one would get near the bush. If he didn't, Smitty knew he faced a long jail term for possession of a still.

One half hour later when Bill, Margaret, and Anna returned from their day's outing, smoke still hung over the valley and there was no sign of Jacob. Smitty explained the little fire while Margaret made coffee and put supper out for herself, Anna, and Bill. Bill had just seated himself, then remembered he had messages for Erie. He had picked them up when he dropped crocks of butter off in Drayton. Handing Erie several slim envelopes, he said, "One's from the peacock, Arthur Moore."

Erie glared at Bill and tucked Arthur's letter in her pocket. The second she opened and read.

"I think I should share this letter with you. It is from Ian Oliver. He wants documentation on my birth. He can't wait too long. He wants to be advised within the week."

Smitty stroked his chin thoughtfully.

"What are you scheming?" Bill asked.

"Who says I'm scheming," Smitty retorted. "Just don't go anywhere tomorrow. Stay around. I might need you. Did Caleb say where he was going when he dropped you off?"

"He didn't tell me." Erie poured herself another cup of

coffee and refilled Bill's cup. "He did say he would be here tomorrow afternoon. We were followed home by those two men that were at the dance. They were on the road into Kitchener, and in Victoria Park too."

"Of course! Caleb's Stuttgard sticks out like a sore thumb. I told him to drive my car. It may look terrible but it's fast."

"He said he'd bring your car tomorrow."

Smitty helped himself to a slice of bread. "After he left you, where did the two men go?"

"Their Ford followed the Stuttgard . . . off in that direction." Erie pointed north.

"He's leading them on a wild goose chase. He'll drive all the way to Collingwood, lose them and drive like a bat to get to Fergus to pick up my car."

Margaret got up to get more cream. "At least they weren't in the area to see the fire. That will give you time to get the still cleared away."

"Cleared away," Smitty spread his bread with treacle. "Not until Jacob comes to see me. That's the only way I found to try to get him to talk to Erie. I know I'm taking a big risk, but I've got to do it. What is everyone doing tomorrow?"

"Anna asked me to take Erie to see the graveyard in Glen Allan in the morning," answered Bill. "I'll be around for you in the afternoon."

"I'm baking," said Margaret, looking at what was left on the table, "and praying."

"I need some time to myself so I'm going to walk the creek," Anna replied. "I love wandering the bank. But I have been kept so busy I've not had a chance to explore it yet. I'll stay away from the bush, Smitty."

Erie had been reading her letter from Arthur. "Perhaps I

should share the contents of Arthur's letter with you too? He writes he is travelling to Toronto on business and he expects to see me there."

"Heavens!" exclaimed Anna.

"Tough beans for me." Bill looked at Erie.

"It's unusual for Arthur to leave New York. He doesn't travel too far unless something big comes along. He does have a broker in Toronto, just like Carliss Enterprises." Erie read again to herself, then said, "He says he'll telegraph me when he arrives and knows what his schedule is. I do find that odd. Why would he come so far, not knowing what he was going to be doing? That doesn't sound like Arthur Moore."

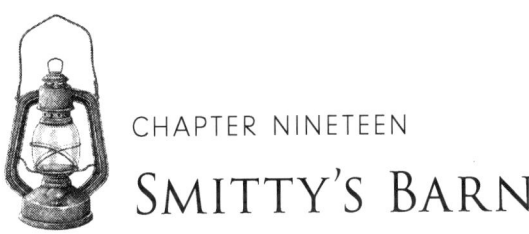

CHAPTER NINETEEN

SMITTY'S BARN

SMITTY'S BARN LOOMED out of the mist, its weathered siding black against the white dawn. The rooster kept up its incessant crowing even though the door to the coop was shut tight for fear of a fox. Smitty, carrying a barn lantern in one hand and two buckets in the other, crossed the wet grass to the building. When he reached the coop, he set the lantern down and swung the bolt on the door.

"If it'll keep you quiet," he said to the rooster, "I'll open it." The rooster crowed its victory and lunged at Smitty. "You keep that up," Smitty sidestepped the attack, "and it's in the stew pot for you."

Smitty threw the contents of one bucket in the general direction of the feed trough, then placed the empty container by the door. Margaret would use it later to gather eggs. Picking up the lantern, he and the dog crossed to the barn. Smitty swung the lantern from side to side, bending occasionally to examine the ground. Before he touched the stable door, he looked closely at the thumb latch. He then ordered the

dog back to the house. Smiling, Smitty lifted the latch and
stepped inside where he was instantly surrounded by cats.

"Get away with you." He pushed them gently away with
his boot. Keeping his back to the door, Smitty stood still . . .
listening. His eyes adjusted quickly to the dark of the stable. The cow moved restlessly at her stanchion and voiced
her displeasure at being tied up. Pigs grunted in their stye.
The horses whinnied softly from their stalls. Smitty held the
lantern before him as he walked between stalls and stopped
when he reached Mildred, the rangy milk cow.

"You're the first today," he said, glancing into the shadows, "and I'm early." He patted Mildred's rump and hung the
lantern on a nail overhead. Lifting a wooden milk stool from
a peg at the side of the stall, Smitty plunked it down and sat
on it. Retrieving a cloth from the bucket, he gently wiped
Mildred's bag while glancing casually down the aisle.

"Now Mildred," Smitty spoke quietly to the cow. "You
and I are going to have an understanding. I'm under and
you're standing." He chuckled at his joke. "I'm going to milk
you this morning, and the cats and I expect a lot . . . no
tricks, you hear."

Smitty glanced at the cats sitting in a row behind
Mildred. "Beggars. Nothing but beggars, all of you." He massaged Mildred's udder for several minutes then put the bucket
under it. Mildred turned her big, brown eyes on him.

"None of that," Smitty cautioned. "Just because you
haven't seen me in a while doesn't mean you need to look
surprised." He pulled a tit. Nothing happened.

"Come on, Mildred. You can do it. Are my hands too
cold?" Smitty rubbed his hands together vigorously and tried

again. A stream of warm milk hit the bottom of the pail. "That's more like it. Four for the bucket. One for the cats." He aimed a stream in the direction of the cats. They all leapt for the white liquid. Smitty laughed. Shifting his eyes to the left, but not moving his head, Smitty said, "You can show yourself, Jacob. You don't need to hide from me."

A man stepped from the shadows. Smitty kept milking, but he watched Jacob's progress down the aisle. "Fancy meeting you in my barn so early in the morning. Is this a social visit?"

"You know why I stand here."

Smitty milked steadily and didn't reply. He glanced up at Jacob.

"Vah ich neht vays, mahct mich neht bays." Jacob moved to stand by Mildred. "Vah ich vays mahcht mich bays. I am very angry, Patrick Smith."

All Smitty could see from his seated position were black boots and pant legs. "Why might you be angry on a fine day like this?" Smitty aimed a stream of milk in the general direction of the cats. It hit Jacob's pant leg. He squeezed again. The action had the desired effect. Jacob stepped back, out of the range of Smitty's liquid weapon. Smitty put his head down and smiled.

"You know the source of my anger . . . you and my broodah, Caleb. Shvehts duhch kay blehch."

"I don't know what you're talking about."

"You bloody well do," Jacob swore.

"Brother Gingerich, such language!"

"Do not call me brother," Jacob snapped.

Ouch, Smitty thought. *He is angry!*

"Look at me, Patrick Smith."

Smitty didn't comply. He wanted Jacob at his level, off-balance, just in case.

"What did you say, Brother Jacob?"

Jacob moved. Smitty stopped milking, ready to act quickly if necessary.

Jacob hunched beside Mildred and repeated, "Look at me, Patrick Smith."

Smitty looked Jacob squarely in the eyes. "What's angering you?" he asked, his eyes never wavering from Jacob's.

"Your still."

"My what?"

"Do not make me repeat myself. I am here to talk about your still and my sugar shanty."

"Too bad about your shanty," Smitty said, allowing himself to relax. "Bill told me about the smoke. He and the ladies saw it on their way home last night. I figured it had to be your shanty. It's the only thing that would burn in that bush."

Jacob had difficulty controlling himself. "How dare you put your still in my sugar shanty?"

"That is the second time you have mentioned 'still,' Jacob. You say there is a still in the shanty?"

"You know there is. And you've been tending it. You got careless and pulled some hot coals too close to my woodpile. The fire started in the kindling. We pulled the pile apart to douse the fire and saved three sides of the shack and your equipment. My firewood's gone and part of the roof's burned."

"You don't say!" Smitty exclaimed, surprised his still hadn't burned. "It's too bad about your firewood."

"That is not the issue," Jacob replied. "The still is of grave concern to me."

"I guess so." Smitty tried to sound sincere. "It's a federal offense to own a still. If you're caught with it, you could go to jail."

Jacob's eyes narrowed. "It is not I who will go to jail."

Smitty stopped milking. "Look at it this way, Jacob. When the feds see the still and they can't find the owner, they'll view your story as highly suspicious. It's on your property. You'll have a difficult time convincing them you're innocent. And, when your own people hear about the still . . . well . . ." Smitty shrugged his shoulders.

"It is not my still," Jacob stated emphatically. "It belongs to you and my broodah."

"Does it now? Has it got my name on it in big, red letters? Does it say anywhere Caleb Gingerich . . . Patrick Smith?"

"It doesn't have to," Jacob replied. "They will take my word for it. I am an honest man. Vahs lehts is, is lehts oon vahs rehchtes, is rehcht."

"So are a lot of bootleggers. The feds hear that story every day."

"Patrick Smith," Jacob rose, "if the inspectors ask to look at my shack, I cannot refuse. The neighbours already have suspicions. Adam turned them away at the gate last night. He lied. He told them we were burning rubbish in the bush. My son's actions tell me he knew there was a still in my shanty."

"Adam?" Smitty reacted with genuine surprise. He had no idea Adam knew of the still.

Jacob stepped toward Smitty. "I demand you dispose of your still. Remove it from my shanty, from my property."

Smitty shook his head. "I'll admit you have a problem. But I'm not going to be caught moving a still. It's in your shanty. You move it."

Jacob paced the floor behind Mildred. "I cannot move a still."

"And you certainly can't be found hiding one," Smitty said, enjoying Jacob's discomfort. He had never seen Bishop Gingerich so flustered before. "The feds will be around for sure. They've been asking questions at the Crossroads." Smitty stood and reached for a battered pie pan in Mildred's feed bin. He set it on the floor and filled it with milk from the bucket. Cats ran from all directions. He put the bucket on the stool and relaxed against the side of the stall.

"I am a farmer. I can't go to jail over a still."

"Patrick," Jacob stopped his pacing. "I appeal to you. I cannot be caught with a still. I am the leader of my people. It would be a disgrace for me, for my family."

"Speaking of family," Smitty interjected. "There's a young lady who's waiting to meet you."

That statement brought Jacob up short. He glanced furtively around the stable. "Dah?"

"Not here. She's at Lilac Hill."

"Why did Anna Carliss bring her back now?"

"To meet you," Smitty answered. "And, to learn about her mother."

"I will not meet her."

"Your option," Smitty said, "but it's unfair to your daughter."

"She is not my daughter," Jacob responded.

"The same as it's not my still," Smitty retorted. "Jacob, come to your senses. She is your daughter, Rachael's child. You can't deny that, just as I can't deny that is not my still. She wishes to meet you, just once before she leaves."

"Nay!" Jacob said emphatically. "I cannot meet her."

"You can't meet her?" Smitty challenged. "Or you're afraid to meet her, Jacob Gingerich. You are very much afraid."

Jacob glared at Smitty who continued to lean against Mildred's stall. He paced again, his hands behind his back, head down. "You do not know what you ask," he said.

"I know very well what I ask," Smitty snapped. "Face reality, Jacob."

Jacob paced again, head lower.

"Tell you what," Smitty shifted position. "I'll remove the still if you will meet your daughter."

"Nay, nay," Jacob said. "Nay."

"You would rather risk a jail term than meet your daughter?"

"There will be no jail term, Patrick."

"Don't be so sure. Just yesterday two sinister looking characters followed Caleb around Waterloo. All it takes is one word. A neighbour who saw the smoke . . . a chance remark by Abraham or Miriam or Salome, and they will investigate the shanty. 'Such a fine man,' your people will say. 'What happened to him?'. . . and Salome, you can't trust Salome to keep quiet . . ."

"Stop!" Jacob stood in front of Smitty. "Do not put me through this, Patrick Smith. Ahlahs hudd ahm ehnd."

"I agree," Smitty said. "Let's end this conversation."

"Nay, nay. Something must be done. I cannot carry on between . . ."

"I told you," Smitty spoke quietly, "I will move the still. But you must agree to meet your daughter . . . tomorrow."

Jacob paced again, an agonized look on his face. "You do not understand what you are asking."

"I know full well what I'm asking. I want you to come

face-to-face with your past. I want you to acknowledge your daughter's birth and Rachael's death."

"I cannot do that. I cannot."

"You can't let this eat away at you all your life, Jacob. You must face it." Smitty stooped to pick up the bucket of milk. "Margaret will want this. Good luck, Jacob. There is no peace for a man who won't accept the truth." Smitty walked past Jacob waiting for a reply.

"Vaw-aht," Jacob called following Smitty. "Vaw-aht. Ich piefdshoon ah vehnich ahnad-shd."

Smitty stopped.

"I . . . I will meet the girl . . . tomorrow if you will remove the still."

Smitty set his bucket down. "We'll shake hands on this agreement, Brother Jacob. A man's word is good, but a handshake seals the bargain. I won't go back on my word. You had better not go back on yours."

"I am not a man to give false words. I will meet the girl tomorrow."

"And I'll remove the still tonight. But you must promise two things. You will not let anyone near the sugar shanty, and if I'm caught, you'll take care of Margaret, should I go to jail."

Jacob answered quickly and sincerely. "I promise both, Patrick." Jacob glanced down at the bucket. "Dahn milch is ahlahs fawah dee cahts?"

Smitty looked at the buckets. It was surrounded by cats. "Shoo! Scat! Get out of there!" Cats scattered in all directions. When he looked up, Jacob was at the stable door. "Erie will understand, Jacob. She has your sensibilities and Rachael's understanding. Just tell her the truth."

"I will send Adam to tell what time. I must speak with Miriam."

Later, with the early morning sun streaming through Margaret's kitchen windows, Smitty retold the conversation, word for word.

Margaret stood at the big wooden table kneading bread dough. "Will he keep his word?" she said as she sprinkled flour on the board.

"He'd better," retorted Smitty, "or I will march Erie over myself."

Margaret kneaded steadily. "What about Miriam?" she asked.

Smitty put his feet on a kitchen chair and leaned back in the one he was seated in. "I have always had the feeling," he yawned, "that you ladies were too hard on Miriam. No one liked the fact she moved in right after Rachael's death, but that wasn't her doing. I figure life with Jacob has not been a bed of roses for the woman." Smitty yawned again. The heat from the stove made him drowsy. He'd had too many sleepless nights recently.

"Speaking of beds of roses," Margaret slapped the dough. Smitty jumped. "Will you give up now?"

Smitty pursed his lips. Margaret slapped the dough again. "Or are you going to wait until you're caught, Patrick Smith? You and I have been through a lot together but this business with the still last night . . . and this whiskey business with Caleb. You're playing a dangerous game . . . and those men hanging around are playing it for keeps."

Smitty stood and put his arms around Margaret's waist. "I'm only doing it for you, girl. I want to build you the largest house in Drayton. I want us to retire with some money. This is no farm. I'm no farmer. You know that. Even Mildred, the cow, knows that." Smitty kissed Margaret on the nape of her neck.

"We had enough money to put the boys through University. It wasn't right they stay up here. There's no future for them here. And it's not right you are living this way either."

Margaret stopped kneading and leaned against Smitty. "I married you for better or worse. I've seen you at your best and at your worst. I'm asking you to get out of the business now. I want to retire too, but not alone. You'll get caught if you carry on. I know it, Patrick. Caleb is clever, but he'll make a slip one of these days that will affect you both. I'll only ask you once, Patrick. There are better ways to make a living." Margaret started kneading again.

Smitty let go of his hold and walked over to the window. Margaret's pie rack stood on a table in front of the screened opening. The sill was lined with geraniums growing in an assortment of odd-sized tin cans. Outside, the late season daisies nodded heavy heads, pears hung ripe on a young tree, and apples needed picking in the orchard. Smitty looked past the orchard to the fields beyond, to the flat clay lands of Maryborough. He couldn't help but think Anna's visit had something to do with Margaret's dissatisfaction. They led such different lives.

"I haven't asked much of you before." Margaret sliced through the rich dough and began forming loaves. "I'm too old for this, Patrick. I don't need a fancy house in Drayton. I can live anywhere, as long as it's with you. Do you understand how much I love you that I'd ask you to get out now?"

Smitty said nothing. He watched as hundreds of small birds swooped over the fields, grouping for their flight south. A hawk circled above them looking for a quick meal. Smitty cleared his throat.

"Call it women's intuition," Margaret said. "If you don't give up associating with Caleb, something is going to happen to you."

"I could do carpentry work. I'm a good carpenter. But don't ask me to give up everything. I would go crazy if there wasn't some excitement in my life."

"I wouldn't tie your hands, Patrick. I'm just concerned about this alcohol business and the men that are involved. They are all gangsters. Now Caleb's gotten Bill involved and he's planning to involve Erie. Stop it now."

"To tell the truth," Smitty said. "It is getting risky. The still has to go first. Caleb and I will move it tonight. I won't set it up again. I promise you that. And, once I'm free, we'll take a trip, maybe to New York or Pennsylvania."

"And the other business?"

"Unfortunately, Caleb needs Erie to assist with that, and I won't desert him now. You don't often call me 'Patrick.' When you do I know you mean business. I will make another promise to you. I will finish this deal with Caleb as soon as I can."

Margaret knew Smitty would keep his promise, but she noted that he didn't say he wouldn't get involved in any more of Caleb's schemes. One battle was won. The war was still being fought.

"Where'll you put the still?"

"Down the old dug well on the abandoned farm. I have been thinking about it for a while now. No one will find it there."

Margaret put her arms out to Smitty. He hugged her.

"There is some risk in getting the still to the farm. We have to haul it out the front gate and take it one half mile down the road. The horses can't outrun the snoopers if they are around with their car."

"Can't you use the car?"

"It would mean transferring the still from the wagon. I'd probably be caught red-handed in my own barnyard. No, it has to be done tonight, by wagon."

Margaret resumed her bread baking again. "Only you, Caleb, and I will know about this," she said. "That's best for everyone."

"Agreed," Smitty said sitting down again. "You have to keep everyone occupied while we're moving the darn thing. Where is Anna?"

"She's coming for lunch before she walks the valley," Margaret formed another loaf and placed it in a greased pan. "And Bill is taking Erie to Glen Allan." Margaret glanced over at Smitty. He was asleep, his chair tipped backward, stocking feet propped up on her baking table.

CHAPTER TWENTY

RACHAEL'S VALLEY

ANNA ATE A GOOD LUNCH then set off to explore the valley. She walked back to Lilac Hill where she changed into comfortable shoes and a pair of Erie's trousers. With some of Margaret's oatmeal cookies in her pocket, she took the pathway down to the footbridge. Instinctively she looked up toward the Gingerich home. She had the uneasy feeling she was being watched. Anna didn't cross the bridge but turned left and walked through knee-high grass alongside the bank of the stream. A gaggle of fat white geese hissed their anger at the intrusion of a human in their territory. Anna walked cautiously through a stand of wild apple and hawthorn trees, pungent with the aroma of small bitter fruits. She followed a cow path which meandered to and fro along the bank. A blue heron, startled by her appearance, flapped his ungainly way into flight.

Thorn trees gave way to a flat, gravel, flood plain. Anna was surprised to see cattle grazing ahead of her. Several strands of wire, hung with grass, the aftermath of high water, barred her way. The stream wasn't wide, so Anna removed her shoes, rolled up her trouser legs and stepped into the cold water. Bottom pebbles hurt her feet as she splashed quickly to the opposite bank. Replacing her shoes, she gingerly stepped over the wire. She walked along the high-cut bank where knee-high grass gave way to waist-high fern. It had been a dry summer. The fern crackled and broke as she pushed through them. She stopped occasionally to examine a pretty leaf, watch an unusually colourful butterfly, or to simply listen to the birds. A blue jay scolded from her perch in a cedar tree. The fern gave way to another area of tall grass. Anna pushed through carefully, looking for wet spots. She eventually came to a small rise of land. *There it is. The trees are taller, but nothing else had changed.* Anna smiled and walked toward the ruin. The rise was ringed on three sides with lilac and honeysuckle bushes. In the middle, almost hidden from view, stood the stone foundation of an old mill, covered with wild grapevine.

Anna, watching for snakes, tugged at the vines. She sat down on the spot she had cleared and faced the stream. A September sky . . . William loved a deep blue September sky. At the thought of William, Anna sighed. *You died four months ago yesterday. Twenty-one years of married life and then you were gone. You would be the first to say life must go on. I am carrying on, but it's difficult. At least Jacob said he would see Erie, William. That is what you wanted.*

"Mrs. Carliss?"

Anna whirled, hand to breast, heart beating quickly. Miriam Gingerich stood before her.

"I am sorry. I frightened you, yet." Miriam looked at her feet. Anna was speechless.

"I am sorry," Miriam said again. "I did not want to frighten you."

Anna shook her head and extended her hand. "No . . . no," she managed to stammer. "Please sit down." She attempted to push more vine off the wall, indicating at the same time Miriam should sit.

Miriam crossed in front of Anna and helped break some of the vine before sitting down. Her black dress and dark blue apron were in sharp contrast to Anna's red sweater and yellow trousers. A prayer cap covered Miriam's blonde hair, while Anna's golden locks were bound loosely in a bun at the nape of her neck.

"I must ask your pardon, for my tongue, when I took Ouma Gingerich from your house. It was not right of me to talk to you in such a way."

Anna, taken by surprise by both Miriam and the apology, said, "You must have been terribly worried about Ouma Gingerich."

"Yah. Since Caleb spoke to Ouma she is impossible. She tries every day to go to your house. Adam or Abraham must watch her constantly."

"She is welcome to come to Lilac Hill; and you are too."

Miriam shook her head. "Jacob won't let me. Ouma is ows dee hiesley; crazy, crazy. Ouma hichd neht may fah-shdahnd we ah shdick fee."

"I don't understand," said Anna trying hard to pick out a few familiar words.

"Ouma has less sense than an animal," Miriam translated.

"Oh, no! Ouma knows what she's saying."

"Ach!" Miriam responded, throwing her arms in the air.

"No, she repeats over and over 'Rachael . . . Rachael.' Jacob laid Rachael to rest twenty years ago."

Neither spoke for a moment then both started at once.

"Mrs. Carliss . . ."

"Miriam . . ." Anna indicated Miriam should begin.

"I saw you from the kitchen. I followed you here. Please listen. Since you arrived in the valley Jacob has been different. He will not eat. He walks the floor. He will not talk." She hesitated, fingering her apron nervously. "And he didn't come home last night after the fire. I haven't seen him today, yet. And the son, Adam? I cannot find him."

"I am sure they're alright," Anna said. "Has Jacob not confided in you?"

"Jacob does not say much." Miriam hesitated again as she spoke. "He is . . . a quiet man. I married him, a quiet man and he has remained so. But it is worse since you came."

Anna cleared her throat. It was now or never. She had nothing to lose by being candid with Miriam. "May I ask a terribly personal question? Was it your wish to marry Jacob? Or was it the wish of his father?"

Miriam was startled and she didn't answer immediately. When she did, she didn't look directly at Anna. "Jacob had two babies to raise after his wife's death. Jacob's father brought me to the house to help. Before Rachael," she fussed with her apron again, "before Rachael there was an understanding. Jacob took me home from sings, but then Rachael . . ." Miriam's voice trailed off. "Rachael was pretty. I was not."

Anna didn't speak.

Miriam turned to look at her. She said solemnly, "Jacob is a good man. He provides for his family. His son, Abraham, is an obedient boy. Adam," Miriam shook her head, "I am afraid for Adam." Miriam rose from the wall. "I have said too much. I must go back. Perhaps Jacob has returned."

"No! Wait! Don't leave!" Anna put her arm out to block Miriam's escape. There was no way she wanted Miriam to leave. Miriam sat down heavily on the wall again.

"Jacob has said nothing about myself . . . my daugh . . . Erie?"

Miriam shook her head. "I knew your name," she answered, "because Adam told me. And there is talk at the crossroads."

"Interesting."

"Perhaps when you leave, Jacob will be again himself? I do not understand him."

"No woman ever fully understands a man," Anna said smiling.

"True," said Miriam "And Jacob is . . . different."

Anna knew she had to trust Miriam. "May I confide in you?"

Miriam faced Anna. "If it will help Jacob to be at peace with himself."

"It might not give him peace, but you will understand what his problem is," Anna answered.

"Where to begin? Where to begin?" Anna pursed her lips, then turned to Miriam. "Twenty years ago, when Adam and Abraham were born, a third child was born to Rachael. That child is Erie, the young lady accompanying me. Erie is Jacob Gingerich's daughter."

"Oon glawblich!" Miriam exclaimed "Oonfahshdehndich! Jacob didn't say."

"Jacob refused to acknowledge the child's birth or to raise her," Anna continued, not understanding Miriam's outburst. "He did this because he believed she caused Rachael's death."

Anna paused, took a deep breath then explained, "In reality, Ouma Gingerich and Abraham Senior caused Rachael's death. Ouma gave the wrong treatment after the twins' birth and Abraham refused to let Jacob send for a doctor."

Miriam listened to Anna, brow furrowed.

Anna pushed on, heart pounding. She couldn't turn back now. "Ouma Gingerich began to act unusual shortly after Rachael's death. The girl child was raised by my husband and I. Rachael was my best friend. Her wee girl grew up to be my daughter. Erie is the mirror image of her mother. That is why Salome Gingerich thinks Rachael has come back."

"Ach!" exclaimed Miriam. "And Jacob suffered because he sees his daughter, but gave her up."

"Not the case. Jacob refused to see his daughter. My letters and pictures were returned. I thought you might have done that. I realize now you didn't."

"He has never met his daughter?"

"Never. And we won't leave Lilac Hill until she talks to him."

"Kinah oon nahrah sawgah dee vawah hied." Miriam shook her head as she spoke. "Ah-ah neht hairicht da-ah moose feelah." She turned to Anna. "Jacob must meet her. He will only have peace when he speaks with her."

"He refused," Anna stated.

"Adam and Abraham, do they know?"

"No," Anna said. "Perhaps it's best they never know. It depends on Erie. It's her choice to acknowledge her family."

"And you?" Miriam asked. "You have raised Erie. Are you not afraid to lose her?"

"Of course I'm afraid. I'm her mother . . . I mean, I feel I am her mother. I'm terrified I'll lose her."

"You have a burden on your heart." Miriam touched Anna's arm.

"I must tell you the rest of the story. You must know all to understand. Rachael Gingerich has an African father. Adam and Abraham therefore had an African grandfather."

"I do not believe!"

"Do you remember Rachael?"

"Yah."

"You saw Erie?"

"Yah."

"You must trust me. I know Rachael's background. What I say is true."

"Jacob married Rachael and he knew she was from a different race of people?"

"Jacob knew of Rachael's father."

"Is that eating his heart too?" Miriam asked.

"I don't think so," Anna said. "But I don't know your church's stand on that sort of marriage. I do know Abraham was opposed to the marriage. I do know Jacob and Rachael were very much in love."

Miriam said nothing for a long time.

"I suspect that is why Jacob won't allow Adam and Abraham to be like other young men in your faith," Anna said.

"That is why! Of course, that is why. And that is why Bishop Gingerich wouldn't allow a doctor at the birthing." Miriam rose from the wall. "I will go," she said. "I will talk to Jacob. Your daughter must meet her father." She stopped talking and both laughed at what she had said. "Erie must meet her father," Miriam corrected herself. "I will send Adam to tell you tonight, if I have luck." Miriam walked away from Anna, then turned back. "Thank you. We are friends?"

"Yes, friends. And thank you. Miriam. Never think you are not a beautiful woman."

Anna waited until Miriam walked from sight. *Doesn't that beat all! How wrong can one be about a person? It wouldn't do to tell Miriam that Jacob would see his daughter. I have a feeling she needs to confront Jacob. Isn't it strange how an enemy can turn out to be an ally . . . and an ally turn into an enemy. What happened to the Jacob I knew; the man that was so kind and loving toward Rachael? The man that would die for Rachael? The man who accepted Rachael for what she was and who she was; the man that defied his parents to marry the woman he loved? I must get back and tell Margaret what's happened!*

CHAPTER TWENTY-ONE
GLEN ALLAN

ERIE AND BILL SET OUT to explore the countryside, a picnic basket tucked under the seat of Smitty's best rig. Erie wore one of Margaret's headscarves to ward off the dust. The horse trotted smartly down the river road, over the bridge, up the hill, and down the other side. Bill reined right onto the main road at the crossroads.

"Wait," Erie grabbed Bill's arm. "Look, there at that small shop."

"The harness shop?"

"The car. I'd know that Ford anywhere. It has a rumpled front end. What is it doing there? Where are the men?"

Bill checked the horse to a walk. "Shall we find out?"

"They know us. They saw us at the barn dance."

"It doesn't matter. We're not doing anything wrong. All I need to do is talk to Brubacher, the harness maker."

"What if they start to ask us questions?"

"We don't know anything, do we? It wouldn't hurt to disguise ourselves a little. If they haven't seen us by now, they might not recognize us. Tuck your hair in a little more. Put the picnic blanket over your knees. Hunch down . . . further . . . good."

Bill maneuvered the buggy into a spot on the far side of the Ford in such a position that Erie's back was to the building. He climbed down and tethered the horse. Scooping up several handfuls of dirt he rubbed it into his pants. Another handful dirtied his shirt. Pulling his hat low he walked into the shop, coming out several minutes later with Brubacher. They walked to the head of the horse. Brubacher checked the harness while both talked earnestly. Brubacher adjusted a buckle here, a strap there, and walked back to the shop. Bill undid the horse, climbed in and drove away quickly. "I hope they don't understand Deutsch. Poor Brubacher had a hard time understanding me. He finally figured out I wanted him to come outside."

"You are getting as bad as Caleb at excuses."

"I had to use some ruse to get him out of the shop. The three were in there alright. They had their backs to the windows. I don't think I was recognized. Brubacher said they asked questions about the fire. Then, they got around to asking about Caleb and Smitty. Brubacher said he didn't say anything . . . no eyes, no ears, no tongue . . . he told me."

"Three," Erie exclaimed. "They've added one since the last time I saw them."

"I'm positive there were three, although Brubacher's shop is pitch black inside and I kept my back to them."

"Can Brubacher be trusted?" Erie removed the heavy blanket and was about to look back when Bill commanded, "Don't let them see your full face. One of them came to the door as we were leaving. As to whether Brubacher can be trusted,

I think so. He won't talk against the bishop. Smitty is well liked too. He'll spread the word that these fellows are making inquiries and the community will clan up. They won't get cooperation around here. Trouble is," Bill slapped the reins over the horse's back, "I think they've got most of the answers already."

"Should we warn Smitty?"

"I'm sure Smitty and Caleb know by now they're in trouble. We'll get home mid-afternoon and we can tell Smitty then. In the meantime, we're on a picnic. Let's enjoy ourselves. I did notice the car was licensed for Ontario, and Brubacher told me one of the fellows was from Hamilton, if that is of any importance."

One half hour later, after a long pull up a steep hill, Bill reined the horse left along the ridge road then stopped. On Erie's right flat farmland stretched to the horizon. To her left, the river valley carved an artistic arch. Although the valley was deep, its banks sloped gradually to the broad flood plain. They were covered with trees and shrubbery which blazed with the colours of an early autumn.

"You have such a far-away look in your eyes," Bill said. "What are you thinking?"

"I feel as though I am somewhere in time where people live by a special clock and do things in their own peculiar way. Things that I fret about don't mean anything here. Who cares who sits beside whom at dinner . . . if nail polish matches dress . . . if one should arrive by taxi or chauffeur—driven car? I worry about stupid things, not realizing a whole world exists where people don't use nail polish or have chauffeurs. It is as though each mile in this buggy is a mile further back in time." Erie pointed to a cluster of buildings down the road.

"That village is so far removed from the hustle of New York City, it's difficult to believe it shares the same continent."

Bill laughed. "You should go one step further and join me in the northern bush." He slowed the horse. "We'll drive through the village, but the cemetery Anna wanted you to see is over here."

The buggy crossed the road and entered a churchyard. Behind the church, Bill reined in, got out, and tethered the horse to the fence.

"Such a pretty view."

Bill gave Erie his hand at alight. "That is probably why your ancestors wished to be buried here." Taking Erie's hand, he led her along a pathway, through a gate, and into the old graveyard. He took a piece of paper from his pocket, consulted it, then walked toward a small hill.

"I've been taken many unique places on dates, but never to a graveyard," Erie quipped.

"Well, this isn't my first choice of location to court you," replied Bill helping her cross a small rivulet.

"I wouldn't have agreed to come but Anna was adamant I see these graves. She thought I'd have a better understanding of my past if I did." Erie looked around her. The road snaked its way through Glen Allan into the valley where an iron bridge spanned the river. A cluster of farm buildings sat low on the hill on the far side. Cattle grazed the flood plain.

"The valley is beautiful," Erie said. "But I'm not here to marvel at the scenery. Who are we looking for?"

Bill glanced at the paper. "It says vanTattan, Scott." Holding Erie's hand, he walked from stone to stone consulting the paper as he went.

"I've found vanTattan," Erie said bending to read a

weathered marker. "William vanTattan, born Africa 1752, died Maryborough 1845. Suzanna Shingler, wife William vanTattan, born Newark 1789, died Maryborough 1861."

Bill stood before another stone. "And over here, James Scott, born Africa 1758, died Maryborough 1847, Marianna Moses, wife of James Scott, born New York 1762, died Maryborough 1848."

"Look at this one," said Erie tracing the lettering on an old marker with her fingers. "Henry Scott, born Africa 1759."

Bill crossed to a moss-covered briar. "Jonathan vanTattan, born Newark 1810, died Maryborough1872. Daniel vanTattan, born Newark 1824, died Newark 1825. Jessica Erie, wife of Jonathan vanTattan, born Newark 1814, died Maryborough 1886."

"You said Jessica Erie. My grandfather was Moses Erie. She must have been a relative."

Bill nodded agreement. "That's what Anna has written. This lady was your great aunt. She says the vanTattan girls married, and that some relatives still live around here."

"Where is my grandfather buried?" Erie looked around her.

"Not here," Bill said. "I know he's buried in Fergus, in the pauper's cemetery at the Poor House."

"Why at the Poor House, and why in Fergus?"

"I must assume he died in the home. I don't know. Anna or Margaret can probably tell you more."

"What were these people doing in Glen Allan? It is so far removed from a city, and from their own people."

Bill led Erie to a low concrete wall. "I understand your grandfather was related to both the Scotts and vanTattans. He was a servant to a Captain Pierpoint and then a man by the name of Webster, James Webster." Bill swept his hands around to encompass the cemetery and valley. "These people came to Maryborough before 1840. They lived in Newark before they moved to Fergus, then here. When I lived with Smitty I remember an old woman that lived near here. Her name was Granny Unger. She would be related to you too."

"Well, I've certainly found family. But, as Arthur would say, they're from the wrong side of the fence."

"Just imagine," Bill continued, "your ancestors were leading civilized lives in Canada when mine were living in hovels in Ireland. Margaret came over in the 1890's. Anna's family came out from Scotland in the 1860's. Your people were in the Americas by 1760 and were well established in Canada by the 1820's. You have nothing to be ashamed about."

"It doesn't matter how long they've been here. Don't forget they were black, and slaves. Their colour wouldn't endear them to many people, would it? And it's obvious they were poor."

"Does that bother you?"

Erie turned to face Bill. "No, it doesn't. It gives me more incentive to succeed. As for being black, I was never naive enough to think I was Anglo Saxon. I used to wake up, look in my mirror and ask myself, 'Erie Carliss, where did you come from?' I thought I was Spanish, Italian, or Greek. Anna was always helping some poor waif on the street. I believed I was one of her charity cases. When Groves and Anna sprung Moses Erie on me, and they did pull him right out of the woodwork, I was damned angry. During a long drive that day I had lots of time to think. My first reaction was to run away and hide. But what was I running from? It dawned on me that I was not angry because of my colour. I was angry because I hadn't been told sooner. If I'd known early enough, my life wouldn't have become so complicated. I would have chosen my friends more carefully. My association with Arthur would be nothing more than a friendship. And Arthur Moore can thank his lucky stars that I have some good Christian morals about me!"

Erie shook Bill's arm. "Think of the scenarios. I go back to New York a Carliss and tell Arthur the truth. Arthur will immediately spread the word. He'll need a good excuse to leave me. He has bragged to so many people that we're getting married. Anna and I will be blacklisted. Carliss Enterprises will suffer. Or, I go back to New York a Gingerich and tell Arthur the truth . . . same effect except that I need not worry about Carliss Enterprises. I won't be involved, and Ian Oliver will have control. Or, I go back to New York a Carliss, marry Arthur and tell him nothing. I take my chances that our first child is not a throw-back to Moses Erie, and I live in fear that someone will 'find out.' "

"Erie," Bill interrupted. "You are forgetting a most important consideration. Do you really love Arthur Moore?"

Erie released Bill's hand and sat quietly, thinking. *Good question. Do I love Arthur? Or am I fascinated by his business sense? Since July and Bill's stay at Seawind, I'm not so sure.* She spoke again, "The longer I stay away from Arthur, the more I ask myself that question. He's fun to be around, but the more I associate with real people, the less I want to associate with artificial individuals." Erie laughed. "To understand 'artificial individual' you must meet Rivona Gilds, or Roosie."

"Where does Arthur stand?"

"Somewhere in the middle, but he has good qualities. I thought you liked Arthur."

"Not bloody likely," Bill said.

Erie thought of Rivona. *Could she crucify me!* "Do you know what the most popular occupation for people of mixed race is in New York City?" Erie asked Bill.

"I haven't the slightest idea."

"Streetwalker, prostitute. That's where Rivona Gilds would expect me to end up if, and when, she hears the news."

"Again, I ask," Bill persisted, "do you truly love Arthur or is it an infatuation with his style of life?"

"His style of life is mine also. It's a heady world when one has money. There's nothing that can compare with high life in New York City . . . London . . . Paris."

"I sampled it. I didn't like it."

Erie gazed down the valley. "Anna and William gave me the world. Money is no object . . . clothes . . . travel . . . cars. I have the best of everything. Yet, looking over this valley I realize I've missed a lot. I am so used to paying for everything, I didn't realize the best things in the world are free . . . fresh air . . . sincerity . . . honest, caring folk." She glanced at Bill. "Last month it was the Cotton Club, one-thousand-dollar gowns, servants, champagne. This week it's snoopers and rum running, mysterious relatives and an interesting bushman to keep me company."

Bill laughed. "You make it sound as though I'm a wild man who just walked out of the bush."

"Admit it. You did. You remind me so much of William."

"That's not good," Bill said seriously. "I don't wish to be a father figure to you."

"No, not in that way," responded Erie. "You have the same qualities I admired in William."

"He influenced my life a great deal too, Erie. Look, I'm not poor and I'm not illiterate. But I am definitely not an Arthur

Moore. I don't own houses, cars, boats." Bill took Erie's hands again. "I am sincere. I am in love with you."

"I will admit," Erie said, "there's nothing backward about you. Would you marry me a Gingerich or a Carliss?"

It was Bill's turn to think. Where did his allegiances lie? Erie had asked him a pretty tough question. "First, you must know your ancestry doesn't matter to me, and I should tell you I love children."

Bill shuffled his feet in the long grass. "As to your question, you were born to Rachael Gingerich. Jacob loved Rachael, and you are the result of that love. Rachael would want you to be a Gingerich. Had things been different you would be. Legally you are Erie Gingerich. Jacob can claim you as such, but only until your 21st birthday. Yet . . ."

"There is always a 'yet.'"

"Anna Carliss saved your life. She raised you as her child. She gave you everything . . . education . . . wealth . . . and most important, love. She adores you. From the moment you were born you belonged to Anna. Rachael asked that she raise you. You had no other mother. You are Anna's life."

"Wait," interrupted Erie. "I have gone over these arguments one hundred times. A simple question, Bill. Who would you choose to be?"

"Gingerich. I would have to say Gingerich."

"That is interesting."

"What you might not know," Bill said, "Is that I was given a choice once. William asked if I wished to take the Carliss name and the responsibilities associated with it. I said 'no.' I preferred to remain an O'Grady."

"How long ago was this?" asked Erie, startled by the information.

"Five years ago," Bill responded. "You were in Europe at the time with Anna."

"And, shortly after my sixteenth birthday he asked me. He must have asked me after you turned him down."

"It appears that way."

"Had you said yes," Erie pondered, "I wonder where my position with Carliss Enterprises would be today."

"Social butterfly," Bill joked.

"You beast!" Erie slapped Bill's arm. "You don't know how much I detest wasting time at tea parties, bridge games, and social chit-chats."

"Don't think for one moment that Arthur will let you pursue a career," Bill retorted. "If he does marry you, knowing all, he'll insist you stay home. You'll not only turn into a social butterfly, he'll make you into a wallflower too. He will refuse to introduce you to certain people, refuse to take you certain places. His family will ignore you, eventually you'll find he has a floosy on his arm—where you should have been."

"Cad!" Erie swiped at Bill again. "He promised I could carry on with a career."

"Promises are meant to be broken."

"What would you do if I married you?" asked Erie, eyes flashing.

"Well," Bill answered. "I wouldn't put you on a street corner to make money for me. I'd hide you in the bush where no one could see you."

Erie stood and landed a well-aimed kick on Bill's shin, then strode defiantly to the buggy.

"I'm joking," Bill said limping along behind her. "Does this mean lunch is off?" He untied the horse and, with some difficulty, climbed into the buggy.

"Are you going to sit there, or are you going to help me up?"

"I'm a wounded man. Give me your hand and I'll pull you up. If I get out, sure as God made green apples, you'll be up and away with the rig." He reached over and pulled Erie into the buggy.

"If I weren't so hungry," Erie glared at Bill, "I would demand you take me right home."

Bill laughed and backed the horse away from the fence. "Let's find a nice spot to eat Margaret's picnic lunch." He reined the horse left onto the dirt road and down through Glen Allan. "Granny Unger lived over there," he said as they passed a little shack on the left-hand side of the road. Truce? I apologize. I did speak out of line." Bill waited a long time for his answer.

"Truce," Erie finally said.

"Can I tell you something?"

"Go ahead," said Erie sarcastically. "You'd say it anyway."

"If you agreed to marry me," Bill stated, eyes on Erie, "I would be so proud of you that I'd introduce you to everyone, the dustman, the mailman, the milk man, the plumber, my banker, the world. The bush is no place for a woman as beautiful and talented as yourself."

Bill detected a hint of a smile on Erie's face. He changed the subject, feeling he'd given Erie enough food for thought about their relationship. "Let's talk about your Uncle Caleb. He's really tempting fate this time. He's been in trouble before and he's always gotten out of it. Smitty's around to rescue him. This time he's involved Smitty heavily in his scheme and they both might get hurt. The dealers in the bootlegging business are rough players."

"Who says these men are dealers?" Erie said. "We know Caleb is involved with booze, but to what extent? Is it small potatoes? Or a large quantity he's handling? Are these snoopers the law? Are they working for the big bosses out of Buffalo, Detroit? Are they working for Rocco Perri out of Hamilton?"

"Hamilton! Brubacher said one man was from Hamilton," Bill said. "Maybe a coincidence? But you've got a point. Caleb has never really said who they are. He called them 'the snoopers.' Are they working for the federal government? As soon as we get back to the farm we had best find Smitty and Caleb. How do you know Perri is based in Hamilton?"

"Arthur told me."

When Erie and Bill arrived back at Smitty's a dirty, green Essex was parked in the barnyard. Caleb came from the house to help with the rig then promptly disappeared. Smitty was nowhere in sight. Margaret said she had no idea where they had gotten to. She sat on the back porch peeling apples. Bill and Erie joined her and eventually found themselves peeling and slicing too.

Margaret was keeping her mind off the situation by preparing to make apple butter. "You just put them into a big iron pot, put the pot over an open fire, add a little cinnamon, some cider, and maybe a bit of molasses and stir for hours."

"Why don't you buy it at the store?" Erie said.

"I sell it to the store. It gives me my pocket money and my apple butter is the best in the district. Look, Anna's coming up the back lane."

Sure enough, Anna was hurrying along, carrying a bouquet of golden rod. Bill ran to open the gate for her.

"Have you seen Caleb and Smitty?" Erie asked.

"No, I didn't. But you won't believe who I did meet. I must tell you the conversation I had."

Anna sat down, breathless. "Miriam followed me to the old mill foundation. She frightened the daylights out of me."

"She had a nerve!" said Margaret, peeling ferociously.

"No, you misunderstood her all along," explained Anna. "She really is a nice person. She knew nothing of Erie's birth, nothing of the twins' ancestry. It seems Jacob hasn't been honest or open with her."

Anna paused for a breath, colour in her cheeks. "At any rate," she continued. "I told her everything. She is on her way to talk to Jacob whom she hasn't seen since the bush fire. I'm sure he'll get an earful."

"Oh, oh!" Margaret said. "There's nothing like the wrath of an angry woman."

Bill rubbed his shin. "I felt it," he interjected.

All three women looked at him and Erie gave him a dazzling smile.

"So, you've talked out of turn, have you," laughed Margaret." You were a bad one for that when you were a young buck around here."

Anna reached for an apple. "We should see results," she said taking a bite. "Miriam will talk to Jacob. He's already promised Smitty he would see Erie tomorrow. Miriam will make sure he carries through with that promise."

Margaret wielded her knife like a weapon. "Smitty always said I'd formed the wrong opinion of Miriam. I just went by what I saw. She is friendly enough at bees and raisings, but she hasn't stepped foot in my door in nineteen years. When old Abraham Gingerich died, she was downright distant to

Smitty. Of course, Smitty didn't help matters. He lit into Jacob about her. But I suppose if I look around, I would find a few people mad at Smitty."

"I hope they don't find anyone today," Bill said. "You don't want anyone talking about Smitty right now." Bill repeated his conversation with Brubacher. "Erie has some suspicions about these fellows, don't you?"

"I just wondered if they were representing the law, or the dealers."

Margaret said not one word. The pile of peelings grew as she worked.

"Jacob actually said that he would meet me? Did I hear you correctly?" Erie asked.

Anna nodded an affirmative.

"At last!" Erie exclaimed.

"He's a quiet man." Margaret put her knife aside and began cleaning up the peelings. "You'll have to ask most of the questions. Come on, Bill. Help me gather these peelings. You can throw them to the pigs. If you ladies want to rest awhile, we'll eat supper around eight o'clock. There will be only four of us. Smitty and Caleb won't be home."

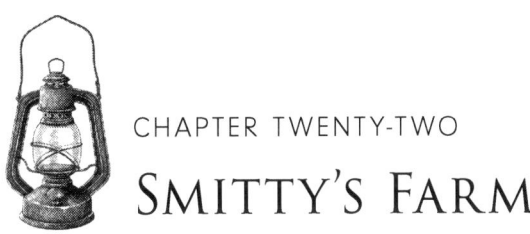

CHAPTER TWENTY-TWO

SMITTY'S FARM

AN OIL LAMP CAST A SOFT GLOW over the small gathering around Margaret's dining room table. Good glasses sparkled in a massive oak china cabinet. The stove, draped for the summer with tasseled velvet, sported a hugh fern. Another fern held a place of honour in a wicker stand before the front window. Large, framed prints of Ireland hung from wire along the picture rail which itself was a repository for knick-knacks. Decorative plates stood side by side along one rail. Smitty's smaller carved wooden objects occupied a second rail. Margaret's collection of salt and pepper shakers and small elephant statuary marched along the remaining two rails. A delicate twig table, covered with an elaborately embroidered cloth and laden with photographs, occupied one corner of the room. An oak bookcase, stuffed with papers and books, stood in another.

The dining room table was covered with white linen cloth and set with Margaret's company dishes. Margaret didn't often have female company. When she did, it was her policy to put her best foot forward. "It was a great meal, Margaret." Bill pushed his chair back from the table. "Good company, good conversation and good-looking young ladies make a man think twice about going back to the bush." He glanced around the table.

"Go away with you." Margaret flushed with pride. "You have inherited your father's Irish blarney."

"Better his blarney, than his vices." Bill laughed.

Anna placed her napkin on the table. "Have you ever thought of asking Smitty to move into town where you could entertain more often?"

"Oh," shrugged Margaret. "He says he's going to build me a house in Drayton one of these days. And we did buy a house in Kitchener once. But I doubt we'll ever move off this farm. This morning he did promise we'd do a little travelling."

Erie entered the conversation. "From what I saw of Kitchener," she said, "it would be a nice place to live."

"Not really," laughed Margaret. "The house Smitty bought is right next to a smelly felt factory."

A felt factory, thought Erie. *I wonder if there are two felt factories in Kitchener or if Margaret and I are thinking of the same building.*

Anna was speaking, wondering about the children Margaret had taken in after their guardian in Fergus died. There was no way the children were going to end up in the Poor House. "Tell me again about Laura and Isobel. They write so seldom."

"Laura is in Saskatchewan with her husband and four children. They had a bumper crop this year. I heard from them three weeks ago. I'll let you read the letter. Isobel is living in Montreal. She just married again. Her first husband died in the war, in France." Margaret glanced at the photographs on the table. "Bill, hand me Sarah and Jennifer's pictures."

Bill retrieved the photographs.

Margaret looked lovingly at both. "Sarah," she said quietly, "died at age six. Jennifer," she turned the second picture around so Erie could see it.

"Such a tragedy!" Anna said. "You wouldn't remember Jennifer, Erie. She lived with William and I for a while. She trained in Rochester, New York and spent two years in England as a private nurse. She met a young man from Fergus in England. They decided to travel home together. They were both lost on the Titanic."

"Such a lovely girl too," Bill added.

"These are the children you raised?"

Margaret nodded. "Between Anna and I," she said. "We took care of them after Mercedes died. Anna took Jennifer and Bill. I took the rest. Actually, the children didn't all belong to Mercedes. She took them in and raised them. Some belonged to her sister."

"Some just arrived," Bill added, "like me."

"I knew part of the story," Erie said. "Bill told me Mercedes was a prostitute. Odd, I know more about Mercedes life than I do Anna's. I know very little about you . . . Mother, and you raised me."

The significance of Erie calling her *Mother* was not lost on Anna. "I'll tell you someday," she said.

Margaret quickly interrupted. "It's unfortunate Caleb and Smitty couldn't join us for supper. They are . . . busy. They wouldn't enjoy this anyway. Smitty would get his fingers in the cups. Caleb would drink from the finger bowls . . ."

Erie laughed heartily. "Caleb is more refined than that."

"That he is," stated Margaret. "But he forgets once in a while and does things for effect. He always comes back to Maryborough in the autumn. It was born into him. He can't leave the country like he left the faith. He comes to help with the harvest. He's as strong as an ox. He does the work of three men."

"So does Smitty."

"That he does," Margaret agreed.

Erie excused herself. She'd been sitting at the table for three hours. Margaret seemed loathe to have them leave. "I'll be right back. The lilac bushes are calling." She let herself out the back door and picked her way through the wet grass to the "thunder hole." Coming out minutes later, she noted the brightness of the moon reflecting in the windshield of the Essex. Erie glanced round the farmyard. On the opposite side of the house to the barn, the orchard stood out against the blue-black sky. *Lovely . . . just a minute . . .* Erie concentrated on the road at the far side of the orchard. She glanced back at the Essex and again at the road. Sneaking across the vegetable garden and alongside the fence, she crouched down and walked as far as she dared. She peeked over the fence and sneaked another several yards. The dog barked in the barn. "It's them!"

The moon reflecting in the windows of the Ford gave Erie a good view of two men in the car. They were parked so that the car couldn't been seen from the house. *Where's the third man?* Erie moved a little closer to the road. *He's hiding in the ditch!*

Erie sneaked back along the fence, keeping low. It helped that the dog barked furiously from his confinement. She was positive she sounded like an elephant in dry bush. She ran across the vegetable garden as soon as she knew she was out of sight of the car, burst in the back door, and ran through to the dining room. She came up short, face to face with Adam Gingerich. She didn't know who was the most surprised.

"What is the matter?" Bill leapt to his feet followed by Margaret and Anna. Adam stood his ground.

"The Ford," said a breathless Erie, "is parked on the road by the orchard."

"No!" Margaret sat down.

Anna sat down quickly too.

Bill was at Erie's side. "May I introduce Adam Gingerich," he said. Adam holding his hat in his left hand, extended his right cautiously.

"Adam, Miss Carliss."

Bill, in making the introduction, alerted Erie to the fact that Adam definitely didn't know they were related.

"Sit down, all of you." Margaret indicated everyone should sit. Erie and Bill did so. Adam remained standing by the door.

"You are sure the car is at the road?" Bill said.

"Yes," Erie replied. "I counted two men in the car and one hiding in the ditch."

"Well, that's that." Margaret threw her hands in the air. "It was bound to happen."

"What was bound to happen?" asked Bill.

"Smitty and Caleb are going to get themselves caught."

Adam moved closer to the table.

"How so?" Anna asked. "Caleb and Patrick are not here."

"They're at the . . ." Margaret hesitated. "They're moving the still."

"Creeps!" exclaimed Bill.

"And they are bringing it through the farmyard."

"Can we warn them?" Anna asked. "They can go out through the Gingerich Farm."

"Risky," Bill said. "That exit might be covered too. And if they are caught on Gingerich land, that implicates Jacob. Smitty wouldn't want that to happen."

Nobody spoke. Nobody moved. The hall clock struck eleven.

"The rabbit," Adam spoke softly, "does not run into the mouth of the fox. He will let the mouse go first. Can't we go first?"

Everyone looked at Adam as though they were seeing him in the room for the first time.

"From the mouths of babes," said Margaret.

"You had better translate for me. I didn't follow the remark," Anna said.

"We send a decoy!" exclaimed Erie. "We lead them away from the farm."

"The Essex." Bill hit the table with his hand. "We take it out."

"What happens if they don't follow?" Anna asked. "There are only two in the car. Will the third man leave too?"

"Big problems when they catch up," said Bill. "And they would certainly leave one behind."

"No problem if a woman's driving," Erie said. "They won't hurt a woman, especially if she says she is only taking a Mennonite friend for a joy-ride . . . at night so no one can see him. And don't underestimate the speed of that Essex!"

"Too dangerous," Bill dismissed Erie's suggestion.

"To whom?" Erie retorted. "I can drive like the devil."

"She can," said Anna. "I've driven with her. She can turn one's knuckles white."

"Mother! What a vote of confidence."

"I'll drive," stated Bill.

"I'll drive," Erie countered.

"Hold it!" Margaret gave both an odd look. "Sibling rivalry at your ages."

"Lover's quarrel," Bill smiled.

"I will ride," Adam said, coming closer to the table. "I cannot drive."

Everyone laughed, breaking the tension in the room.

"Good boy," Margaret stated. "Erie. You drive the Essex. They'll believe your story. There's nothing in the car that will incriminate you."

"When she gets caught?" said Bill.

"As Erie said, don't underestimate the Essex," Margaret cautioned. "It's a fast car. It has been modified."

Margaret turned to look at Bill. "If the ruse works Bill, you go to Smitty immediately. Give them a hand. Get them out of the area quickly. Warn them about the fellow in the ditch. Anna, you and I will go about our business as though nothing is amiss. We'll do the dishes and keep the lamp burning in the dining room."

"The moon's up," said Erie. "They're not going to follow a girl who gets into a car. We have to make this look good."

"Clothes," Bill said. "A change of clothes and some odd activity in the yard."

"There are some work clothes in the back hall." Margaret left and returned with an armful of work clothes. "Come into the hall to change in case they're watching the window."

Erie emerged dressed in coveralls and rough shirt, her hair hidden under a cap.

Adam stood by patiently.

"The plan," Erie said, "is that Adam and I will walk to the car. I'll back it up to the stable door. We'll both get out and go into the stable. We'll carry a few things to the car, get in, keep the lights off, pull onto the road, and away we go."

"Don't let the dog out," Margaret cautioned. "He'll go after the fellow in the ditch and the men will know they've been seen."

"What if their car stays behind?" asked Anna.

"They'd be fools if they did," said Bill "But if they do, I'll go warn Smitty anyway and we'll prepare to fight our way out—three on three."

"Don't let it come to that. It's not good to get Caleb and Smitty involved in a fight."

Margaret disappeared into the kitchen and returned with a key. "You'll need this. You won't have any problems with the car. It works beautifully."

"Are you ready, Adam?"

"Yes," Adam placed his cap on his head.

"Well, let's go."

Anna hugged Erie. "Please, be careful. You don't know the roads."

Erie kissed Anna on the cheek. "Don't worry," she said. "Adam does."

"Take care, child." Margaret said, squeezing Erie to her.

"I will."

Bill stood in line. "I'll go," he said. "The roads will be safer and so will you."

"Just give me a hug," Erie laughed. "Don't let Smitty or Caleb do anything rash. Come on, Adam."

Adam obediently followed Erie out the back door. They crossed to the Essex. Erie climbed in and slammed her door.

She looked around for Adam and heard tapping on the window.

"I cannot get in," he said. "I do not know how to open the door."

"Oh fun," Erie muttered reaching to open his door. She pushed the starter and the engine turned over nicely. "Sounds good," she said. Putting the car in reverse, she backed to the stable door. At the sound of the engine starting up, the dog barked furiously.

"Adam. When I stop we'll get out. We have to get into the stable without letting the dog out. When we're inside we'll tie him up and load a few things into the car. We have to make it look like we're taking something away from the barn."

Adam nodded. "The dog obeys me," he said. "I'll go first and tie him up."

Erie stopped the car, showed Adam how to get out and they both exited the vehicle. While Adam sneaked into the barn and tied the dog, Erie opened the trunk. She looked through to the front seat. She hadn't noticed before there was no back seat. "Where . . . ?" Suddenly the truth dawned on her. "A rum-runner!" she exclaimed. "This car is a runner."

Ten minutes later, with an assortment of feed bags, buckets, tools, and Mildred's milk stool in the car, Erie eased the engine into gear and drove down the laneway. She didn't look back, but she knew there were three faces at the dark parlour window. She hesitated at the end of the lane so the men in the Ford could see the car fully. She turned right onto the gravel road and shifted gears.

"Watch the other car," she ordered Adam. "Let me know if it's following us."

"It's coming," Adam said, his body turned to look out the

back window. "I can see it. It has passed the gate. It's moving faster."

"Good," Erie gave the car a little gas. It responded nicely.

"It is coming faster." Adam warned.

Erie geared up and pushed the gas pedal. The car shot forward. "Modified," she laughed. "This car can fly!" She pushed the pedal again and geared up once more. The chase was on! Who was chasing her, Erie didn't know. But, they would have quite a ride on their hands if they stuck with the Essex.

"Right . . . right," Adam shouted. "There is no more road. Right!"

Erie made the turn . . . barely.

"Give me more warning, Adam."

"I have not been this road yet," Adam shouted as he clung to the door.

"Great!" Erie muttered. "Flying blind!"

Twenty minutes after the cars left, Smitty, Caleb, and Bill brought the wagon through the farmyard and turned left onto the road.

"Watch the ditch," Caleb hissed. "Both sides of the road." He chucked to the horses, working the reins.

"There!" Smitty whispered. "To the left, in the ditch."

Caleb slapped the reins hard on the backs of the greys and ducked behind the still's copper boiler.

"Down, keep down."

Smitty and Bill were already lying flat on the wagon, hanging on for dear life. There was a dull thud on the front board.

"He plays for keeps!"

"He is running after the wagon," Smitty said. "The darn fool. He can't outrun a team of horses."

"Well, he'll have a long run," Caleb replied. "And he can't aim well when he's running. You alright Bill?"

"Why do I get myself into these messes? It is so peaceful in the bush. Bears don't shoot."

Down over the bridge the greys ran and up the other side. Caleb stood up as best he could on the swaying wagon. Bill and Smitty stayed down.

"One hundred yards is his best," Smitty observed. "He's way back there somewhere."

Across the main road and back on the concession line, Caleb reined the greys to a slow trot, then turned right. Smitty jumped from the wagon and opened a gate letting the team through. He closed the gate and jumped on again.

"We'll drop this still in the well. That won't take too long. Bill and I will walk back to the farm. We'll be back there about three o'clock. Caleb, you take the team down to the bridge construction above Fergus. Exchange the greys for one of Charlie's older teams. Leave the wagon. Bring back the oldest wagon Charlie has. Make sure it doesn't have a bullet hole in it." Smitty chuckled. "If you drive out the back forty, you should make it down there, exchange the horses and be back here before six in the morning."

"If the fellow shot at us," asked Bill, "I wonder if they'll be trigger happy with Erie and Adam."

"Nah," said Caleb. "This snooper's an import. We must be causing some big waves, Smitty. It's time we shipped everything out."

CHAPTER TWENTY-THREE

HOMECOMING

AN EARLY MORNING SHOWER dampened everything. Water dripped from the eaves of Smitty's front porch. Cobwebs hung like jeweled nets from the trumpet vine. Because of the mist, it was difficult to see any distance.

"A Scotsman's mist wets an Irishman to the bone," said Smitty, pacing the length of the porch . . . back and forth . . . back and forth, passing Bill pacing in the opposite direction. "Where is she?"

"Sit down, both of you. You are making Anna and I nervous." Margaret's hands were busy darning, but her eyes were on the laneway.

Caleb lounged against a porch support. "I wonder how far she got before she was stopped?"

"Don't know," Smitty muttered. "When do you figure we'll have a visit?"

Caleb looked at his pocket watch. "Before noon. Let's hope Erie and Adam get back before then. Is everything fixed?"

"The still's down the well. The team of greys are at the

bridge site. Charlie took the wagon on down to Fergus. His boys will switch the boards. They'll burn the one that has the bullet hole in it. His team is grazing in our pasture with Mildred. His wagon is by the barn. There's nothing amiss."

"Except Erie," said Bill peering into the mist.

"And Adam," added Margaret.

"Jacob isn't going to be pleased we kidnapped Adam." Caleb laughed and the sound seemed to echo down the lane, returning with a feminine quality to it.

"Erie?" Smitty called into the mist. "Is that you? Adam?"

Two figures appeared.

"Erie!" Bill leaped over the railing and ran across the lawn.

Erie and Adam looked up, startled. Adam held a large piece of paper. Bill grabbed Erie and swung her off her feet. "Are you alright? They look okay," Bill shouted.

"Stop yelling," Margaret commanded. "The neighbourhood will hear you."

The three walked to the veranda, Bill with an arm around each.

"Where is my car?" Smitty asked.

"Your car? The first thing you think about is your car?"

"I asked if you were alright first," Smitty said.

"We are just fine, aren't we Adam."

Adam grinned. "Erie Carliss and I had an exciting time. Such a car for such a ride!"

"Exactly where is my car?" Smitty asked again.

"It's in a field up there somewhere." Erie waved her hand in a northwesterly direction. "We ran it out of gas and off the road. If you're going to run liquor, Patrick Smith, you keep a full tank of gas—maybe an extra tank wouldn't hurt. Shame." Erie laughed at the look on Smitty's face. "Here," she pulled a piece of paper from her coveralls. "This is the man's name. He says you can have your car for a bottle. You might offer to repair his fence too."

"Great heavens!" Smitty said glancing at the paper. "She parked in Tommy Johnstone's hayfield on the other side of Blyth."

"You ran it over a fence?" asked Caleb.

"Not over," said Adam. "We went through the fence. There is just a little damage."

"We didn't have time to find a gate," said Erie dryly. "Oh, am I hungry!" She sat down on the top step. Adam joined her. "Adam, show them what is hanging all over the countryside."

Adam gave Caleb a grimy sheet of paper.

"Well, look at this . . . a wanted poster . . . 'information leading to the arrest of those involved in the manufacture of illegal spirits, a fifty-dollar reward.'"

"Who's behind it?" Smitty asked? "It can't be the Government. They're too involved in the sale of the stuff."

"Women's Temperance League of Perth County," Caleb read from the poster. "It wouldn't be the authorities. They're making too much off the bootlegging business. They wouldn't put out a reward for anyone. They'd have to arrest half the Cabinet."

"Then who was the fellow that shot at you last night?" questioned Margaret.

"Maybe he was the law," Caleb said. "We might meet him today. All the activity last night will bring company before noon."

"And who were the goons that chased me?"

"Dunno," Smitty answered quickly, glancing at Caleb. "Haven't got a clue."

"Maybe some big shot from the sleazy side of the tracks?" Erie asked.

"Dunno," Smitty said being deliberately evasive. "Margaret, make these young people something to eat. Tell us how you got to Blyth?"

"Don't say a word until I get back." Margaret disappeared and returned shortly with a tray laden with bread, butter, jam, cheese, apple pie, and tall glasses of milk.

"Erie, are you really alright?" Anna asked.

"Except for being very tired, I'm fine, Mother." Erie smiled at Anna. She made sure that she'd emphasized the word *Mother*.

"What happened after you left?" Caleb sat beside Adam on the step.

"You must congratulate your mechanic. That Essex is a flying machine. The Ford was good, but the Essex always had the edge, until we ran out of gas."

"They caught you."

"They did not catch us." Adam chuckled. "We caught them."

"Begin at the beginning, please," said Caleb.

Anna buttered bread, spread it with jam, and gave Erie and Adam each a piece.

"Butter one for me too," said Smitty. "I need some fortification. Anxiety makes a man hungry."

"We left the farm," Erie ravenously ate her bread, "and drove up the line then turned abruptly right. At the next road over, turned left again. Two roads up . . . left . . . two up left . . . then right. Adam got pretty good at scouting the corners. He learned to give me plenty of warning. We nearly lost your car only once. Two deer bounded right in front of us. I slammed on the brakes and skidded right. The snoopers kept right on coming. They couldn't see the deer. We just missed the animals and the snoopers were within twenty-five feet of us. Adam was ready to get out at that point. I nearly had to pry his fingers off the door when we finally hit the haystack."

"You hit a haystack."

"Be thankful we did," Erie said, "or we wouldn't have had anything to hide the car in. Johnstone helped us with that chore this morning. After the deer, I just put the pedal to the floor and we tore along. These snoopers didn't want to catch us as much as follow us, I think. When I realized that, I really concentrated on driving. That is when the Essex proved itself. I held it at a steady speed and then . . . sputter . . . sputter . . . We looked for a place to park. I didn't have much choice in the end. We coasted down a hill, into Johnstone's laneway. When I saw the culvert, I turned sharp left. I didn't expect a fence. But we sailed right through and into a soft pile of hay."

"Ja, it was hay," Adam said. "Smack the car went, right into the stack."

"I shut the car off and we sat. The Ford came over the hill and went right on past. Adam and I raced for the fence. Adam scuffled our tracks and we pulled the wire together. Johnstone just rolls it back and forth to get in and out of his field, so it wasn't attached permanently. We didn't damage the car much. We heard the Ford coming back and laid down by the fence in the high grass. It passed. We finished doing the fence and went back to the car. Adam threw armfuls of hay over the back end. The next time the Ford came through, it had its lights on. We were away from the car, behind another stack . . . ready to run. The Ford slowed down and looked hard at Johnstone's lane, but it didn't stop. It didn't come back, so we climbed into the car and slept. Johnstone found us early this morning."

"His dog found us," Adam said.

"We explained we were joy-riding. But he laughed and helped us hide the car. He gave us the note, hailed a friend heading for Milverton with milk, and we were on our way home. We got some interesting questions, but Adam had an answer for all of them."

"I quoted proverbs," Adam said, "to everyone that did not speak our language. We rode in the back of a truck, yet. But four miles back, he put us out. Amby Martin gave us a ride here."

"He was very nice," Erie said, handing Adam a glass of milk. "He asked if my family came from here. Or if I had relatives living here." She looked at Anna as she spoke. "Of course, I said no."

"Old Man Martin's son," said Caleb, "the Coffin maker."

"He did ask if we were related." Adam looked at Caleb. "I answered I was not because Miss Carliss came from New York City to visit with Mr. Smith. He did ask peculiar questions."

"Amby Martin let us off at your gate," Erie said yawning. "I told him I'd given Adam a joy-ride and we had a little accident."

"I must go home now." Adam stood. "Fahdah will be angry with me."

"Do you want me to go with you?" asked Caleb.

"I will go myself." Adam answered.

"Tell him you were with Miss Carliss," said Anna, feeling sorry for Adam. "He might be a little less harsh with you."

"I will tell him I was helping Patrick," Adam answered quietly. "He will throw his hands in the air and walk away."

Smitty laughed. "I can't be that bad. Thank you, Adam. I appreciate what you did for me." He shook Adam's hand.

Caleb placed his arm around Adam's shoulders. "Good fellow," he said.

Bill shook his hand warmly. "Thank you for accompanying Miss Carliss. I felt very assured with you in the car."

"Erie said we would do it again." Adam laughed. "She has invited me to travel to see her. She said someday we will drive again and perhaps fly up in the sky too."

Erie stood and impulsively hugged Adam, who was startled then pleased at the gesture. He hugged back. "I will come see you before I leave Lilac Hill," she said, then stepped away from Adam.

"Don't forget Fahdah will visit you today at Lilac Hill at two o'clock. That was the message I brought last night."

"I wouldn't miss that meeting for the world," Erie said.

Adam pulled his hat from his pocket and stepped off the porch. He paused briefly at the back gate to wave.

"Brave young man," said Caleb. "I wouldn't want to face Jacob."

"He's my brother!" Erie said. "I didn't tell him. Caleb, please give him direction. Don't let him do anything rash. He is such a fine young man, so gentle. He idolizes you. Remember the mistakes you've made. Don't let him repeat them, please."

"I'm a fine role model," Caleb said.

"Come on." Anna went to Erie. "Margaret and I are going to put you to bed, you poor dear." They each took an arm and lead Erie inside.

Smitty sat on the steps. Caleb and Bill joined him.

"That woman has guts!" Smitty exclaimed.

"That woman is suspicious," Caleb countered.

"That woman is beautiful!" said Bill. "I'm surprised she didn't let the snoopers catch her and ask them questions. You want a piece of pie? There's some left."

"Oh, oh, here they come." Caleb was on his feet looking down the lane.

"Margaret," Smitty called.

Two men in a buggy appeared out of the mist.

"I should've made bets," Caleb observed, consulting his watch. "It is eleven thirty-five."

With his foot, Smitty pushed the tray back on the veranda where it might not be seen. "Margaret!"

Margaret appeared in the doorway and, surveying the situation, quickly removed the tray.

"Act natural," Smitty cautioned. He stepped off the porch to greet the men. "Constable, good day."

The constable tipped his hat and introduced Mr. Richardson, Government Agent.

Richardson extended his hand. Smitty shook it firmly, noticing it was calloused and dirty, not a government hand. "Constable, you know Caleb Gingerich, brother of Bishop Gingerich."

Caleb shook hands with both the constable and Richardson.

"Bill O'Grady down for a visit from New Liskeard."

Bill shook hands with both.

Formalities over, Smitty asked the questions. "Are you just passing through?"

"I'm here on business," the constable replied. "Richardson claims you have a still. He wants to make a search of your property. As you know when I have a request such as this, I have to comply. Here are the appropriate papers."

Smitty accepted some legal looking documents, glanced quickly at them then said, "Go ahead. Feel free to look anywhere. But, before you do, answer me one question, Richardson. Are you the fellow that shot at Caleb last night?"

"Shot?" the constable exclaimed.

"Shot," Smitty repeated. "Caleb was taking my team and some farm equipment down to Yatton, and some darn fool shot at him. Fortunately, it missed by a mile. He heard it whine past the wagon."

"I heard it hit the wagon," Richardson said. "This pair of beggars had a team of greys and a still on the wagon. I saw it."

"You carry a gun?" the constable asked Richardson.

"I do."

"Well, don't use it around here," the constable snapped. "There's no need. I don't want innocent citizens getting killed."

"I'm dealing with criminals." Richardson gave all four men an icy stare.

"Look," the constable advised. "Clean up the King Government before you come shooting around here. They're taking money and goods right and left and turning a blind eye to prohibition. Don't come out here causing problems. This King graft business has been in all the papers."

"I don't know any King," said Robertson. "Let's take a look, shall we?" Richardson stepped from the wagon. The constable followed. Caleb tethered the horse to a gate post.

"If you don't mind," said Smitty, "we'll just sit on the front porch until you're finished."

"Can we get to Bishop Gingerich's bush from here?" Richardson asked.

"Difficult," Smitty answered. "There was a washout at the gully crossway back in July. No one had time to fill it in."

Smitty, Caleb, and Bill retired to the porch. The constable and Richardson headed for the barn. "Wait until they open the door," Smitty chuckled. "The dog hates strangers and he's loose in the barn now." His remark was followed by fierce barking and hollering.

"Call off the dog, Patrick."

Smitty whistled and the dog raced to the porch where it lay down beside him.

"Creating a washout was brilliant if I do say so," Caleb said. "It took most of the morning, but it looks like it happened a month ago . . . even to grass hanging from the side. After Richardson sees it, he will realize a team and wagon couldn't get through."

"I figured we were found out," Smitty said, "when Adam and Erie came to the barn. We were right above them. The still was there most of the afternoon. Boy, it was hard sitting in that barn, knowing they were having a good meal at the house."

"The constable won't be difficult," observed Caleb. "But can you believe the other one? King, be damned. He didn't know King was Prime Minister of Canada."

"He doesn't work for the government and he isn't Canadian."

"I'm constantly amazed," exclaimed Bill, "at what you pair know."

"You have to understand that half the Province is turning a blind eye to bootlegging. Every red-blooded man is involved. The government doesn't care. They're in it too. The

Prime Minister, King, has been advised over and over again about the corrupt government he's running, but he doesn't listen. Mark my word. He'll be forced to act soon." Smitty stroked the mongrel's head.

One half hour later Sherriff and Richardson returned.

"Can we offer you some coffee?" asked Margaret.

Both men declined. Richardson looked perplexed.

"Richardson says you were driving a team of greys."

"My team is in the pasture with Mildred, the milk cow. They were brown the last time I looked at them."

"Is that your wagon?" Richardson asked.

"Yep," Smitty replied.

"Bad washout," the constable said. "You'll have to call a bee to repair that before winter."

"A lot of work," said Caleb. "It will be a lot of work."

"Where did you deliver the equipment?" Richardson asked.

"Yatton," replied Caleb. "There's an auction down there this morning. Caleb consulted his timepiece. "Lunchtime," he stated. "There was a sale in aid of Farmer Wilkes you know . . . the fellow that was burned out. Everyone donated something. They just dumped it off in the past couple of days. Money goes to Wilkes."

"Any more questions, Richardson?" The constable was anxious to get away. Richardson shook his head. "In that case, we'll be going." The constable tipped his hat. "Sorry to have bothered you fellows."

"Nice meeting you, Richardson." Smitty extended his hand. Richardson reached for it. The dog growled. Richardson tipped his hat instead. "You won't get away with it," he said looking from Smitty to Caleb to Bill.

Caleb clenched his fists.

"Have a nice day, gentlemen." Margaret stepped out where she could be seen and stood beside Caleb, her hand on his arm.

The constable tipped his hat to Margaret and climbed into his buggy.

"I don't like it," said Caleb. "A fool like that carrying a gun."

"Well, you're both getting out of the business now," stated Margaret. "And it's none too soon. Fifty dollars is a lot of money. Fifty dollars is a fortune when eggs are only fetching ten cents a dozen. Someone's going to turn you in."

"Clever way to catch a criminal," observed Caleb. "Have their wife or child rat on them. That poster explains why rumours are flying around about us."

"This temperance movement is all hell-fire and brimstone," muttered Smitty. "It fires women up to save the world from the ravages of drink. But they can't save the world from the ravages of war. Most of the fellows dependent on drink are the men who fought in the Great War. They are only drowning their memories."

"Just finish this job quickly," said Margaret.

Erie slept through everything. Her last thoughts were about her father whom she would meet at two o'clock.

CHAPTER TWENTY-FOUR

The Gingerich Farm

A THUNDEROUS ROAR WOKE ERIE. Lightning flashed again and again as thunder rolled across the sky. Lace curtains billowed with the violence of the wind. Someone rose and closed the window.

That's right. This is Margaret's bedroom. She missed two o'clock. What was she to do at two? Meet her father. It's pouring rain. It must be night it is so dark out. Two o'clock.

Another flash of lightning crackled through the air, followed by a thunderous roar of thunder. The ground shook. Erie sat up in bed, terrified.

"It is just a storm. It will be over soon." The voice belonged to Anna who sat by the side of the bed. "I didn't forget," said Anna soothingly, "that you don't like thunderstorms. I've been here since it began."

"What time is it?" Erie pushed her hair out of her eyes.

"It's one-thirty."

"I'm not late then."

"No, you'll be on time. I ran to Lilac Hill and brought a dress for you. Margaret's ironing it. Come, get up. I'll do your hair. You must look good for your father."

Erie sat on the edge of the bed, reluctant now she was awake to take the initial steps to ready herself for the meeting.

Thunder rolled down the valley.

"You can't postpone it. Sit before the mirror. We don't have much time. The worse of the storm is over."

Erie, wearing one of Margaret's voluptuous white cotton nightgowns, obeyed. Anna left the room and Erie heard her call to Margaret to bring hot water and a lamp. It was, Erie conceded, very dark in the room.

A particularly vicious bolt of lightning sizzled through the atmosphere, hit close by, and shook the house. Thunder rattled the windows. Erie jumped and screamed.

"That was a little too close to be comfortable with," said Anna coming into the room again. She crossed to the window. "Patrick and Caleb are heading for the barn. Perhaps it hit one of the rods."

Anna found a hairbrush on the dresser and drew it through Erie's thick, black hair. "Shall I put it up? Or shall I pin it at your neck. Or do you wish it braided?" She made fixing hair seem like the most natural thing to do during a vicious storm.

"Whatever you think best, Mother."

"At the nape of your neck," said Anna. "Your mother always wore her hair up. It's best you keep yours down when you meet Jacob."

Margaret arrived, dress in hand. Bill followed behind with lamp and pitcher of water.

"Was the barn hit, Margaret?"

"I don't think so. The men went to check. But something close-by was struck. I could smell sulphur in the air."

"Smitty and Caleb left the baby behind." Erie smiled. "He's protecting the women," Margaret laughed. "Bill, go downstairs and leave us women be." She poured hot water into a flowered ceramic basin, handed Erie a fragrant soap, and stood by with towel on her arm.

Erie washed quickly. "The rest will have to wait," she declared, drying herself. "I miss my bath the most. How can you stand it, Margaret?"

"It isn't hard," Margaret replied. "In the summer I bathe at the river. I even own a bathing costume. In the winter, we bring a horse trough into the kitchen. It becomes a permanent fixture from November to April. We fill it up with hot water and have a merry splash. We put canning kettles on the stove to heat enough water for it."

"Do you ever dream about hot running water?"

"There's no sense in dreaming about something you can't have; although I'll appreciate the convenience when I finally get it."

Erie sat patiently as Anna did her hair. She then stepped out of Margaret's nightgown and into underpinnings and the pretty cotton dress Anna chose for her. "If the rain doesn't let up, Jacob'll be late for his date. Who is that?"

Margaret went to the window and threw it open. "It's Miriam. What . . . ? " She listened then shouted, "Go! Patrick and Caleb are at the barn. We're coming!"

"What's wrong?"

"Jacob's barn is burning. It was struck by lightning. We have to help." Abandoning the bedroom, all three women ran downstairs. Bill was already in the yard. Smitty burst through the back door and reached for his heavy boots.

"We've got shovels, buckets and rakes," he shouted. "We'll run through the valley. You bring whatever you need. Bill is hitching the horse. Come round by the concession road as fast as you can."

"Where's Miriam?"

"Caleb's bringing her to the house."

Smitty disappeared out the back door as Caleb came in the front, supporting Miriam.

"Margaret . . . Anna!" he called. "Take care of Miriam. She was in the barn. She's badly hurt."

Anna went to Miriam, put an arm around her shoulders and helped her to a chair. Sitting by her, Anna reached for her hand. Miriam, vacant eyed, pulled it away.

Bill, who had come through the door with Caleb, was pressed into service.

"Put these in the laundry baskets, over there." Margaret emptied her cupboards of salve, lard, baking soda, baked goods, butter, coffee. "Take the baskets to the buggy."

"Margaret," Anna called. "Look at Miriam's hands and arms."

"Burned," said Margaret, assessing the situation quickly.

"She was untying the horses," Bill filled in the details. "A ball of lightning ran along the stanchions and burned her."

"She's in shock, poor dear," declared Margaret. Miriam was oblivious to all the attention she was getting.

"Bill, help Anna put her in the spare bedroom upstairs. Anna," Margaret sorted through her medicine chest, "put this on her hands and arms. Don't rub it in. Cover the burns lightly with cheesecloth. It's in the dining room cupboard.

Sit with her. Keep her comfortable. If I'm not back in three hours, change the dressing. I'll send someone to fetch the doctor from Drayton. Let her sip water, but only if she asks. Don't let her out of bed."

"Can you manage?" Erie asked Anna.

"I will be perfectly alright. Go with Margaret."

"Bill," Margaret was in command. "After you've put Miriam upstairs, run through the valley. I'll handle the horse and buggy. We'll get there as fast as we can."

By the time Margaret finished packing supplies, Bill was out the door. Margaret drew a sweater over her shoulders, threw one at Erie, and they hurried to the wagon. Thick black smoke filled the valley. The rain had ceased, but a fresh wind blew from the west.

"Climb in," said Margaret. "I'm much better at driving a horse than a car." She let the horse canter down the lane, but on the concession road she whipped him into full gallop. As they neared Jacob Gingerich's farm they joined a steady stream of horses and wagons coming from all directions.

The fire burned so hot the horses had to be tied way down the lane. Hungry tongues of fire leapt to the sky, flamed by the wind. Men ran in the direction of the barn. Women ran to the house, carrying bundles under their arms. Margaret entered Miriam's kitchen, a laundry basket in her hands, and surveyed the situation. Oume Salome sat in one corner keeping everyone at bay with her babbling. Adam and Abraham weren't in sight, obviously at the barn.

"Miriam id doh?" asked one of the women.

"Miriam is Vay gahdoo," answered Margaret.

Erie arrived with the last of the laundry baskets.

Handing salve and lard to a Mennonite woman, Margaret

gave instructions in Deutsch for its use. Several women hurried out.

"That's for the men in case there are burns," Margaret explained to Erie. Turning to the women in the kitchen, she began giving orders, "Brohd, boodah, kays, shmoh-gah dah." She began cleaning the kitchen table.

Apparently, Margaret Smith has the respect and attention of these women, thought Erie. She moved around Miriam's kitchen in charge of everything. The women listened and obeyed her. Of course, there's no other woman in the house, except Miriam, who would normally be in charge.

"Rachael . . . Rachael," Ouma Salome set up a wailing in her corner. She tried to get out of her chair.

Activity stopped. All eyes were on Erie.

"Go to her," said Margaret in a whisper. "Sit with her."

Erie walked hesitantly toward the old woman, whose arms were outstretched, waiting to envelope her. "Grandma," she murmured feeling trapped . . . frightened. She looked back to Margaret for encouragement. Margaret nodded and broke the silence in the room by saying, "See huhd hawah off dee tsoong—Grandma has hair on her tongue."

The women giggled and went back to work.

As Erie approached Salome, the wailing ceased. Watery eyes followed her steps. Arms were still extended. Erie stood before Ouma Salome, then sat down on the floor beside her. She reached for her grandmother's hands.

"Rachael," Salome said softly. She managed to free a hand and she stroked Erie's hair.

"Rachael," said Erie holding a boney, arthritic hand, "is here for you."

Tears ran down a weathered, wrinkled face. The hand

moved from Erie's hair to touch her cheek, her eyes, her nose, her lips. The fingers were gentle, caressing.

Erie didn't move, nor did she relax her grip on Ouma's hand. Above the noise in the room, the crackling of the fire and shouting of the men could be heard.

Ouma muttered in Deutsche. Erie didn't understand, but looked up and smiled. The hand again moved to caress Erie's hair. Eventually the hand ceased its caressing and rested in Ouma's apron-clad lap. In the chaos of Miriam's kitchen, Ouma Gingerich slept.

Erie gently removed her hand and went to look for a blanket to cover her grandmother. Not seeing anything suitable in the kitchen, she stepped into the back hall, nearly colliding with a young girl coming from a storage room.

"A blanket?"

The girl pointed toward a door.

Opening the door, Erie stepped into an area which resembled both a kitchen and a sitting room. Beyond the cookstove a door led to a second smaller room, a bedroom. Erie entered it. Returning to the main room with a quilt, Erie was puzzled. She noticed steps leading to a second floor. Compulsively, she looked up, then ascended. She opened a door and stepped into a storage area full of trunks, boxes, ropes of onions and bundles of drying herbs.

I shouldn't be here, she admonished herself. *On the other hand, I was born in this house. I am a daughter of this house.* Boldly now she walked across the room, opened a second door, and found herself in the upper hall of the main house. Bedrooms ran along front and back walls. The hallway had a door at one end in which Erie stood and a window at the other which looked out over the orchard. Shivering, Erie walked toward the central stairway.

Bedroom on left . . . men's, she observed glancing through partially open doors. Bedroom on the right, men's. Bedroom on the left, men's. *Strange.* Erie walked past the stairway and stepped up to a closed door on the right. She turned the handle. It opened into another bedroom, definitely that of a woman. The next door on the left opened into a storage room. The last door on the right was locked.

Hearing voices, Erie quickly went downstairs. At the bottom she found two women ripping a sheet.

Erie hurried into the kitchen, covered Ouma carefully with the quilt then went to help Margaret.

"Why are they ripping the sheet?"

"One of the men got a beam on his leg. They're wrapping it with clean cloth. They'll take him to the doctor in Drayton. I told them to send the doctor to our farm when he's finished."

"What can I do to help?"

"Butter the bread. Pass it along to Alena and Hester."

Erie joined the line, slicing when necessary and buttering. She watched both Ouma and the fire. Most of the able-bodied women had gone outside to join the bucket brigades.

Smitty came in, accompanied by Adam. "He has a coal in his eye," Adam said.

"A speck of dirt," corrected Smitty. "My eye is not large enough to hold a coal."

Margaret sat him down and looked into the eye. She took a handkerchief from her pocket, then poured a little hot water into a bowl. She dipped the cloth and gently wiped Smitty's face around the eye.

"How bad?" she asked, looking into the eye again.

"The barn's gone. Horses and cattle are out. Most of the pigs were caught in the fire. Harness is gone. Season's crops are gone. Hand tools are gone. Machinery was outside for the most part. We managed to draw most of it away from the barn. We are wetting down the drive shed and outbuildings. Water had to come from the stream, bucketed up the hill. The well's running dry."

"Erie, do you have a clean handkerchief?"

Erie searched a pocket and found one.

Margaret took it, twisted one corner tightly and held Smitty's eye open. She touched the corner of the cloth to the corner of Smitty's eye socket. "Got it!" she said triumphantly. "Does that feel better?"

Smitty blinked. "It does."

"Sit. I'll clean the rest of your face." Margaret gently wiped Smitty's face with the wet handkerchief. "Do be careful," she cautioned. "Don't play hero."

"Miriam played hero. She was burned, yet she led all the horses out. Then she ran for help."

Smitty stood and kissed Margaret on the cheek.

Margaret, blushing, rejoined the women around the table. "It's strange," she whispered to Erie. "Except for the pictures on the wall and decorations around the doors and windows which aren't here, nothing has changed in this room in twenty years. Dishes are in the same place. Towels are in the same place. Pots and pans are in the same place. There is no new furniture and the old is still all in the same place."

"Does Jacob have people stay here?" asked Erie. "Do they all sleep upstairs?"

"Odd question," said Margaret looking at Erie.

"Does he?"

"Ouma Gingerich lives in the doddy haus downstairs. Either Adam or Abraham sleep in there at night so she won't wander. Jacob and Miriam sleep upstairs. So do Adam or Abraham and a hired man when they have one. It is a big house to use only three bedrooms upstairs. These houses were built for large families. Why do you ask?"

"Are you sure about the sleeping arrangements?"

"Well, I can't be absolutely sure. I don't live here. That's the way it should be. Why do you ask?"

"Just something I saw. It isn't important. What will Jacob do about his barn?"

"The community'll rally around him. People will take his cattle and care for them until he raises another barn. Some will give of their crop. Others will donate time. As soon as the rubble cools, there'll be a bee to clear the old barn away and to build a new one. It's not the material things one loses that hurt. Jacob'll be out there now thinking of the hours of work he and his sons put into the harvest."

"It isn't fair that I'm here," whispered Erie. "What if my . . . Jacob . . . came through that door with soot in his eye? He should not meet me in front of all these people, not after the fire."

"You're right." Margaret went to the stove. She dumped a pound of coffee into a large preserving kettle full of boiling water, cracked several eggs into the pot and moved it from the hot fire.

Coming back to the table, she said, "We can't leave Ouma here either. The men won't have time to care for her tonight." Giving instructions to Alena, she motioned that Erie should follow her. In the main room of Ouma's doddy house,

Margaret outlined her idea. "We'll take a change of clothes for Ouma, walk her to the buggy, load her in, and you will drive to the farm."

"I can't drive a horse and buggy."

"You don't know until you've tried. Just let the horse do the driving. That animal has enough sense to head for home. Get Anna to help put Ouma to bed in the room behind the parlour."

"I don't understand a word she says, except 'Rachael.'"

"She'll do anything you want her to. Now let's find her clothes."

"Look upstairs," said Erie. "Third door on the right."

Margaret looked puzzled.

"This is Miriam's room," Erie explained. "These are Miriam's things. Look at the name on the trunk in the bedroom, the name in the Bible, the articles of clothing on the bed."

Margaret went into the bedroom. "Can you beat that!" she said coming out. "Ouma must sleep upstairs. Jacob and Miriam in the doddy house. Strange."

Erie showed Margaret Ouma's room. They chose a few articles of clothing Salome might need.

Downstairs Erie woke Ouma gently. She spoke to her in Deutsche. Ouma let herself be dressed in a shawl and led to the side door.

"I will walk you to the buggy and see you on your way." Margaret walked on one side of Ouma, Erie on the other.

"I'll come home with Smitty. Can you manage supper?"

Erie nodded. She looked toward the fiery ruin of the barn. "Which is my father?"

Margaret stopped. Ouma stood patiently between them.

"Over by the gate," whispered Margaret. "He is the tall man, greying hair, back to us, head bent."

My father, thought Erie, looking intently through the smoke at the man's back. A lump in her throat prevented her from speaking again.

"Let's get you on your way before he looks around." Margaret started walking again. She kept herself in Jacob's line of vision. He might see her or Ouma, but he couldn't see Erie. "You'll meet him, Erie. I'll bring him to the house tonight. We have his wife and mother. He promised you. Up, Ouma. Climb into the buggy. We'll tuck you in." Margaret freed the horse and handed Erie the reins. "Don't be afraid. Just don't whip the reins. Keep them slack. He'll go for the home farm." She stood in the laneway until she saw Erie turn onto the concession road.

CHAPTER TWENTY-FIVE

THE QUEEN'S HOTEL, TORONTO

ARTHUR PACED THE FLOOR of his suite at the Queen's, a drink in his hand. "Look, Perri. I've been here for two days and I haven't been told anything. My time's valuable. I can't sit in this hotel room forever. I have business back home to conduct. Thank God you sent this little liquid diversion or I would have gone quite mad. At Costello's request I've ventured no further than the hotel's dining room. I feel like a prisoner. I want an explanation."

Perri sat in a leather chair, legs crossed, smoking a cigar. "I told you, Arthur. We expect to have the shipment ready... shortly. We're working on it now. It shouldn't be more than a day or two more. Surely, you can humour us that long."

"Is the shipment as big as you indicated?"

Perri nodded.

"And, I get seven percent?"

Again, Perri nodded.

"Two days. That's all I'll wait. Not a day longer."

Perri puffed on his cigar.

"You want me to send you a little entertainment?"

"Not of the variety I assume you're talking about."

"That's right. You are engaged to that Carliss woman."

"Erie Carliss. We're announcing our engagement soon."

"Costello tells me she is visiting relatives here?"

"She's staying with friends of the family, Patrick Smith, near Drayton."

"Ah, yes, Patrick Smith."

"You know him?"

Perri shrugged. "I've heard of him. Did your fiancée speak about a Caleb Gingerich?"

Arthur thought for a moment. "No. That name was never mentioned. Look, why all the questions about Erie?"

"No reason. I just liked what I saw at the Cotton Club. She's a classy woman." Perri rose to leave. "I'll wire you instructions. Whatever I tell you, follow it to the letter. The success of this operation depends largely on your participation. If you run out of private stock give Bessi a call in Hamilton."

"I'm only staying two more days."

Perri retrieved his hat and cane. "Remember, follow my instructions to the letter."

"If I don't wish to?"

"You can leave anytime, Arthur. But, from past experience, I know money talks. And we're talking big dollars. Good day."

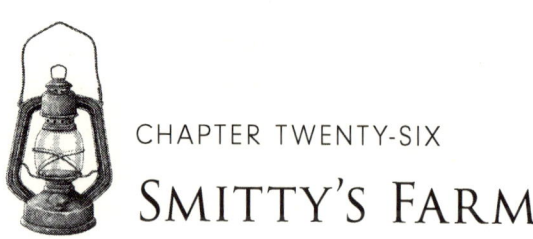

CHAPTER TWENTY-SIX

SMITTY'S FARM

ANNA AND ERIE HAD THE TABLE SET, soup simmering on the stove, meat, potatoes, and squash in the oven. The only thing that was missing were Patrick, Margaret, Bill, and Caleb. Ouma Gingerich sat by the stove, the dog curled at her feet, a kitten asleep in her lap. Her eyes followed Erie everywhere, but she said not a word.

Anna stirred the soup pot and tasted the concoction. "I've never made soup," she said. "For that matter, it has been years since I've cooked. But I think we've done an excellent job of the meal. We're almost domesticated!"

"I'm rather enjoying this," Erie said. "Didn't you find that it was tedious having someone wait on you on occasion?"

"Speaking of waiting on a person, that doctor said Miriam can have some soup. We'll have to feed her as her hands and arms are bandaged," Margaret said.

"I'll do it. It will give me a rest from grandmother's eyes." *Also,* Erie thought as she gathered tray, bowl, spoon, and napkin, *it'll give me the opportunity to speak with Miriam alone.*

Anna patted Ouma's hand. "She sure likes looking at you, doesn't she? I wonder what she's thinking. She's not fussing with her basket of scraps anymore."

Erie filled the bowl and slowly walked up the dark stairway. Peeking into the bedroom, she noticed Miriam's eyes were open. "Supper. Doctor's orders." Erie setting the tray on a table, helped Miriam to sit up by propping pillows behind her back.

"I am just a bother," said Miriam.

"You are not. Let's try to eat." Erie put a napkin around Miriam's neck and sat on the bed.

Miriam smiled. "Just like a baby, I am."

"If we do this right," laughed Erie, "you will eventually consume a bowl of Anna's soup. If we do it wrong, the bed will eat the soup."

Miriam giggled.

"Open wide," said Erie. "Let me know if it's too hot."

Miriam did as she was told, swallowed a spoonful and said, "Is good. Is very good."

"I'll give your compliments to the chef. Are your hands and arms sore?"

"Yah," Miriam answered between spoonfuls.

"You were a brave woman, Miriam. I dread storms and fire. You stayed in a burning barn to rescue the horses. I admire your courage."

"I just heard the horses and couldn't let them die."

Spoonful by spoonful the soup went down. "Some more?"

"Mayn," answered Miriam. "I am full, dahgn-gaw."

"Do you feel like talking?"

"Yah," Miriam lay back against the pillows. "Is nice to be with women. I do not live with women."

"Grandmother Salome lives with you."

"Yah," Miriam said. "Crazy Grohs Moodah. Is she alright, yet?"

"She's sitting by the stove in the kitchen watching me like a hawk. She has said nothing to either Anna or me. She was searching through a basket of scrap material that we had to bring with her, but she's stopped doing that. She's just looking at everything and everyone in the kitchen."

"Grohs moodah's gvild . . . gah visah, her memory is in the basket. She thinks you are Rachael. She was looking for a scrap of Rachael."

"At least she's quiet. All the way here she said . . . 'Rachael . . . Rachael.' Margaret told me the horse would head home, but she forgot that horse's home was miles away from here. Between steering the horse in the right direction and Grandmother's jabbering, I had quite the ride." Erie made herself comfortable in a chair by the bed. "Anna told you everything?"

Miriam nodded. "And I talked to Jacob. I was so angry." Miriam turned her head from Erie.

"I apologize for causing friction between you and my father. I did not mean to step between . . ."

"Nay," interrupted Miriam. "It is not you between. It is Rachael. She has been between us since we married. The marriage should not have been. He has not let her go." Miriam looked at her bandaged hands. "Yet, Jacob is a good man."

Erie cleared her throat. "It's not good, is it Miriam? Father has not been a husband to you. You raise his children, care for his mother; yet you are not as husband and wife. And he is keeping the house as it was when Rachael was alive, isn't he?"

"Yah." Miriam bowed her head. "I live with Rachael every

day. My fahdah said Jacob's grief would pass. It has worsened each year."

"No one knows but yourself," said Erie. "You have treated Jacob well. You know that an unconsummated marriage is no marriage even in the eyes of your church."

"Patience makes the world," said Miriam. "Yet, I am forty-two and I have no children of my own. Because I have no husband, I will have no children."

"Don't say that, Miriam."

"Nay." Miriam shook her head. "All is dead. Jacob is dead . . . as Rachael is dead. He has never . . . I have never felt his arms. He does not show his feelings."

Erie rose and walked to the window. *It's not over,* she thought. *Not by a long shot! Father has been so unfair to Miriam. He must be totally unfeeling. He has to be made to understand what he has done to this woman by keeping my mother's memory alive, and by refusing to admit to himself she died.*

"You are the only one that knows," said Miriam. "I did not even tell your mother, Anna. You understand your father?"

"I don't understand him at all. I'm simply Rachael's child, his child. I didn't know he was a . . . sick man." Erie crossed to the bed again.

"He is not Grahngk. He grieves, yet."

Erie changed the subject. "Here, let me make you comfortable. Your hair has fallen." Erie took a brush from the dresser and gently drew it through Miriam's blonde hair. She brushed it to the side, over Miriam's shoulder. "Just a moment." She rummaged through a box on the dresser and found a piece of blue ribbon. She tied it in Miriam's hair.

"Ribbon is not right."

"Ribbon is alright," said Erie. "I did it. You didn't. Sleep

Miriam. I'll bring Jacob to see you when he comes." She bent and kissed Miriam's pale cheek.

"I accept you as my daughter," Miriam smiled at Erie.

"Now I have three mothers."

"Erie," Miriam spoke softly. "Do not expect your father to . . . Jacob will not . . . he does not give affection easily."

"Don't worry Miriam. I understand he has a conservative nature. You sleep to gain the strength you'll need to face him. He needs you now more than ever. But don't bend to him anymore. Let him know your feelings too." Erie paused at the door. "Whatever the outcome of my talk with father, I'll keep your secret. It's between you and I."

"And God," said Miriam. "I speak with God."

"And God," said Erie. "He must know too." Walking down the stairs, Erie mentally added Patrick and Caleb to the list of people who knew Miriam's secret. Caleb would have to know. He'd stayed at Jacob's, and Patrick would be clever enough to figure out what was going on.

In the warm kitchen, Ouma dozed with the dog on the floor beside her. Anna sat at the table holding a letter. She looked up when Erie entered. "While you were upstairs, Mr. Wilson delivered this." Anna passed Erie an envelope.

"A letter from Arthur." Erie wiped her hands on her apron and sat down. She tore the envelope open and read quickly. "He is staying at the Queen's in Toronto. He wants me to leave a message at the hotel giving a day when he can come to Maryborough. Or, if that isn't possible, he wants me to meet him in Toronto."

"Are you prepared to meet him?"

"No."

"Then I'd leave a message that you'll meet him at the

hotel. If you don't wish him to come to Maryborough, don't invite him."

The dog left Salome and ran to the door. Someone tapped on the kitchen window.

"They're back." Anna rushed to her feet. Ouma woke with a start. The stamping of feet heralded the arrival of four tired, grimy people.

Anna tipped the dirty dishwater down a drain, where it gurgled into a drywell. She refilled the pan with hot water from the kettle.

"Wash up and then we'll serve up supper."

Margaret sat down and leaned back in a chair, eyes closed. "I have never felt so tired."

Ouma Salome watched everyone, mumbling to herself.

"Did Jacob not come?" asked Erie.

"He's waiting by the drive shed. He wouldn't come any further. He says he'll stay at the shed. If you want to meet him, you have to go to him."

"I'll do that." Erie stood, making room for one of the men to sit down. "Should I take a lantern?"

"Jacob has one with him."

Caleb put his arm across the kitchen doorway, blocking Erie's exit. "He has just lost his barn."

"Caleb. I'm not insensitive to Jacob's situation." Erie waited for Caleb to lower his arm. He did so, patting her on the shoulder.

"Then go to your father."

Erie approached the drive shed hesitantly, understandably nervous. Would he even be there? He must have extinguished the lantern. She couldn't see a light, and no one stood by the door.

"Jacob . . . Father? I can't see you. Where are you?" Erie was fifteen feet from the shed when Jacob stepped out of the shadows.

"I am here."

In the moon's light Erie perceived a suggestion of Jacob's face and shirt. *If he wished to see me, he would have left the lantern on. Do I shake his hand? Do I speak to him first? The closer I get, the more I can see of him. He appears to be looking at my face.* Erie stopped five feet from her father. Jacob stepped back.

He doesn't wish for me to get too close, Erie thought. She spoke, "I am glad to meet you, at last."

When Jacob didn't speak, Erie continued, "I'm sorry about your barn. It's a crushing blow for you." In the awkward silence that followed, Erie knew Jacob was scrutinizing her. She moved a step closer.

He's a handsome man, but shorter than I thought he would be. He's older looking than Caleb. "Can you rebuild?"

"Yah, we will have a barn before winter." Jacob's voice was deep, his Deutsche accent heavy.

There was another long silence, which Jacob finally broke. "I did not wish to meet you."

"At one time I didn't want to meet you either. But I am here and the meeting is taking place."

"You have not asked why I refused to meet you."

"I think it is because, to you, I am a painful reminder of my mother. My being here is as though she has come back into your life. In reality, Father, she never left, did she."

"Nay. Do not speak so."

Erie stepped closer. If she wanted to, she could have reached out and touched Jacob. "So, now I am here, what do we say to each other?"

"It is right you came. William told me you would come."

"I arrived earlier than you expected."

"Yah." Jacob's right hand came up as though to touch Erie, but he caught himself and put both hands in his pants pockets.

I wanted him to touch me, Erie thought. *I fully expected he would.*

"You are as tall as she. Your hair is as black as hers. You are as my Rachael was."

"I am your daughter. I may look like my mother, but I am not her."

"Is so," answered Jacob.

"I do understand your feelings, Father. I've lost someone I love too."

"You could not understand how much of a loss . . ."

"That was a long time ago and you must begin again."

Jacob turned away from Erie. "I know now I have been wrong. You had to come to show me the wickedness of my ways."

"I came to meet my father, not to destroy him. And I can't believe you have done anything wicked." *It isn't right*, Erie thought, *for me to discuss personal problems with the man. They are between he and Miriam.* "I am not going to wreak havoc with your life. I can leave just as quietly as I came. I won't tell anyone that I'm your daughter. That is up to you to do so, if you wish."

"That is right," said Jacob. "It is as I feel. Do you leave soon?"

What a blunt question. He has just met me and he is asking when I'm leaving. Am I that much of an intrusion on his life? Does this man have no feelings? "You do not get off so lightly," Erie said. "Before I go, I have several favours to ask of you."

"If I feel I can fulfil them I will," Jacob said.

Erie took one more step toward her father. "I want you to take me to mother's grave."

"Nay, nay," said Jacob. "I cannot do that."

"I can get Smitty or Margaret to take me, but it is only right that you do. It's simply a matter of you driving me to your meeting house to see a headstone. If you don't want to be seen with me during the day, we can go at night."

Jacob coughed and turned his back to Erie. "What is your second favour?"

"Light the lantern so that I might see more than a shadow of my father."

"Is that important to you?"

"Yes."

Jacob struck a match and reached to light the lantern he had hung on the door. He turned toward Erie and stepped back so that the full light was on his face. "Am I what you expected?" Jacob was crying. A surge of pity overcame Erie. She wanted to go to him, to put her arms around him. Instead, she started to cry too. "Can I ask one more favour?"

"If you must." Jacob had not moved. His eyes were riveted to Erie's face.

Erie wiped her eyes with a handkerchief. "Will my father give me the satisfaction of putting his arms around me, just once, please?"

Jacob shuffled his feet in the dirt. He then reached to touch her lightly with his right hand. "Do not cry. The sorrow is not yours. It is mine." Slowly he raised his left arm and Erie stepped into her father's embrace. Jacob held her tenderly, like a babe in arms. "This is the first time I have held my dadah."

Erie was too overcome to reply. When her father's arms tightened around her, she felt a peace in her soul.

When Erie returned to the kitchen, Bill offered his chair. He pulled another up beside her. Erie reached for his hand under the table and held it tightly. She caught Anna's eye and nodded slightly to let her know she was alright.

Grandmother Salome sat between Anna and Margaret, pushing her food around her plate.

"I was saying," said Smitty, "I'll have to get up earlier in the morning. We brought some of Jacob's milk cows home to keep Mildred company."

"Your milk stool is north of Blyth," Erie reminded him. "Where are Adam and Abraham?"

"They stayed at the house with a few of their neighbours. They'll watch for flare-ups. The wind is down, but if it freshens during the night, sparks could light the house. I heard Jacob going through the back hall. Is he coming to eat?"

"He will come soon," Erie said. "He's gone to Miriam."

"Ouma Salome," Anna touched her arm. "You're not eating."

Salome looked at Anna and whispered, "Rachael's kinde." She pointed a boney finger at Erie. "Is Rachael's kinde." She bent her head and began pushing the food around again. "Rachael is dohd."

"Perhaps we should put her to bed," said Anna.

"No." Ouma Salome spoke in a firm voice. "I will eat."

Caleb, Smitty, and Margaret looked at each other.

"Now, that is a change!" Caleb exclaimed.

Ouma Salome looked again at Erie. "Rachael's kinde?" she asked.

"I am Rachael's child," Erie said.

Ouma glared at everyone round the table and lapsed into silence while she ate. Occasionally she lifted her head to look at Erie.

"Did Jacob?" Smitty asked.

"Shh. We have a lot to talk about, Smitty." Erie picked up a spoon. "But this is not the time nor the place." Bill squeezed her hand under the table.

Margaret spoke, rather ordered, "Smitty, you and Caleb sleep at Lilac Hill tonight. Bill and Jacob can share one bedroom here. Anna and Erie will take the other. I'll sleep in the back room with Ouma."

"No," Anna said firmly. "You'll sleep in your own bed tonight. I'll watch Ouma."

Ouma Salome spoke clearly. "No one sits me."

"Just in case you need something during the night," Margaret said. "We don't want you to wander away."

"I am not kinde," Ouma Salome said. "She is a kinde." She pointed at Erie.

"Such a change. Ouma doesn't usually speak. She hasn't said so much in ten years. There is an old saying 'a loosened tongue—a loosened mind.' "

"Perhaps a sign of progress," said Anna. "She now knows Erie is Rachael's third babe." Jacob suddenly appeared in the doorway. Smitty leapt to his feet. "Sit here, Jacob. I'll get another chair."

Anna hustled and set another place. Jacob wearily sat down. "Miriam is asleep, like a baby."

Ouma Salome spoke, "Jacob. Is Rachael's kinde?"

"Yah, Moodah. Is Rachael's kinde."

"Is neht Rachael?"

"Nay," answered Jacob. "Rachael is dohd, forever yet."

"Is so," said Ouma Salome, matter-of-factly. "Is so."

CHAPTER TWENTY-SEVEN

SMITTY'S BACK PORCH

ANNA SHIVERED AND REACHED for the wool blanket she'd used as a cover. Remembering where she was, she looked to see if Ouma Salome was still asleep. As quietly as she could she extricated herself from the lumpy, upholstered chair that Smitty had put in the room for her. She stretched, tiptoed to Ouma's cot, and tucked a corner of the quilt in. Anna slipped into her shoes and, wrapping the blanket around her, went to sit on the back porch. The front door was locked, for the first time in history, Margaret had said. If Ouma wandered, the only way she could get out was past Anna.

The storm had broken the hot sultry weather. Anna stretched several times, enjoying the cool breeze, then sat in the rocking chair. The ruins of Jacob's barn glowed on the opposite side of the valley, the acrid smell of burning wood carrying for miles.

"You couldn't sleep either?"

"Goodness!"

"I startled you." Erie sat in Smitty's chair wrapped in a quilt.

"I didn't expect anyone else to be up in the middle of the night."

"There are more than us up," said Erie. "They didn't see me, but I noticed Caleb and Smitty leave with the team and wagon."

"They're probably going to get the Essex. But why would they choose to do that after such an exhausting day? Where's Caleb's Stuttgard?" Anna said.

"Some of the questions I intend to ask if I can get Caleb to sit down long enough to talk to me. If he wants Carliss Enterprises to invest their name in his project, I need answers, and soon."

"One never knows what Caleb and Smitty are up to."

"Margaret must get so exasperated."

"Margaret knew who and what she was marrying. But she didn't count on having two to ride herd on. She's proved to be a good match for both of them. You might have noticed."

Erie laughed. "She certainly doesn't take a back seat to anyone! Anna, do you feel like a mother-daughter talk?"

"Perhaps it should be friend to friend. I think it's time we talked seriously, Erie. You have at least seen your father."

"I did, but he was so upset about the fire, he didn't say much. I did most of the talking. He answered a few questions, and he finally did agree to take me to the cemetery."

"Why do you wish to see your mother's grave?"

"Remember when I went to State College, I roomed next to Alica Griffith?"

"Yes."

"Alica was adopted. She was forever searching for her mother. She knew her father was dead. Finding her mother became a passion for her, no . . . an obsession. She was consumed with the desire to meet her mother. I was convinced she was crazy. One day I asked her what she would do if she found out her mother had died. She replied that if she could see the grave, her search would be over, and she'd ask no more questions."

"Did Alica find her mother?"

"She did. She persisted and bothered people until she came face to face with her. She wished afterwards she hadn't. Her mother wanted nothing to do with her. Alica said it would have been better if she'd been shown a grave. After I see my mother's grave, I'll close one chapter in my history."

"You told me last night that Jacob was reluctant to take you."

"He tried to persuade me that I didn't need to go. From the way he acted, I don't think he's visited the site for a while himself. I finally said that if he didn't take me, I'd approach Adam."

"Would that have been fair to Adam?"

"I was only bluffing. I'd never have approached Adam. After I spent one night talking and listening to Adam, I realized that I didn't want to interrupt his life. Although we have the same parents, and are of the same coupling, we're of two separate cultures. Jacob has left little room for flexibility in Adam and Abraham's lives. Adam lives in awe of Caleb and Smitty. They are like gods to him. I'm afraid they've influenced him too much. As for Abraham, I haven't even met the fellow."

"I don't think Adam is happy in his faith."

"He lives around it. He needs someone to talk to. Mother, he is such a gentle and kind fellow."

"Jacob hasn't allowed either to court?"

"Adam tells me that Abraham is seeing a girl who is not of the faith. What is their church's stand on marriage of questionable colour?"

"Miriam said she knows of no situation where that has happened."

"Except in the case of my father and mother."

"I wonder if Abraham would leave his faith to marry?"

"Adam says the girl might join the faith."

"That won't work," Anna said. "You know the results of your mother joining their community. She was accepted by some, rejected by others."

"Perhaps it's different now. My father was such a fool," Erie said. "Why didn't he leave the faith?"

"You must understand the extent of his love for Rachael and his respect for his father. Respect plays an important part in a Mennonite's life. The two emotions were in complete conflict with each other in Jacob's case. His love for Rachael was all consuming. His respect and obedience to his father began the day he was born."

Erie walked to the steps. "I've been thinking a lot about my situation. I feel I belong to you because you raised me. Yet, when Jacob held me briefly, I knew I was his child and it was right that I met him. Not until I experienced being held by my father did I realize there was a bond stronger than the love you and William gave me. It is 'blood love' for want of a better name."

"Blood ties are strong ties," Anna said. "I wish you had experienced your mother's love. I couldn't give you that bond, but in her place, I gave you all the love I knew she would. I never knew the joy of being held by a mother or father. I envy you the moment you had."

"You do know how I felt."

"Completely."

"Then you'll understand what I'm going to say next."

"I'll try." Anna leaned forward in her chair.

"I came to Maryborough a Carliss. But I will leave Maryborough a Gingerich. William was grooming me to take his place in Carliss Enterprises. Not many women have the privilege of entering high finance and I was thrilled to have the opportunity. I was annoyed to find out the job had been offered Bill before it was offered me. Obviously, William was looking for someone to take over."

"He was, just in case . . ."

"Now I'm upset. Was I on a waiting list for a crown and throne?"

"Don't be upset. If I explain to you why William was so obsessed with finding an heir, you might understand and change your mind about your surname."

"I'm listening."

"William loved children and so did I. But, as fate would have it, William had an unfortunate accident while riding a bicycle. As a result, he couldn't father children. This happened shortly after our marriage while Bill and Jennifer lived with us. William accepted them as his own. When you came into our lives, he was euphoric—a baby for him and I to adore, and raise. But, because we raised Bill and Jennifer, he felt an obligation to them. He offered each the Carliss name and its inherent responsibilities on their sixteenth birthday. He felt that with the name, went the responsibility. And rightly so, it did."

"That makes sense. What happened?"

"Jennifer wished the name, but would not assume any responsibility. Bill wanted neither. He told William that, twice . . . after his sixteenth birthday, and again just before your sixteenth birthday. You were in line for the crown. You were the only person worthy of it. William wasn't disappointed in either of them. From the beginning he adored you, and he knew you were his successor."

"Why, then, did he offer the position to Bill twice—asking Bill to take the Carliss name?"

"Because he wanted heirs apparent who would carry the Carliss name. If Bill agreed to adoption by William, his children would carry the name. The problem is that Ian and I can find no papers that indicate you were ever registered as a Carliss, or a Gingerich. It doesn't matter really. Your children will carry the name of the man you marry, if you marry."

Erie walked the length of the porch. *If I marry Arthur Moore, Carliss Enterprises will eventually be part of the Moore empire. Regardless of who I marry, the name won't survive. If I don't marry . . . that is a different story; also, if I choose to be officially adopted by Anna . . .*

Erie stopped walking and said, "I'm leaving Maryborough a Gingerich because I won't ask anyone to lie for me. But I would appreciate you and Ian Oliver initiating adoption proceedings immediately because I want to be known as a Carliss."

"William would be pleased," said Anna, clapping her hands together. "I wished you to choose Gingerich. He wished you to choose adoption."

Erie turned to look over the valley. *That is one decision made,* she thought. *Now I must deal with Arthur.* "What am I going to do about Arthur?" she said aloud.

"Why did he come to Toronto?" Anna asked. "It seems odd that he would make the trip north when all his dealings are in the United States."

"He negotiates shipments from Canada. He told me he often deals with Canadian companies, just as Carliss Enterprises does. He buys a lot of grain . . . Erie walked the porch again, deep in thought. *How stupid I am! Why indeed is he in Canada!* She whirled around to confront Anna. "Our gypsy days are over, mother. We're heading home. As soon as I finish my business with Caleb, we're going back to New York."

"Don't you want to stay longer, perhaps to visit Toronto with Bill?"

Bill, my dear Bill, Erie thought. *How long have I known I'm in love with Bill?* "If I decide not to marry Arthur, would you be upset?"

"Not in the least," Anna smiled.

"And what would happen if I decided not to carry on with Carliss Enterprises? What if I decided eventually to sell most of Carliss Enterprises?"

"Ian Oliver is a very capable man. He has been my financial advisor for years. I'm sure he can give you good sound advice. He won't let you jump in, or out of anything."

"You are a brick, mother."

"And you are an exceptional young lady, Erie Gingerich Carliss, just like your mother."

Erie kissed Anna's cheek. "Why don't you get into my bed. You look as though you haven't had too much sleep. Ouma was hard on you."

"Are you not going back to bed?"

"Not right away. I think I'll wait to see if Caleb and Smitty come back."

CHAPTER TWENTY-EIGHT

LILAC HILL

ERIE WAITED ANOTHER bone-chilling hour on the porch before she wrapped the blanket around her, and, barefoot, walked to Lilac Hill. She preferred her own bed at the cottage to Margaret's hard horsehair couch. She wanted privacy to do some serious thinking. In the east the sky streaked with the first signs of morning, but the night was still dark enough she had to be careful where she put her feet. She grimaced with pain when she stepped on sharp stones. Hot spots glowed in the barn ruin. Lantern light shone from Miriam's kitchen window.

There is no rest for the wicked or the weary, thought Erie as she washed her feet in the rain barrel. When she entered the cottage, she noted that neither bed had been slept in, but from the dirty dishes on the table, Smitty and Caleb had made coffee.

Not a bad idea. Erie talked to herself as she changed into shoes and clean cloths. She felt the stove. It was still warm.

Lifting the lid, she blew on the grey ash and was rewarded with a small flame. She quickly added wood shavings then several small pieces of kindling. When the kindling flamed up, she added a large piece of maple and shut the lid.

Everyone's trying to control a fire across the valley and I'm trying to light one here. Erie rubbed her hands together over the stove. Now for the coffee. Filling the pot with water, Erie guessed at the amount of coffee, then set the pot on the fire. She sat at the table, feet on a second chair, eyes closed. The room began to lose its chill as the coffee pot boiled. Remembering coffee should never boil, according to Bill, Erie rose and moved the pot to the back of the stove. Because her back was to the windows, she didn't see Margaret until the door opened.

"May I come in?"

Although Erie was startled, she had the presence of mind not to show it. "Please do. The coffee's ready, I think. What are you doing up at such an ungodly hour?"

Margaret, in old house dress and rubber boots, entered the cottage. She slipped the boots from her feet while Erie got a pair of slippers from Anna's bedroom.

"I had to show Bill how to milk the cows before I came.

"You have Bill milking cows?" Erie grinned.

"He used to do a good job of milking. But recently he's lost his touch."

Erie poured each a cup of coffee. "It's pretty strong and there is no milk but here's some sugar."

After checking the fire, Erie sat down, thinking as she did so that she was becoming pretty adept at living in a primitive environment. "Are Smitty and Caleb back yet?"

"No," said Margaret. "And that worries me. I didn't want

them to go last night. They were both so tired after the fire. It's raw energy that keeps them going."

"Did they go for the car?"

"That they did," answered Margaret. "But they had other business too. I heard them leave and I heard you get up. I waited until now to come to talk because I also heard Anna and assumed she was speaking to you. I hope you don't mind my bothering you. I want to talk with you about Caleb's latest venture."

"I think you should talk to Smitty and Caleb about it."

"I have," said Margaret. "But the situation is to the point where I need your help."

"Is Bill involved at all?"

"As far as I know, only to the point of helping with the still."

"Exactly what are we talking about?" Erie asked. "Caleb will say only he needs the Carliss Enterprise name. He hasn't explained anything to me, although I'm beginning to piece a lot together."

"It's a dangerous scheme. I really began to worry when I found these."

Margaret gave Erie several slips of paper.

"If Jacob's barn hadn't burned, I never would have found them. They were tucked in behind the box in my medicine cabinet. They are in Caleb's handwriting."

"One is simply a compilation of figures," said Erie.

"Well, look at the other paper."

"Rocco Perri! Why has Caleb got Rocco Perri's name and a number of addresses?"

"You know Rocco Perri?"

"Passing acquaintance," answered Erie. "He was in the

company of Frank Costello at the time. How is Caleb mixed up with Perri?"

"If he is," said Margaret, "Patrick is too, and that gives me the chills."

"The two men in the Ford," asked Erie. "Are they Perri's men?"

"I know they're working for the distillery, so they're not Perri's men."

"And what might they want?" asked Erie.

"Whiskey," answered Margaret. "They're looking for their whiskey."

"Rocco Perri is a nasty man. He's the bootleg king of Canada and he controls drugs too."

"Caleb wouldn't ever get mixed up with drugs."

Erie looked at the papers again. "Anyone who hangs around with Frank Costello is bad news. Rocco Perri's girl-friend, Bessi Starkman, is vicious too." She left the table and walked to the window overlooking the valley. "This house Smitty bought in Kitchener . . . you mentioned it was next to a felt factory. Do you still own the house?"

"Smitty had it put in Isabel's name, the Isabel that we raised with Anna's help."

"And the felt factory?"

"It doesn't manufacture anymore," Margaret said. "It's a warehouse for a licensed distillery."

"What about Baeker Vinegar? It's a warehouse for booze too?"

"As far as I know it is," answered Margaret.

"Might Isabel own property close by that warehouse?" Erie pushed for more information.

"No," replied Margaret. "But Laura, another of our chosen

children, owns a small building that is back-to-back with the Old Vinegar Factory."

"Smitty gave Laura the money to buy the building?"

"No, Caleb gave her the building as a present when she was married."

"Next to two distillery warehouses are two properties that are accessible to Caleb and Smitty," mused Erie. "And in those warehouses . . ."

"Whiskey," a male voice said.

Both Margaret and Erie jumped.

"Barrels and barrels of uncut whiskey," the voice continued.

"Smitty, thank God you're back." Margaret went to embrace Smitty.

Erie crossed quickly to the stove and threw the two pieces of paper into the flames. She turned, saw Caleb behind Smitty, and said, "Both of you, sit down. I'll make another pot of coffee. We'd better talk and you have to be honest with me."

Wearily, Smitty and Caleb sat at the table. While Erie busied herself at the stove, Margaret rinsed cups.

"The car's back." Smitty unlaced a boot and removed it slowly. "Caleb's Stuttgard is here too. He labouriously removed his second boot.

"It's been a long night." Caleb struggled with his heavy boots then opened the oven door. Both men drew their chairs up to the stove and propped their feet on the open door. The room quickly filled with the odour of wet, smelly socks.

"Have you figured it out yet?" Caleb yawned and looked at Erie. "An intelligent girl like yourself should have most of the answers by now."

"Almost," answered Erie. "You're clever, Uncle Caleb. I have to hand it to you. It is an imaginative scheme."

"To survive, one has to be both clever, imaginative, and a little mad." Caleb laughed. "Tell me, what have you deduced so far."

"You're stealing uncut whiskey from the distillery warehouses," began Erie.

"Correct," said Caleb.

"You, of course, have accomplices to help you with that. You certainly need inside help at the warehouses."

"Correct again."

"To disguise the thefts," continued Erie, "you're replacing the barrels of whiskey you steal with barrels of water."

"Smart girl."

"I assume you're exchanging barrel for barrel."

"An excellent deduction."

"You operate a few stills around the countryside and sell the rot-gut they produce to pay the people that are helping you."

"Right on track."

"And you are selling the good uncut whiskey."

Caleb raised his hand. "Not yet," he said.

"Where's your storage? How do you transport the whiskey from warehouse to storage?"

Neither Caleb nor Smitty answered.

"Look, if you're not selling it, you're storing it," said Erie. "That's why the snoopers are tailing you."

"You can't even prove we're stealing it," Smitty said.

"They are reasonably sure or they wouldn't waste their time on you. All they need is to find you with some of the distillery's barrels. They weren't after a still the other day. They were looking for stolen barrels of whiskey."

"Perhaps you've gone too far this time," Margaret said. "The snoopers have been pretty persistent. They're not going to be forgiving men if they find you out."

"Neither will Rocco Perri," interjected Erie, watching Caleb. Her statement got the desired reaction. Both Caleb and Smitty sat up smartly.

"What do you know about Rocco Perri?" Caleb demanded.

"I've a passing acquaintance with the man," answered Erie. "He'll be involved if it's whiskey. My guess is he's looking for your cache too."

Caleb smiled.

"Not because they want to buy it," continued Erie. "If he can find the cache, he'll steal it from you, no questions asked. Where does Carliss Enterprises fit into this scenario?"

"Documentation," said Caleb. "We have to move the whiskey and we need documentation to get it across the border. Carliss Enterprises ships grains, livestock, ore, vinegar across all the time. We need appropriate customs forms with your signature for a number of carloads of vinegar to Chicago, vie Windsor."

"What is your usual procedure with illegal liquor?" asked Erie.

"It's quite legal for an American Company to buy liquor from a Canadian distillery," explained Caleb. "Usually an order is placed with a brewery or distillery from a U.S. firm or company. A Canadian contact or company picks up the order at one of the breweries or distilleries with the proper customs forms. The order clears customs alright, then just disappears because it can't legally land in the States. Some gets through and lands on the shores of Lake Erie or Lake

Huron. Other shipments don't get any further than the outer harbour before they're taken down the lakeshore and end up in Ontario."

Erie, listening closely, said, "You're clever enough to cut out the middleman. You've been stealing barrels of whiskey right out of the warehouses. You can't have someone place an order for it with you because you aren't a distillery or a brewery. You have to ship it out of the country disguised as some other commodity."

"Correct," said Caleb, slapping his knee.

"How many barrels?"

"The equivalent of one thousand, two hundred," answered Smitty. "But they're not all from this area. We've been working on this one a long time and we've a huge network of people . . ." He didn't elaborate.

"Uncut?" asked Erie.

Smitty nodded.

"A trustworthy buyer in Chicago? No trace back to you?"

Caleb nodded. "A cash deal. But we have to move it now to make the deal. It's about time, the snoopers are getting too close."

"What would Carliss Enterprises percentage of the profit be?"

"Ten percent," said Caleb. "Cash payment."

"Where did you say all this whiskey came from?"

"Toronto, Hamilton, Kitchener. Our fellows even tapped one of Perri's sources, big time!"

Erie groaned. "You two are sitting on dynamite!"

"It started small," Caleb said. "It just grew and grew. It's alright, Erie. We haven't seen Perri's men around here. We set them on the wrong trail months ago. But you're right, he's not looking for the few barrels he lost; he's looking for the entire cache, if indeed he is involved," Smitty said.

"It is a good investment for Carliss Enterprises," Caleb interrupted. "We want to use your name and documentation. There's no danger on your part, just a telephone call to get everything in order. Your name is clear at the border. Carliss has always had a good name with Customs. We can get the shipment out of the country and retire on the money."

"How soon," asked Erie.

"We have three days," replied Caleb removing his feet from the oven door, "before we lose our opportunity to get across at Windsor without close inspection. The snoopers will know what we're up to if our names show on any paper-work, let alone if we show our faces near the border."

Erie paced the floor between stove and door, hand to chin. The money meant little to Carliss Enterprises as it couldn't show on the books. Caleb was in big trouble if he couldn't get the shipment out of the country quickly. And Rocco Perri was somehow involved.

"You are discussing stolen goods," cautioned Margaret. "If the box cars are examined, Carliss Enterprises will have some explaining to do. Their name is on the documents."

"The Company can deny everything. They can say they have been set up. It happens all the time," Caleb countered. "But you must be aware of those risks. William took them all the time."

Erie stopped pacing. "You can't hold the shipment any longer?"

"It's too big and someone's talking. We have to move

everything out of Canada. Our market is in the United States. That's where it has to go. We're already moving everything to one central location, a bit at a time."

"I can write the agent," said Erie. "I have dealt with him on many occasions."

"Does he know your voice on the phone?"

"Yes."

"Call him. Don't send a telegram. Don't write. I'll pick up the documentation personally in Toronto."

"But," Erie raised her hand, "Margaret's right. We're talking about stolen goods. What if I choose not to co-operate?"

"You wouldn't be your father's daughter . . . I should say William's protege, if you did. We do have alternative plans. Although a lot more dangerous for us, we can possibly get the shipment across without your assistance."

"False papers about a distillery, false invoices, false customs papers . . . you'd be caught for sure."

"Understand Erie, we're not praying on honest men and innocent companies."

"Twenty percent," said Erie. "I wouldn't consider getting Carliss Enterprises involved in this scheme for less than twenty percent of your profit, cash."

"Come now!" exclaimed Caleb. "We have others to pay."

"I stand to lose my import privileges and you've no choice but to move the whiskey across the border within the next three days. I'm not a push over, gentlemen."

"Can you conscientiously involve Carliss Enterprises in this?" asked Margaret.

"You'd be surprised how much graft and corruption takes place among the financial wizards of the world. I see little risk for Carliss Enterprises if Smitty and Caleb have 'fixed' the border. We buy raw materials from Canada all the time. The risk is entirely on the shoulders of Caleb, Smitty, and their henchmen. They must load the cars in such a way that the barrels remain undetected. They must trust their cohorts along the way to ensure there's no slip-up or tell-all. They must know the risks associated with flirting with Rocco Perri and the mob."

"Twelve percent," bargained Caleb. "That's the best offer I can make."

"I'm not interested in twelve percent."

Caleb looked at Smitty. "Fifteen percent." Caleb stood. "That is the final offer. You are the limit, girl. You know you have us against the wall."

"You can always go with your second plan," Erie said. "And, I'll forget we had this conversation."

"Let's shake hands on the deal."

Caleb extended his hand. "Fifteen percent it is, on my handshake."

Erie shook hands with both men. "Can I borrow your Stuttgard? I'll go to Kitchener to call Toronto. I don't imagine there's any privacy near any phone in Drayton."

"Bill can drive you. Go to the Waterworks. Ask for Lloyd. Introduce yourself. Tell him you want to use his phone."

"Lloyd," said Erie. "The Waterworks."

"I'll give Bill directions." Smitty pulled on his boots, stood up, and stretched. "I'm starved. Let's go wash up, eat, and have a good sleep."

"One thing," Caleb said. "Anna and Bill aren't involved in this. Neither are Jacob Gingerich or his boys. They know little. This conversation was between the four of us. Keep it that way."

"Agreed," answered Erie. "I don't feel Anna should be placed in such a dangerous situation. As for Bill, I don't believe he isn't more fully involved."

Caleb shrugged then laughed. *Clever woman*, he thought looking at Erie, *William chose his successor well.*

Margaret and Smitty set out for the farm, leaving Caleb with Erie. She gathered a change of clothes for Anna before joining him on the porch. He took her hand and helped her down the steps.

"I have nothing but admiration for you, Erie. I'm proud to be your uncle."

"And I applaud the ingenuity of both Smitty and yourself," answered Erie. "But you're living a hazardous life."

"My curiosity is aroused," Caleb said. "How do you know Rocco Perri?"

"I've met him," Erie said. "I spent part of one evening socializing with him. But I've got to tell you that while you and I were in Victoria Park, I was sure I saw the woman I know as Bessi Starkman watching us. Bessi was at the Cotton Club with Perri. Remember I asked if you knew her, but I didn't explain at the time why I asked?"

Caleb stopped walking. "Bessi Starkman is Rocco Perri's woman," he said quietly. "Are you sure it was her?"

"I'm positive. I don't forget faces."

Caleb whistled. "So we might be in trouble yet. She's as involved in the business as he is."

Caleb drew a deep breath and began walking again, hands in pockets. He kicked a stone ahead of him until he lost it in the tall grass. "There is a young man," Caleb said breaking his silence, "who wishes your Arthur Moore would dig a hole somewhere and disappear into it."

Erie laughed. "I've wished in the past several days the earth might swallow Arthur too."

Caleb stopped walking again and touched Erie's arm. "You can't mean that."

"No," Erie hung her head. "That would not be the proper solution. I have to talk with Arthur."

"Bill loves you. Surely you must realize that."

Erie smiled at Caleb and glanced across the valley. "My values have changed. There's such a difference between the way people live in New York and here. Arthur would be a 'fish out of water' in Maryborough. After the initial shock I had when I arrived, I can truthfully say I'm enjoying myself. I enjoy the city too. But I realize now I surrounded myself with a false sense of values. I'm beginning to question the genuineness of people I associate with, and the whole way of life they represent."

"You knew no other way," Caleb said. "You were raised among wealthy people. I admit I have associated with the sort of people you're describing, and I find some of them obnoxious. But then I was raised a country boy."

Erie laughed and said, "You haven't seen my 'city side.' I can be as vampish as Rivona or as demanding as Mrs. Moore."

"I believe you can," Caleb said. "But your personality is tempered with your mother's qualities—patience, kindness. And I know that in subtle ways, Anna never let you get out of hand. You may have been born of this valley, Erie," Caleb placed his arm around his niece, "but you are certainly not going to die in this valley. You have a brilliant mind and you're going to use it."

"As far as Arthur is concerned, I should be at home having children."

"And Bill?"

"I'm totally confused. I thought I loved Arthur. I think I'm in love with Bill. I'm not sure what love is now."

Caleb let go of Erie and scuffed his feet in the dirt. "You're asking the wrong fellow about love. I've never really loved anyone. I was foolish enough once to think possibly Anna might look at me, more than once. But she didn't, and I didn't pursue the issue. I was young and I was Mennonite."

"You did know her as a young woman, didn't you?"

"Yes," replied Caleb, "and Rachael too. Think of it. If Jacob hadn't married Rachael, I would have asked for her hand. I might have been your father."

Erie impulsively hugged her uncle and kissed his rough cheek. "You rogue!" She laughed, then became serious. "Anna and William were inseparable. They lived only for each other. Anna will never marry again. Do you want some advice to the lovelorn?"

Caleb smiled broadly and nodded.

"Write to her often. Visit her. But don't ever force yourself on her in any way. She will be your best friend, but she will never consider marriage."

"Advice well taken," said Caleb. "Now can I offer you some?"

"Go ahead."

"Marriage is not a joke. You must marry the right man. Marriage is a total commitment to each other. Arthur Moore might be the best man for you, but if he's condescending in any way towards black persons, you will eventually feel that. Bill might not be perfect, but he is Anna's half-brother and was raised by Anna and Margaret, two of the most sensible women I know."

"I understand what you are saying," said Erie, taking Caleb's arm.

"It's just sound thinking," Caleb said. "But sometimes the heart rules the head. Let's change the subject. I'll fill you in on details of our scheme. You must commit all instructions to memory. We want nothing written down that can be traced back to you. I'll never let you get yourself into a dangerous situation."

"Gallant words," said Erie, "especially if you are dealing with Perri's men too. As soon as you make the phone call, your involvement is over. I suggest you leave Maryborough as soon as you can. Take Margaret with you. I don't want her around if fireworks start."

"Margaret won't leave Smitty."

"I know that," said Caleb. "But if you plead hard enough she might change her mind."

"What can I plead?"

"Think of something," Caleb answered. "Even if you persuade her to go to Toronto with you for several days, just get her away from the farm until the shipment is over the border and into the buyer's hands."

"I'll try." Erie suddenly stopped, grabbed Caleb's arms, and said, "Have I been stupid?! Of course, Arthur Moore is in Toronto waiting to do the same thing for Perri as I'm doing for you. Perri's onto you, Caleb! Arthur's waiting for the word on how much and what port of exit."

"Figured as much," said Caleb. "Don't worry yourself about it. Arthur's not a problem."

CHAPTER TWENTY-NINE

KITCHENER

BILL PARKED THE STUTTGARD on Frederick Street as Caleb had instructed him to do. After assisting Erie from the car, he walked in one direction while Erie stood for some time admiring winter coats in the window of a dress shop. She casually looked around to see if she was being followed, then began to walk in the opposite direction of that which Bill had taken. Several blocks east she stopped before a wooden door, read the sign, and entered. A middle-aged man shuffled out of the dim interior and introduced himself as Lloyd. Following Caleb's instructions, Erie asked to use the phone and was shown into a dimly lit back office. The door closed behind her and she was left alone to complete her business. Twenty-five minutes later she stood beside the Stuttgard waiting for Bill, who appeared eventually, several packages in hand. He opened the door for Erie and said, "I walked blocks before I found the book shop Caleb said was 'just around the corner.'"

"Perhaps we parked on the wrong street?"

"He distinctly said Frederick Street, beside that dress shop. At any rate I'm famished. Let me take you to lunch."

"A capital idea," said Erie relieved the operation had gone so smoothly. The necessary papers would be ready for Caleb to pick up in Toronto tomorrow, after she'd signed for them.

"Let's try the Walper Terrace. I understand it's the best in town."

"Are we dressed for it?" Erie said. She'd tried not to dress too conspicuously.

"You look stunning. I'll have to bluff my way through."

Erie blushed with the compliment. Arthur threw them out like pennies. Bill's compliments came few and far between, but were most sincere. Bill drove to King Street and parked near the hotel. He looked around before giving Erie his arm. They walked around admiring various shop windows before they entered the Walper's lobby. Although they didn't have a reservation, they were immediately seated in the dining room. One waiter took their order, while a busboy hovered close by.

"Caleb told me you were leaving Maryborough," Bill said as soon as they were left alone.

"I think it's time I went home. Anna has had enough of a holiday too, although she'll miss Margaret. By the way, she'd like Margaret to come with us, at least as far as Toronto."

"Margaret won't go."

Erie rearranged her napkin several times. "Can you talk to her? Possibly suggest she go to see her boys? Anna and I would stay with her as long as she wanted to visit. I want to meet her family. And you live there too, when you're not in the bush. You could show me your city. We could all go together tomorrow."

It didn't take Bill long to respond. He'd been trying to get Erie to Toronto for a while. Now was his golden opportunity. "I'll talk to Margaret. You can stay with James and me. Perhaps Frank has flown in. I have a large house with lots of room. You can stay as long as you like." Bill became quite enthusiastic about the idea. "I can take you around Toronto. You can spend some time with Anna's friend, Mr. Osler. I believe there's an invitation on my desk to a play at Chorley Park next weekend that we can attend."

"How, pray tell, might I explain your undivided attention to dear Arthur who might also be in Toronto?"

"We'd make a cozy group," Bill laughed. "Anna, Margaret, Arthur, you and I, because I won't let you out of my sight."

Erie said softly. "Arthur is usually an understanding man, but you tend to bring the nasty side of him out, especially when you insist on holding my hand, like you did in Maine, as you're doing now."

"Sorry. I just cannot control my hands."

"You'll have to learn to. Soup's on its way." Erie's hand suddenly tightened in Bill's. "And so has Rocco Perri."

"What?"

"Rocco Perri and Bessi Starkman," she whispered. "They're being led to our table, right behind our waiter."

"What the hell!" Erie squeezed Bill's hand to silence him.

Perri and Starkman stood beside the table. Bessi was dressed theatrically, her jewelry flashy and expensive. Bill stood to meet them.

"Miss Carliss?" Perri bent to kiss Erie's hand. "What a pleasure." Rocco was smooth, his voice like oil on water. "We haven't met," he said to Bill, "Rocco Perri."

Bill shook hands.

"And my wife, Bessi."

"My pleasure," said Bill. "You will join us, of course."

While Perri consulted a gold pocket watch, Bill was trying to recall the stories he had heard about the pair.

"We've another party to meet, but we can join you for a few moments. It isn't often we meet such a notable young lady in Kitchener."

Perri's Italian accent complimented his dark Mediterranean complexion. Although his compliment was for Erie, the gangster's attention was on Bill. "I don't believe I've seen you before. What business are you in?"

"Mining," Bill answered truthfully. "I'm a geologist, actually more of a prospector at the moment. I'm usually in Northern Ontario, but came down to see Erie."

Perri nodded then addressed Erie. "And what brings you from New York to Kitchener?"

His method of questioning was blunt. Perri's black eyes searched Erie's face, commanding her to answer.

"I am . . ." Erie began, looking away from Perri and into Bessi's steely eyes.

Bill cleared his throat. "It's really a private matter," he said. "She came to see her fiancé."

"Ah, yes, Mr. Moore, isn't it?"

"I'm her fiancé, not Mr. Moore," said Bill. He received a well-placed kick on his ankle and tried not to grimace. He squeezed Erie's hand, hard.

"I don't quite understand." Bessi's voice was soft, unlike her penetrating eyes. "I was given the impression you were engaged to Mr. Moore."

"No doubt . . ." Erie managed to utter before Bill continued, "You see, Erie and I have known each other for years. We saw each other last at William Carliss's funeral, but we always kept in touch. When I heard she was coming to Maryborough to visit old family friends, I came out of the bush at New Liskeard to meet her. We had some unfinished business—after Maine." Bill squeezed her hand again.

"In the short time we've been together in Maryborough, Erie realized she'd made a mistake promising to marry Arthur Moore. We love each other, don't we dear?"

Erie lowered her head and landed another well-placed kick on Bills ankle.

"Is that so?" said Perri, scrutinizing Erie.

Erie raised her head and met Perri's eyes. "If Bill says so," she said. "Arthur, dear fellow, doesn't know yet. He will be terribly upset."

"I'm sure he will," said Bessi. "I dumped a man once, literally had him dumped."

The crudeness of her remark brought an icy stare from Perri and a smile from Erie. "Then you must know what I'm going through," Erie said, wondering if Bessi was capable of any feelings at all.

Bessi nodded and said, "You visiting friends around here?"

"Yes, friends."

"Miss Carliss, are you familiar with a man named Caleb Gingerich?" Bessi came right to the point of their unexpected visit.

"I am. Caleb Gingerich is . . ."

"Her uncle," Bill came to Erie's rescue. "Is he a friend of yours?"

"Unlikely," retorted Bessi.

"You're telling me you're related to Caleb Gingerich?" Perri turned on Erie.

"It's a subject we don't discuss much." Bill was the one to answer again. "He . . . Erie's mother knew Caleb before she married William Carliss." Bill winked at Perri.

"Knew?" Perri's brow furrowed in thought. "Knew . . . oh, I get you. As in the biblical sense."

Bill grimaced with pain as Erie's shoe connected again.

"Ah," said Bessi. "A blot on the family."

Bill coughed and answered. "You might say that."

Erie bent her head, an action seen by Perri as one of extreme embarrassment.

"Bessi says things she doesn't mean," apologized Perri.

Erie shook her head. "It's alright, Mr. Perri. But, please, mother would be devastated if word got around."

Rocco raised his hands. "I'm a gentleman," he stated. "That's your business, not mine."

Now it was Erie's turn to attack. She saw an opening and took advantage of it. "Didn't I see you in Victoria Park several days ago, Bessi? I was going to introduce you to Uncle Caleb, but you left so quickly."

Bessi hid her surprise well. Perri cleared his throat.

Erie pressed on. "Perhaps you didn't see me. But I saw you. I couldn't imagine what you were doing in Kitchener. This is such a small conservative city. I didn't think there'd be anything of interest here for you."

"We have friends here too."

"Do you know Patrick Smith?" Erie was not backing down from the Perri's.

"I've heard the name," Perri said evasively.

"My mother and the Smiths are friends. Mother owns a summer home in Maryborough which the Smith's care-take."

"I didn't know there were any summer homes in Maryborough," Bessi sniffed.

"Mr. Perri," Erie turned her attentions and beautiful eyes on Rocco. "Could I ask a favour of you both? Of course, Arthur doesn't know about Bill. Not too many people do. I would like to tell him personally. When you see him, if you see him before I do, please don't mention you saw us together. He is in Toronto, you know."

"You . . . you have my word," answered Perri. "Rocco Perri's word is good."

"I understand it is," Erie oozed charm.

"And you, Mrs. Perri?" Erie faced up to Bessi.

"That's your business, not mine. You'll have the chance to speak to Arthur Moore before I see him to . . ." Bessi caught herself. "Before I would ever see him." She covered her slip nicely.

Erie smiled at both. "You are so understanding. These trysts hurt everyone. I am sure you know, Mr. Perri. You did stay at Lucky Luciano's apartment several times while in New York, didn't you? Arthur mentioned you came and went a lot from his building."

Perri, looking uncomfortable, cleared his throat then took an elaborate gold watch from his pocket. "If you will excuse us." He started to rise.

The maître d' hustled to the table. He seemed in a hurry to rid the dining room of the pair.

"It has been a pleasure." Erie extended her hand but remained seated.

Bill rose, shook Perri's hand, and bowed slightly to Bessi. "It's not often I meet such a refined and lovely woman," he said. "The pleasure was mine."

As soon as Rocco and Bessi turned their backs to leave, Bill summoned a waiter, handed him a dollar bill, and said quietly, "Tell me if they leave the building with anyone. If they leave alone just nod from the doorway."

The waiter took the money and walked to the entrance of the dining room. He disappeared for several minutes then returned to the entrance where he nodded to Bill, then went about his business.

"Phew!" said Erie. "To what do we owe that visit?"

"I apologize for the lie. We were treading on thin ground with those two. We needed a good believable story. My ankle is sore!"

"It would need to be such a story. And I don't know if Bessi bought it."

"Sure she did," said Bill, sipping his soup, "and she'll waste no time getting the word back to Arthur Moore."

Erie leaned back in her chair and sighed, "I'm going to be in fine shape to go with my father tonight. The whole purpose of this trip was that I should meet him. I've somehow got distracted. The visit has been overshadowed by the most bizarre incidents."

"Marry me and I'll protect you from everything, and everyone."

"Marry you and my life will be one of constant turmoil, especially if we live anywhere near Caleb and Smitty." Changing the subject she asked, "Will you travel to Toronto with Anna and I tomorrow?"

"Yes, and I'll definitely try to persuade Margaret to join

us. If Rocco Perri is heavily involved in some deal with Smitty and Caleb, she might be in danger if things go wrong. This time I think those two have taken a larger chunk of the pie than they can eat!"

"They're up to their necks in it," Erie said. "Can we leave? I know we haven't had a proper lunch, but I suddenly don't feel hungry. And I have to speak to Caleb."

Bill summoned the waiter. "I've lost my appetite too. Having to say Bessi Starkman was refined and lovely choked me right up. You can bet we'll not leave this hotel without a shadow. Let's make it look convincing."

"Surely they won't follow us to the farm?"

Bill dropped his napkin and signaled for the bill. "Sure they will. And they are probably grilling some poor shoe-maker over by Frederick Street. I knew I was being followed."

"Goodness," said Erie. "Was I?"

"No," Bill answered. "I had the common sense to watch when you left. I noticed when I got out of the Stuttgard that a car had pulled up behind me. I saw the same car on the road in from Maryborough. I made sure they followed me. The men figured you were shopping for clothing. Thank heavens you stopped to look in the shop window. I knew I wasn't on any particular mission for Caleb, so I reasoned you must be."

"This situation is getting more sinister by the moment." Erie shook her head in disbelief. "Let's go. I'm going to send a telegram."

"To whom?"

"To Arthur Moore. I'm asking him to come to Drayton on the noon train tomorrow. We'll be leaving on the early morning train to avoid him."

"I'll bet Perri miscalculated," Bill said. "He figures everything will happen here in Maryborough when it's really coming off in . . . ? "

"I've no idea where it's coming off," Erie said. "Let's find the telegraph office. We must assure that Arthur is in Maryborough both tomorrow afternoon and evening."

"Will he come up here for you now?"

"I'm going to sign the telegram Rocco Perri, and you're going to pay the telegraph officer heavily for not telling the name, if the tail asks."

CHAPTER THIRTY

GINGERICH'S FARM

SMITTY BENT TO CHECK that the dragging chain was firmly attached to the blackened beam. His face was dirty with soot and streaked with sweat. The team, smelling the acrid smoke and feeling its heat on their flanks, stomped nervously. Caleb held them in firm check, alternating between soothing words to the team and intense conversation with Smitty. Not far away, Elmer Brubacher and Milo Horst bent to a similar chore. Jacob's neighbours had rallied to clean up what they could of the smouldering ruin. Some beams were drawn away from the barn. Others were thrown in to be consumed in a controlled burn. Arran Gingerich, a cousin of Jacob's, was in charge of the crew.

After a good sleep and their noon meal, Smitty and Caleb drove Miriam and Ouma Salome home, then joined the gang.

Anna and Margaret were already at the Gingerich farm. They made Miriam comfortable and were preparing huge jugs of hot coffee and molasses drink for the crews. Occasionally, Caleb saw Anna carrying pitchers of drink, walking between the house and the table set up in Jacob's orchard. He remembered that the first time he saw her, she was carrying a jug of the same brew to the men in the back field at the Gingerich home farm.

Despite the fact that the day was cool, clothing stuck to his body in the intense heat. Once, Anna came to the fence with a change of shirt for him and Smitty. The dry flannel was appreciated, but within the half hour it was soaked again.

Caleb looked around the barn yard. Confidentiality was easy to obtain even though the snoopers had followed them from home and were parked out on the road. No one worked within hearing distance of he and Smitty.

"I figured Perri was snooping again," said Smitty giving the beam a kick. "The constable did some checking on Richardson after I let it slip that he had a gun and fired it. He didn't like the idea of anyone carrying a gun in his territory. The authorities don't have a Richardson working for them up here. The only conclusion I can come to is he is being paid by Perri."

"Perri had a nerve approaching Erie," said Caleb keeping an eye on both the team and a huge beam leaning dangerously over the one they were working on. "He's here for one reason only. If he finds the cache before it's shipped, he'll take it. Erie believes Arthur's in Toronto to provide the necessary papers through his broker for Perri, just as she's doing for us."

"He won't find the cache unless someone talks, and there are few of us know where it all is and when it will move out." Smitty yanked the chain.

Caleb firmed his grip on the reins, chucking quietly to the horses who pranced nervously when a small timber crashed nearby. "Those fellows aren't giving us much room to maneuver, are they? They're making it difficult for me to get to Toronto to pick up the papers. Perri's men will be watching both of us. I'm surprised they aren't here too."

"They might be," said Smitty assessing the situation overhead. "You realize, if we pull this beggar out of the way, the big center one is going to come down?" Smitty pointed to the offending beam hovering precariously overhead. "And if that one goes, God knows how much will follow. I don't know what it's holding back, more beams . . . grain . . . hay? Once you get the team moving, keep them going."

"I figure," said Caleb, "if I hike them up and to the left, I can get the beam out without causing too much of a commotion. I'll just drop the center beam and some hay, maybe a little wall too."

"If your theory doesn't work," said Smitty, "you won't have to worry about Toronto. You'll be under a ton of grain and beam."

Caleb shrugged. "What'll it be? Straight ahead or left?"

"Straight out and run like hell! I'll attach another chain to this clunker." Smitty hunched to work at the chain.

"If you can't get the papers and deliver them, I can't either. Who can?"

"None of our men," Caleb answered. "They're all known. Erie volunteered. But I don't want her or Anna involved. And now they know Bill. That leaves Margaret. She's the only one we can trust."

"I don't want her involved." Smitty rose slowly so as not to startle the horses. "The chains are solidly attached."

Everyone knows Margaret, thought Caleb looking toward the orchard where several women worked around the table. Margaret Smith with her red hair and colourful cotton dress stood out among them . . . as Margaret Smith, Catholic . . .

not as Margaret Schmidt, Mennonite. Caleb laughed. The horses jumped.

"Careful," warned Smitty. "The team's spooked today."

"Remember the time we dressed Margaret as a Mennonite and sent her along to Jacob's on Halloween? He didn't know her. We went to two . . . three places and she fooled them all?" Caleb said.

"Yes."

"Would she do it again?"

"Why?"

"To get the documents. She's our only choice. If she won't do it, the deal's lost."

"I'll have to ask her," said Smitty. "She just might if she thought it would end our scheming once and for all. No one would give a fig about an old Mennonite woman, would they?"

"Not if we're causing a diversion here in Maryborough." Caleb eyed the beam, still figuring it was best to pull slightly left.

"I'll ask her," Smitty said. "Now, let's see you move this piece of wood without killing yourself."

"You want to take the reins?"

"It's your party. What are we going to do about the snoopers and Perri?"

"You figure that one out," said Caleb. "It's your turn to come up with a solution."

"Are you ready?" Smitty stood back to survey the situation one more time.

"I am," said Caleb. "Just go move Elmer and Milo back. I don't want anyone hurt."

"Maybe a little to the left," Smitty observed. "And get yourself out fast!"

"I'll be running right beside the team."

"Nell is the least skitterish. Run on her left side."

Caleb stepped carefully across the chains as the horses pranced and snorted. "Steady, steady."

Caleb held even pressure on the reins as he maneuvered himself into a more favourable position. "Give me a wave when everyone's clear."

Smitty walked over to the first group of workers and spoke to them. All three moved among the crew to pass the word. Soon, men and teams were clear of the north side of the barn. John Martin and Smitty walked to the back lane. If the horses bolted, they would go in that direction.

Caleb calculated his risks. Watching for Smitty's signal, he planned his strategy. He gathered the trailing reins in his right hand, controlling the team with his left. When Smitty's arm came up, he whipped the reins over the backs of the horses bringing the ends down savagely like a cat-o-nine tails. The action had the desired effect. The team bolted forward. Caleb sprinted to grab Nell's harness. Holding on with his left hand he struggled to mount the horse, but failed. Holding tight, he slapped Nell hard with his free right hand. Nell, terrified, snorted and lunged left, pulling her teammate with her.

With a roar the large beam gave way, bringing stone wall, smouldering hay, and smaller beams with it. The hay, exposed to oxygen, exploded into flame.

The team ran wildly down the orchard lane dragging the beam and Caleb with them. John Martin leapt for Nell's head as the horse passed the orchard gate. Smitty lunged at the opposite horse's halter. Together they brought the team to a halt. Caleb fell to the ground, gasping for breath, his left-hand bleeding profusely. He instinctively rolled away from the animals' hooves. When his vision cleared, he looked up into the face of Anna Carliss who had dropped to her knees beside him. She gently lifted his hand and placed it on her white apron. Smitty was beside him too.

"Caleb, are you alright?"

Caleb closed his eyes. *Heaven*, he thought. If only his hand didn't hurt so much, he would be in heaven. A cool hand stroked his forehead and he heard the renting of cloth. Opening his eyes again he saw Margaret kneeling beside Anna, strips of white cloth in her hand. Anna's hand was on his forehead, her eyes searching his face.

"Answer me!" Smitty bellowed.

"Go away," moaned Caleb. "Your bellowing would bring a man back from the dead."

"He's alive," declared Smitty.

"Of course, I'm alive. What happened at the barn?" Caleb struggled to rise.

"Lay still," commanded Margaret. "Let me finish wrapping your hand."

"Do you hurt anywhere else?" asked Anna.

"My heart," muttered Caleb. "Everywhere," he answered loud enough Anna could hear him. He focused on the sky behind Anna and saw a large plume of smoke. "Brought some hay down, did I?"

"The rest of Jacob's barn," replied Smitty. "That center beam had a lot of rubbish behind it. There won't be any more cleaning up today. If you'd gone straight you would have been dead now." Smitty gently assisted Caleb to sit up.

"Please do be careful," said Anna. "He might have broken a bone."

"Or two . . . or three," said Caleb.

"Can you stand?" Margaret's matter-of-fact question put everything into perspective.

Caleb glanced at the crowd that stood around him. "I can't disappoint my fans. Help me up, Smitty. Anna, you steady my left arm and hand. It's sore. Bliss," he whispered to Smitty.

"Onto the porch with him," said Margaret.

A sharp pain shot up Caleb's left leg. He gasped for breath, then said to Smitty, "Carry me."

"Be damned," snorted Smitty, thinking Caleb was joking.

"Smitty, carry him if he asks." Anna anxiously watched Caleb. "He might be badly hurt."

"If I carry him, you'd have to let go his hand," Smitty replied, smiling at Caleb.

"Hell, I'll walk."

"One foot in front of the other. Easy does it." Smitty placed his left arm behind Caleb's back, giving him a poke as he did. With Smitty supporting him, Caleb eventually made it to Jacob's porch where he was lowered into a large wooden chair. One of the women had already laid a blanket in the chair. Another drew up a milk stool and lifted Caleb's left foot to it. A quilt appeared and was tucked around him.

Anna went into the house.

"You darn fool!" Smitty said. "Walking just so Anna could hold your hand. Your leg's hurt, isn't it? I didn't notice until we started for the house. I'm sorry. I thought you were joking when you asked to be carried. I could've done it."

"It's my ankle or foot," said Caleb, grimacing with pain.

Anna returned with a basin of water, bandages, and a can of ointment. Margaret followed her. Examining the hand, Margaret made her diagnosis. "There's skin off everywhere and two deep gashes. You must have hung on to the horse for dear life."

"It was my life, dear lady," answered Caleb. "I tried to mount Nell, but she was moving too quickly. So, I hung on knowing if I dropped to the ground I'd be hit with the beam. Would you check my left foot?"

Margaret gave Anna instructions on cleaning and bandaging Caleb's hand, then she unlaced his boot. The ankle was so badly swollen she couldn't remove the shoe.

"Jacob will have to cut it off."

"The foot?"

"The boot," said Margaret. "A joker to the end, aren't you, Caleb. If he's careful, it won't hurt. Jacob can snip the stitching."

Smitty went to find Jacob while Margaret checked the leg, then removed Caleb's right boot.

"If I'd known we were going to undress," joked Caleb, "I would have worn clean socks and underwear."

"You always had a keen sense of humour," said Anna carefully washing the hand.

"It helps in situations like this."

Jacob arrived and went to work. Even though he tried to be gentle, the pain was intense. Caleb closed his eyes so that Anna wouldn't see it in his eyes, but she sensed his suffering and wiped his forehead with a damp cloth.

"So I burned the rest of your barn, Jacob."

"Is so," answered Jacob. "But had to be done, yet. You are a foolish man, my broodah You could have killed yourself."

"All in my day's work."

"You take risks," admonished Jacob.

"I've no one to worry about me," Caleb answered truthfully. "I'm only a threat to myself."

"Ach," said Jacob snipping carefully, trying to cushion the foot and ankle on his lap. "You should have married. A good wife, and you will settle down. Is that not so, Mrs. Carliss?"

Anna smiled and thought of Jacob's two wives. "Loyalty and love can have a great effect on some people," she said. "A good wife must be balanced with a good husband."

"Well said!" Caleb patted Anna's arm with his free hand.

Jacob bent over the shoe and said nothing. He snipped and removed bits of leather until Caleb's foot was free of the boot.

"I'll fetch Margaret." Anna rushed into the house. Jacob cautiously snipped Caleb's sock. "Your ankle looks like a plump goose, broodah."

"There's no sense in doing things half-way. If I'm going to sprain my ankle, I may as well break it instead."

"What's this about broken ankle?" Margaret said, coming toward Caleb. She wiped her hands on her apron, eyed the purple, swollen ankle and said, "Jacob, go to the icehouse. Bring what ice you can find to the porch. Anna, ask Miriam what pillowcase we can use." She bent to take a closer look at Caleb's foot. "Wiggle your toes."

Caleb did as he was told with great effort and pain.

"Did you hear anything crack when you were running?" Margaret gently touched the swollen mass.

"No. I was too busy trying to mount Nell."

"Well, you're not going anywhere for a while. I'm pretty sure it's broken in several places. And, by the way," Margaret looked toward the kitchen door, a man your age should not be wearing his heart on his sleeve. You behave yourself around Anna, you hear?"

Caleb smiled. "I hear. But I do like her holding my hand."

"She'll be holding your foot if you don't watch your tongue," replied Margaret.

Caleb laughed and said, "You sure have a way with words, Margaret Smith. Where's Smitty?"

"The last time I saw him, he was walking out the laneway."

"Take a peek around the corner and tell me if he's talking to the snoopers."

Margaret did as she was told and said, "He's got his foot on the running board of the Ford and he is indeed chatting up the snoopers. The car's pulled right into Jacob's lane. There's a small crowd gathering round it. It's sure a curiosity for them. Wait a minute. Jacob's appeared. He's waving his arms. He must be ordering the car off the property. Now he and Smitty are walking to the house."

Eventually Smitty sauntered up onto the porch.

"What are you up to?"

"Cat and mouse," said Smitty. "I was just speaking with the mice." Seeing Anna approach, he continued. "I was just saying to Caleb that Jacob doesn't need to worry about mice in his barn for a while. They'll be heading for the house. We'll have to find him a couple of cats." He winked at Caleb. "Tonight, we round up some cats."

Anna looked quizzically at Smitty. What on earth was the man talking about.

Margaret entered into the conversation. "Caleb won't be looking for cats or mice for a while. We'll pack this foot and ankle in ice if there's any left, then you take him home, Smitty. Get Adam to help you. Put him in the room downstairs." She glanced at Anna. "Do you wish to be his nursemaid? He'll demand everything!"

"Erie can take care of Caleb. I'll stay here with you."

"Don't I get a say about my private nurse?"

"No," answered Margaret. "Just mind your p's and q's. Smitty, don't let him put any weight on that ankle or foot. We'll have to send for the doctor."

"I'll send Bill in the Stuttgard . . . for the doctor . . . and a few cats," Smitty said.

"What are you talking about, Patrick Smith?"

Adam arrived with a milk pail full of chipped ice.

"Margaret, tell Anna how to care for Caleb's ankle," Smitty said. "Come look at Nell with me. I think she's lame."

"Putting a horse in front of an old friend," snorted Caleb. "You might ask after the welfare of Mrs. Schmidt too."

"Put the ice in the pillowcase. Place it carefully around the ankle and foot. Adam, you help Mrs. Carliss. Hold your Uncle's hand for her."

Adam looked puzzled.

Caleb laughed. "Go get me a cup of coffee, lad. Don't mind the chatter of this woman."

Anna busied herself with the ice. "What is going on, Caleb? Erie's so secretive. Smitty is positively insane. He's talking rhymes."

"It's the full of the moon," replied Caleb. "The harvest moon affects people in different ways. Haven't you heard the tale of the cat and mouse and the harvest moon?"

"No, I haven't heard it and I don't believe I want to," replied Anna.

"Good. I haven't heard it either, and my ankle's hurting so much I can't make up a good story."

"I'm not a good nurse," Anna said. "I'll try not to hurt you, but your ankle looks so dreadful."

"I promise I won't scream," bribed Caleb, "if you promise me you will go out to dinner with me the next time I visit New York City."

Anna blushed.

"I will scream in absolute pain."

"I'll join you for dinner," capitulated Anna, "but not in New York. The next time you're in Camden, Maine, we will certainly take dinner together."

"Very clever woman," said Caleb. "You know I have never been to Camden. It's a bargain. Sometime in the spring, perhaps?"

"Yes," answered Anna. "That would be nice. Camden is lovely in the spring."

Anna gently applied the lumpy pillowcase to Caleb's ankle. Caleb bit his lower lip and grimaced. To keep his mind off the pain he concentrated on Smitty's *cat and mouse*. What was the man scheming?

"... in the morning."

Caleb was brought back to reality by Anna's voice. "You knew Erie and I are leaving on the early morning train tomorrow?"

"I didn't know that," lied Caleb. "I was under the impression you were leaving in the afternoon."

"Erie thought it best to leave on the early train. Would you take care of Arthur Moore, if and when he arrives?" Anna, not seeing Caleb's grin carried on, "Erie doesn't wish to meet Arthur so soon after speaking with her ..." Anna looked around the porch. "Father."

"Understandable," said Caleb, knowing the real reason Erie didn't wish to confront Moore. "Don't worry, Anna. If Arthur Moore shows up in Maryborough, Smitty and I will be perfect gentlemen to him. We'll treat him like one of the family."

"I trust you to be a gentleman, Caleb Gingerich, and to put him on the train back to Toronto in one piece."

"We won't do anything . . . much, Anna. We won't even mention Bill. He's heading back to Toronto too."

Anna smiled wryly at Caleb. "It's perfectly alright to mention Bill around Arthur Moore. Actually, mention him as often as you wish. Just, don't give the man the notion we are barbarians right out of the Canadian woods. Remember, Erie and I must live in New York and associate with people of Moore's silk."

"Where is that written in blood?" asked Caleb. "I'm not a betting man . . ."

Anna laughed. "I dare you to say that with a straight face."

"I bet you," Caleb emphasized his offer by slapping his left leg with his good right hand, a gesture he regretted immediately. "I bet you . . . another dinner that Erie and Bill O'Grady marry and live in Toronto."

"I wouldn't take you up on that bet," said Anna, "because I'd lose. Oh, Caleb. I can't influence Erie's decision in any way, but I do hope she sees the inevitable."

"Everyone else does. It's only a matter of time before she does too."

Anna got to her feet and wiped her hands down her apron. "I'd best go see to Ouma Salome and Miriam. Margaret and I will be home in time for supper."

"What about you, Anna? Will you live in New York? Won't you be lonely without Erie? Won't you consider . . ." Caleb wisely held his tongue.

"Wouldn't I consider moving to Toronto if Erie married Bill?"

"Yes."

"Time will tell," answered Anna. "Time has a habit of telling all, doesn't it?"

Caleb nodded and closed his eyes. Anna took that as a sign he was tired and left so that he might sleep a little before he was moved.

When she left, Caleb opened his eyes again and looked over Rachael's valley to Lilac Hill.

Oh, for one moment of my youth again, with the wisdom of the years I have lived. If one could go back and change time and circumstances. It's time I left this valley for good too. Caleb closed his eyes again. *Once Smitty and I are free of this business venture, I'll settle down . . . no, slow down. Settle is too permanent a word. Jacob is settled. I'd have to be around horses. I understand horses. And I'd have to be somewhere near Anna. Just close enough I could keep an eye on her and perhaps visit once in a while. But I wouldn't make a pest of myself.*

When Smitty and Adam came for Caleb, they found him asleep, a smile on his face.

"Let's go see the women," said Smitty. "With that kind of smile on his face, he's having sweet dreams. It's not fair to wake him."

Turning from Caleb, Smitty thought, *I must be getting daft, worrying about disturbing Caleb's sweet dreams.* "Come on, Adam. Let's go look for a pork sandwich."

CHAPTER THIRTY-ONE

THE GRAVEYARD

THE MOON WAS A HUGE YELLOW GLOBE low in the sky on the eastern horizon. The road was a pale ribbon lined with the silhouetted shapes of trees and buildings. Lights twinkled from houses and barns that Jacob and Erie passed. Leaves and dry grasses rustled in the slight, cool breeze. Jacob kept the horse at a neat gait. The harness, devoid of bells or brass, slapped gently against the sides of the animal. Buggy wheels ground over gravel road. Dogs barked as they passed.

Jacob, hat pulled firmly over his ears, said little. He did answer any questions asked by Erie, but he didn't initiate a conversation. Erie, enveloped in a large black shawl, looked as bleak as the night landscape. "You will be cold," Jacob had said, giving her the shawl. She accepted it realizing that without it someone might recognize her and think it strange Jacob had her in his buggy. She had pulled the shawl around her head, hiding herself in it for comfort. For the few hours she had alone with her father she would have consented to wear a sackcloth, had he handed her one.

So far she had ascertained they had five miles to travel, that Jacob told no one where he was going and that he seemed relieved she was leaving Maryborough so soon.

On the loneliest stretch of road, with not a house in sight, Jacob pulled to the side at the crest of a hill. By the light of the moon, Erie could see tombstones and wrought iron fencing. By the time Jacob alighted, Erie was out of the buggy and at the horse's head.

"This is not what I expected, Ja . . . Father. I understood your cemeteries were devoid of ornamentation."

"This is not a Mennonite burial ground, daughter. It is a Catholic cemetery."

"My mother was Catholic?"

"Yah," said Jacob.

"But didn't she take your faith."

"Yah," answered Jacob softly.

"Why then is she buried here and not at your meeting house? You won't be buried here."

Jacob didn't answer. He took Erie's elbow to help her up the hill. At the entrance, he hesitated, then placed himself between the cemetery and Erie. "Why did you wish to come here?"

"I only have my mother's grave. I have no pictures, no memories, no letters, only a tombstone."

Jacob's head fell to his chest.

"You have not erected a tombstone?" Exasperated, Erie threw her hands into the air. "Father, it is as though you wished to forget her. You have buried her five miles from home, with not a headstone to her memory."

"You did not have to come here." Jacob looked at his daughter and then to the ground.

"We both had to come here."

His next question took Erie by surprise as it came from a man who professed pleasure she was leaving. "You would consider returning to your people?"

"If I did," said Erie. "you would have to acknowledge my existence. You would have to explain your actions twenty years ago. You would have to accept my children, be they black, white, brown; and you would have to look at me every day, a physical reminder of Rachael."

"Yah." Jacob was short on words.

Erie whirled to face him. "You are prepared to do that?"

"If I must," answered Jacob. "This is your right as my daughter."

"I will not exercise that right. I am flesh of your flesh, blood of your blood, yet I am not one of you. I would wrong . . ."

Jacob interrupted, "You would wrong no one. I've been very stupid, mie dihchdah. I know it now. I did not listen to my heart. I was influenced . . . nay, that is not vawah. I allowed myself to be led by mie fahdah. He was a grehfdich mahn. He was a religious man. He was right as he read it in the bible . . . as he explained it to me. Caleb questioned Fahdah and left. I did not. Until now I did not understand Caleb's decision. I believe now he made the right choice."

"No father." Erie reached to touch Jacob. "Caleb may have made the right choice for himself, but not for you. Mother would not have lived one moment longer if you had left the faith. Do not question your religion, only how you interpret your teachings, or how your father managed to influence your views. Perhaps some of his influences were wrong, but not all of them."

"How can I speak to my people now? I have wronged Miriam, wronged you, wronged your broodahs."

"You can advise as you always have, with sincerity and honesty. You must right the wrongs in your private life, consummate the marriage between Miriam and yourself, allow my brothers to marry, allow me the freedom of knowing you as a friend and to love you as a daughter. Father, look at me."

Jacob lifted his eyes to Erie's face.

"I will not disturb your life. I will leave as I came . . . a friend of the family. Seven people know the truth. As much as I would like my brothers to know, they will never be told by me. I could not adopt your ways. Neither should my brothers try to adopt mine. They are honest, naive young men. I envy my brothers for their simplicity of life. They must stay in the faith, Father. And you must turn your love to Miriam. Give her the love you have denied her."

"You know . . ." Jacob seemed annoyed and couldn't finish his sentence.

"Miriam didn't tell me," Erie said quickly. "I'm clever enough to know that separate bedrooms mean separate lives. While I was at your farm on the day of the fire I noticed. I also wondered why a healthy woman like Miriam didn't have children."

"Enough!" said Jacob sternly, Jacob the Bishop talking.

"No, not enough!" retorted Erie. "Miriam loves you. She loves children. You have deprived her of that special gift between man and wife. Do you know what women would do in the city under similar circumstances?"

Jacob remained silent and Erie let the subject drop. He had gotten the message.

"Show me mother's burial place."

Jacob led the way, past well-kept granite and marble headstones in the small cemetery to a spot at the back where a huge wild rosebush grew.

"This is it? No cross, no indication of who . . . where . . . when?"

"It is here, somewhere here." Jacob was down on his hands and knees ripping away at the grass.

"Father, what are you doing?" Erie dropped to her knees by Jacob.

Like a madman Jacob began ripping at sod and roots. He began to sob.

"Father, please!" In desperation Erie began digging too, uprooting small clumps of grass and weed. Her fingers touched something cold and hard. She recoiled in fright.

"Ach," sobbed Jacob. "It is here." As he ripped furiously at the overgrowth, the full moon shone on the back of the sobbing man on his knees by the wild rose bush.

"Look, duhchdah. Look."

Jacob fumbled for a small packet of matches, lit one and held it close to the ground. His free hand cleared dirt from a flat object. Once cleared, he ran his fingers over cold metal, urging Erie to do so to. Lettering was raised on a metal plate and could be read easily by sight or feel.

"I made it in the blacksmith shop without Fahdah knowing," Jacob sobbed. "I brought it here one night and buried it. I planted a wild rose near it because Rachael loved wild roses. Fahdah never knew."

"Rachael Gingerich," Erie read slowly, running her fingers over the metal lettering. "Wife of Jacob Gingerich, April 21, 1905."

"Because of Anna Carliss, you are not buried here, child.

I did not bury you with your moodah. I gave you to William and Anna Carliss . . . in Pennsylvania in 1913. After William visited the farm to ask if he and Anna could adopt you, and I said no, I decided I would go to Pennsylvania to get you. I'd refused William's request; therefore, I must have wanted you myself, I thought."

"Why did you say no?"

"I do not know. I believe it was because you looked like Rachael." Jacob sobbed as he spoke. "Anna Carliss saved your life while I did not care whether you lived or died. I blamed you for Rachael's death for many, many months. I did not know . . ."

"You gave me to William and Anna?" Erie held her father's trembling hand. "What do you mean?"

"I got to the gate at the Bedford Estate in Pennsylvania and saw you playing with the other children. You were laughing and chasing a kit . . . a beautiful, little, Rachael child . . . Rachael's legacy. My eyes told me all. You had everything I wanted for Rachael. You were surrounded by love. You had freedom. You were as Rachael wished you to be, as she should have been. You would never be tethered by four walls and rules. You could never be Jacob Gingerich's child, fitting into Jacob Gingerich's life. Your mother . . ."

Jacob sobbed uncontrollably. "Your mother, my Rachael, came to our home as a high-spirited young girl. I can see her now . . . listening to my father's teachings . . . working with my mother. She never questioned. She always obeyed. But, as I grew to love her, I realized she had lost that spirit. She became more Mennonite than my sisters who always questioned our ways. She spoke intelligently with Fahdah about our teachings and she joined our faith to marry me. I thought if I married her, she would be free. I could open a window and let her be free." Jacob reached to touch Erie's long, black hair.

"I forgot Fahdah," he said quietly. "It was I that could never be free. He taught me well, did Fahdah. He saw in Rachael a threat to me. It was fine when she just lived with us, but when we loved, Fahdah began to turn from her. He held her race against her . . . her religion against her . . . her dedication to Mother against her. He did not live by his own teachings. Rachael loved him in spite of his anger. She loved him too much. He held that against her. He loved her not enough."

Jacob reached to touch Erie's face. "We married against his wishes, but with Moodah's full blessing. Mother Salome was a wise woman, with a spirit as high as Rachael's. She saw in Rachael the young woman she had once been. Fahdah had chosen Miriam for me a long time ago. While Rachael was alive, she was my strength. With Rachael I could manage Fahdah. I thought he would grow to love her as I did . . . as Moodah did. As soon as Rachael died, my spirit died too. I didn't blame myself for its death. I blamed you . . . I blamed Miriam. I hardened. I became Bishop Gingerich, son of Bishop Gingerich."

Jacob absentmindedly stroked Erie's hair. "I watched you for a long time at the Carliss Estate; then I turned my back to you and walked away. I put you out of my life. I could not put you in a box. I could not extinguish your love of life . . . your freedom to live. You became William and Anna's child. I thought no more of you. I had nothing more to do with the Carliss family. I made my house a shrine to Rachael. Miriam could not move a thing that belonged to Rachael. She could not sleep in the same bed . . ."

"Father, father," Erie flung herself at Jacob and he held her close to him.

"It was the right thing to do." Jacob cried. "Anna Carliss loved you as the daughter she could never have."

"And you loved me, father." Erie's tears mingled with those of her father. "You loved me enough to give me freedom. You must now give that love to Miriam. It's not too late, Father. Release Miriam from the prison you have placed her in. Love her as you loved Rachael. Remember Mother, but love Miriam too."

Jacob and Erie clung to each other for a long time before Jacob finally said, "Leave me for a while, child. Leave me with Rachael."

Erie kissed her father's damp cheek and rose to her feet. "I will stay by the buggy, father."

She walked slowly through the damp graveyard to the gravel road where she stood holding the horse's halter. "Bill," she murmured. "I hope you are at Smitty's when I return. I do need you now."

From the cemetery an unearthly wailing rose to meet the full of the moon. Jacob was finally making peace with Rachael and himself.

Erie shivered and pulled the shawl closer about her. Looking up through tear-filled eyes, Erie saw a brilliant star shooting across the western sky.

The full moon that shone on Erie and Jacob brightened the backyard at the Smith farm. Caleb, supported by Smitty, labouriously made his way from the outhouse to the porch.

"How long are you going to be laid up?" questioned Smitty, taking care to support Caleb properly.

"As soon as my hand heals and I can use crutches, I won't be such a burden. I don't like being babied any more than you like doing it."

"Come now. It all depends on who's doing the babying, doesn't it? I don't mind helping an old friend. You would do the same for me."

The two stopped for a moment so Smitty could adjust his hold. A brilliant star shot across the heavens.

"That was a beauty!"

"Just Rachael showing her love," said Smitty. "It looks like we're in for a meteor shower. There's all kinds of them up there."

Caleb glanced up. "The Irish and their superstitions," he said.

"It is not a superstition. It is a custom. There is a big difference between a superstition and a custom."

"What will you associate me with when I die" Caleb shifted his weight on Smitty a little. His ankle was paining terribly.

"A thistle," said Smitty, "of a clump of burdock . . . something obnoxious."

Smitty started to walk slowly again. "This isn't just a little break, is it?"

"Doc says it's bad. I have to see a specialist in Toronto as soon as I can."

"You haven't said much about my scheme." Smitty changed the subject.

"It's hair-brained," said Caleb.

"But will it work?"

"You're forcing their hand," warned Caleb. "And I can't help you. I'm a sitting duck with this gimpy hand and foot."

"It will work. Trust me," counselled Smitty. "Margaret has agreed. Adam is primed. Bill issued the invitation. Moore is playing right into our hands."

Caleb leaned heavily against Smitty to hobble up the steps. "I reserve judgement, Smitty. This has got to be the riskiest set-up you have even conceived."

"What is there to lose?" asked Smitty.

"A life. If someone is carrying a gun, we could lose a life."

"The snoopers don't carry guns. Moore won't have one. You and I don't own one."

"That leaves Perri's men," countered Caleb.

"They are the unknown factor," admitted Smitty. "But they'd be darn fools to show their weapons in such distinguished company."

"I wish I weren't such a cripple. I can't help you if anything goes wrong, and I got you involved with this in the first place."

"Don't worry. Nothing will go wrong. But this is the last time. I've decided I'm not going to get involved in any more schemes. What about you?"

"I haven't decided where I'll lay my hat yet or what I'll do."

"I'll bet it will be somewhere near Anna Carliss. You don't stand a snowball's chance in hell of courting her, Caleb Gingerich."

"I've been warned about that at least three times. There's no harm in trying, is there? Maybe the chase will keep me out of trouble."

"Anna needs someone to watch out for her. You're just the fellow. But trouble follows you wherever you go, Caleb. You generate it like heat."

"What are you going to do, Smitty?"

"I don't know," Smitty said. "I promised Margaret that if she got involved this would be the last. You know what I'm like Caleb. I would go crazy sitting around a house doing nothing."

"Margaret is well aware of your needs too. She won't let you sit. Take her advice. Do what she says. Women's intuition! You know, Margaret says she wouldn't be surprised if I end up with a permanent limp because of this break."

Smitty shook his head. Margaret's intuition was usually correct. He had never known a time she had ever been wrong.

CHAPTER THIRTY-TWO

LEAVING MARYBOROUGH

THE LAND LAY BEJEWELED under a heavy dew. Sunlight sheathed everything with droplets of liquid crystal. Such a beautiful day made leaving Lilac Hill all the more difficult. The Smith household stirred early. Smitty drove down the back lane to pick up Anna and Erie's luggage. The back seat of the Essex had been installed making it a respectable family car once more. Anna cried when she closed the door to the cottage. She made Smitty promise he would paint it and do some repair work. Smitty made her promise she would not leave it twenty-one years before she came back. Erie stood on the porch looking toward her father's home. When at last she was rewarded by the sight of figures standing on the porch, she waved frantically. Jacob and Miriam waved back.

"Aren't you going over to say good-bye?" asked Smitty.

"We said our good-byes last night," Erie responded, giving no explanation.

"Oh, how I hate to leave this valley," Anna lamented.

"This is twice I have left Lilac Hill in the autumn. The first time I was a bride."

"And the second time?"

Anna smiled and said, "I am leaving a much happier woman than I came. The past two weeks have been . . . invigorating."

"What about you, Erie?" Smitty put an arm around his cohort.

"I can't pick my life up where I left it off. But I'm going back to New York. I've a lot to think about and I want to spend some time with Mother . . . Anna."

"Let's go have breakfast."

"We'll walk and meet you at the house. How is Caleb this morning?"

"He's in extreme pain. We have to get him to Toronto as soon as possible."

"Can't he travel with us?" asked Anna.

Smitty hedged and finally said, "He says he wants to have his car in Toronto. He wants me to drive him down. It will be tomorrow before I can do that."

After Smitty left, Erie and Anna walked as far as the wooden footbridge.

"Will you ever come back to Rachael's valley," Anna asked.

"Only with children of my own who must know the truth. And only at the proper time in their lives."

"There may never be a proper time," said Anna.

"That depends on the child. Will you ever return, Mother?"

"If Lilac Hill remains mine," replied Anna. "If Smitty sells his farm, I have instructed him to turn Lilac Hill over to Miriam Gingerich."

"Not to Jacob or Caleb?"

"This is a woman's retreat," answered Anna. "It is a lover's rendezvous. Oh dear! My memories of this place. We had better go."

Breakfast was a jovial meal with Caleb and Bill's cavorting which livened the affair. Margaret outdid herself, hot scones with Miriam's wild bramble jelly, summer sausage sent over by Jacob, egg toast, maple syrup, and steaming coffee.

"You promise to join us in Toronto tomorrow?" said Anna for the third time to Margaret.

"I will meet you at your hotel for lunch at noon," promised Margaret. "We'll spend a delightful week in the city. I can't leave today. I want to check on Miriam and Ouma."

"No harm will come to you ladies. I'm travelling with you." Bill smiled at Anna and winked at Erie.

"That's akin to putting the fox in the henhouse," Smitty snorted. "You'll see Caleb the day after tomorrow too."

Leaving the farm was difficult. Margaret and Anna had a good cry, even though they knew they would see each other in a day's time. Bill was put in charge of a picnic basket Margaret had packed for the train ride down. Sandwiches were wrapped in good white linen napkins because she had an aversion to brown butcher's paper.

Smitty hurried everyone to the car. As the Essex vanished down the farm lane in a cloud of dust, Caleb clung to the door of the Stuttgard for support. Smitty purposefully drove the long way into Drayton so Erie and Anna could catch one last glimpse of the Gingerich farm, the river valley, and the Catholic cemetery. They were early for their train, so they stood chatting on the platform, watching other people arrive.

"See that fellow, over there, the one in overalls?" Smitty

said quietly to Erie, nodding at a man lounging against a wagon. "He's following you. He'll board the train and ride to Toronto, beady little eyes on you all the way. My shadow's not too far away either. Didn't you notice we had company on the sideroad?"

Erie nodded.

"Act natural. Keep him interested in you. But don't go near the broker in Toronto. Don't let him notice anyone else on the train. Be the center of attention, even if you have to faint in front of him."

"That ploy is so old-fashioned."

"Well, how am I to know such things."

The train was pulling in when an elderly, stoop-shouldered Mennonite woman stepped onto the platform.

"Mrs. Schmidt," Smitty doffed his hat to her.

Bill, Anna, and Erie busily gathered their hand luggage.

Smitty gave Anna and Erie a bear hug before they were whisked on board by Bill.

"Don't cry!" Smitty called. "We'll see each other again soon."

Anna was too overcome to say anything.

Smitty assisted Mrs. Schmidt aboard. The old lady immediately took a seat on the opposite side of the aisle to Anna, Bill, and Erie.

Glancing out her window, Erie caught sight of a dark-clothed man standing alone in the shadow of the station.

"Father," she whispered. She clutched Bill's hand. "Father has come to see me off."

Erie waved but knew Jacob Gingerich would not acknowledge the gesture. She leaned against Bill, glad he was with her and understood what she was going through. Bill put his arm around her.

Mrs. Schmidt piled the seat beside her high with bags and proceeded to knit.

"All aboard," called the conductor again. The train pulled out of the station, heading for Fergus and Guelph. Erie watched her father until she could no longer see him through the window.

Bill comforted Anna. "You'll see everyone again. Don't take parting so hard."

When Erie noticed the man in overalls coming down the aisle, she whispered to Bill. "Smitty says that fellow is following me. I'm to keep him busy."

The shadow motioned to the Mennonite woman to move her bags so he could sit down. She upbraided him in Deutsche and shooed him away. He chose a seat directly behind Erie.

Anna watched the landscape for a long time before she closed her eyes.

Bill and Erie kept a lively conversation going about stocks, mining, real estate, and world events, until the fellow rose to use the facilities.

"Has he got something to do with my mission last night?" asked Bill.

"What was your mission?"

"Smitty said I was drumming up a few cats. In reality, I delivered a message to a blind pig in Kitchener which had connections with someone . . . don't ask who." Bill shook his head. "Shh . . . he's coming back."

Another long interval of useless conversation took place. Anna woke up and smiled at Mrs. Schmidt. "I marvel at how some people can knit anywhere. I can't knit on a moving train. I get ill. She is such a sweet lady, isn't she?"

"I'm surprised she's on the train at all and travelling alone."

"Mennonites can use the train, especially if it's an emergency. You wouldn't expect them to drive to Toronto by horse and buggy," said Bill. "She's probably going to Pennsylvania. The conductor will make sure she gets to the right connection in Toronto. What are your plans when we reach the city?"

"I have some business on Bay Street," said Erie loudly. "Some banking to do, some papers to fill in, and then we'll meet James and Frank." She winked at Bill.

"James has been expecting us," said Bill. "You have everything ready to give him?"

"Did you telephone Frank we were coming?"

"Everything has been arranged. One shipment has already arrived."

The shadow craned his neck for a look-around.

Anna seemed perplexed. "Would you care for a short walk down the aisle?" Bill asked. "Perhaps to stretch your legs after your sleep?"

Anna accepted the invitation.

The shadow stayed with Erie. When Anna and Bill returned, Anna winked at Erie, acknowledging that she had been briefed on the situation. Thereafter the three kept an animated and ludicrous conversation going. Erie was sure the shadow was writing everything down. Mrs. Schmidt slept.

Below Guelph, Bill announced he was hungry. "Let's have Margaret's lunch."

Erie unpacked the basket, handing Anna and Bill the linen-wrapped sandwiches, cheese, and apples. "It was kind of Margaret. She sure knows Bill's fantastic appetite." Erie unwrapped a ham sandwich. Having said that she remembered the Mennonite woman and wondered if she might want a sandwich. Margaret had packed far too many.

Old Mrs. Schmidt was busy unwrapping her own sandwiches. She glanced quickly at Erie before whisking her own linen napkin out of sight.

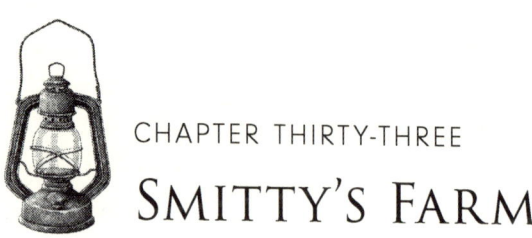

CHAPTER THIRTY-THREE

SMITTY'S FARM

THE ONLY LIGHT in the Smith house came from an oil lamp in the middle of the kitchen table. The dog barked his displeasure at being tied up in the barn. Adam Gingerich worked among the cows, milking and bedding them for the night. Occasionally he looked out the door to see if a lamp had been placed in the back kitchen window.

"What is going on?" hissed a plaid-shirted snooper peering over the shoulder of his companion. Both were crouched in the long grass by the orchard fence where they had an unrestricted view into the kitchen.

"Nothing. The dog's tied in the barn like Smitty said he would be. That fellow they picked up at the train station is sitting at the table with them doing something. I can't see what."

"Smith said to show up at eight o'clock."

"I smell a trap," the second snooper in the black shirt said.

"So do I. But we can't afford to ignore his invitation. We have watched these two for months and have nothing concrete on them. How do we know they're responsible for the missing whiskey?"

"Come now," said black shirt. "We know they're behind the thefts."

"We can't prove it," said the first. "We only have hearsay." He stood and brushed dirt off his pants.

"Time to go calling."

"What if it's a trap?" asked black shirt.

"Those two haven't got a full can of brains between them," answered plaid shirt. "They're farmers dabbling in something they shouldn't be. They're working for someone else, maybe Perri. I think they'll try to bribe us, cut out their boss. If they're doing that, how are they going to move the whiskey? They'll offer us a cut if we help them. They might even offer to sell it back to the distillery."

"What's our answer?"

"Depends on the offer," said plaid shirt. "We're working for the distillery, but the pay isn't that good."

"I still think we should have armed ourselves," muttered black shirt.

"They're foolish," said plaid shirt, "but they're not stupid. And we're not out to kill anyone, you damn fool. We're looking for missing whiskey. Come on. Keep a sharp eye for trouble."

The snoopers walked across the lawn and knocked at the back door. Smitty answered immediately and had them inside quickly so they wouldn't notice a light now on in the barn.

"Gentlemen, this is Arthur Moore of New York City." Arthur stood to shake hands.

The snoopers exchanged glances. "First surprise," muttered plaid shirt.

"Arthur is here on both business and pleasure," said Caleb. "He is engaged to my niece, and he is looking for Rocco Perri."

"Second surprise," muttered black shirt.

"I'm sure you have met Caleb Gingerich."

Caleb nodded, his bandaged left hand on the table, partially covered by his right.

"Third surprise," muttered plaid shirt.

"I beg your pardon," said Smitty. "You're doing a lot of whispering."

"How did your friend hurt himself?" asked plaid shirt.

"At the Gingerich farm yesterday afternoon," answered Caleb. "I tried to outrun a horse."

"Sit down, sit down," Smitty offered chairs. "Care for crokinole? We were initiating Arthur into the honourable game."

"We didn't come for crokinole."

"No crokinole? How about a cup of coffee?"

"We'll have a cup of coffee." Plaid shirt looked around the kitchen before sitting down. "Nice house, Smith. Where's your wife?"

"Helping the neighbours," answered Smitty. "Mrs. Gingerich isn't well. She was injured in the barn fire, you know."

"I heard," said black shirt.

No sooner had coffee been poured than a knocking came at the front door. "Must be city people," said Smitty. "No farmer comes to the front door." Smitty lit a second lamp he happened to have handy. "If you will excuse me?" Minutes later he returned to the kitchen leading two dark-suited men. "Arthur, I think these men are looking for you."

"Rocco's men," black shirt hissed to plaid shirt.

"Sorry gentlemen, I can't introduce you because I don't know your names," Smitty said.

"Introductions aren't necessary," snapped one, a short man in stature but very muscular in appearance. The other was tall and thin.

"Sit down." Smitty set the lamp he was carrying on the windowsill facing the barn. "Join the party."

"Aren't you late?" said Arthur Moore. "You were to meet me at the station at one o'clock. Fortunately, Patrick and Caleb came along and introduced themselves. I would have stood around for a long time, and I'm not used to being kept waiting."

The snooper glowered at the henchmen, who in turn glowered at Moore.

"You may as well sit down, gentlemen," Arthur said. "Mr. Smith will pour you some coffee."

"That's stretching it," said Caleb referring to the word *gentlemen*, but placing the inference on the coffee. "Smitty. Make another pot of coffee."

"Are you going to stand all night?" Arthur asked. "Or are you going to take advantage of the hospitality."

The two reluctantly pulled out chairs and sat down, one on either side of Moore, but made sure they weren't near the snoopers.

"Obviously, you got the note." Smitty deftly poured cups of coffee, then placed cream and sugar in front of the pair.

"You play crokinole?" asked Caleb.

"We play for keeps," said the short man.

"We only play for pennies," Caleb replied smoothly. "That way no one loses his shirt."

Smitty glanced at Moore's men, shrugged, and said, "How about a game of poker?"

"Some other time. Look Mr. Moore, if you are ready, we'll leave now."

"Where might I be going?"

"The word was to pick you up . . ."

The back door creaked. All four men stiffened. Caleb noticed the short man reach to his jacket.

"Adam," said Smitty breaking the tension. "Come in, lad. Are the chores done?"

"Yah," answered Adam. "The cows are milked. The pigs slopped. The horses ae fed."

"Good boy," said Smitty pulling out a chair beside him. "Join us. Have some coffee. These four gentlemen are visiting . . . Mr. Moore, Caleb, and I." Smitty gestured as he introduced the men. "We don't often get company in the middle of the week. There's no cookies, Adam. Margaret hasn't baked yet."

Adam doffed his hat and sat down.

Caleb hadn't moved one finger since plaid shirt and his companion arrived. A cup of coffee sat beside his right hand untouched.

"You play crokinole?" asked Smitty.

"Yah," replied Adam picking up a black chip. He placed it on the board and with a flick of his finger, sent it sailing into the opposite side where it struck the edge.

Arthur's friends jumped.

"Bad shot," said Caleb. "Try again."

Adam reached for another chip.

"You've travelled around here a lot, lad," the plaid-shirted snooper said. "Have you seen anything unusual lately?"

"What is unusual?"

"That's what I asked you."

"I don't think the young man comprehends what you mean," said Arthur. "The fellow means have you seen anything different or out of the ordinary recently."

"Ah, I have," Adam replied playing with a chip. "One of Amsy Martin's cows had a two-headed calf."

"Not that unusual," said plaid shirt. "I mean strange men around, things going on late at night, old buildings being used again."

Adam fired off another shot. It scooted onto the board and almost made bullseye.

"Good shot!" observed Arthur.

"When I was with Fahdah today we saw some things that were different."

"Like what?"

"Mrs. Schmidt was travelling on the train. There must have been a death in her family. And we saw freight cars."

"What's different about freight cars?" sneered black shirt. "You see them on the line everyday."

Adam shrugged and picked up another chip. "I have not seen them on this line before."

"That's interesting," said the tall man.

"Doesn't mean a thing." Smitty picked a chip and flipped it onto the board. "What's a few freight cars on the tracks."

"They were on the old spur line," said Adam knocking Smitty's chip away from bullseye and scoring one himself.

"Bravo!" Arthur removed the chip.

"Where is this old spur line?" plaid shirt said taking a sudden interest in crokinole. He picked up a chip, aimed and let fly. The chip shot across the board and bounced out onto the table.

"Too much finger," said Adam. "At the cheese factory."

"Adam," Caleb said. "Maybe the men don't want to hear about the freight cars."

"On the contrary," said plaid shirt. "Where is the cheese factory?"

"At Walkerton."

"Anyone for more coffee?" Smitty asked.

"Cut it, Smitty. Did you notice any activity around these cars?" Plaid shirt toyed with a chip.

"They were loading up, yet."

"Loading what?" the short man demanded. "For Christ's sake, stop playing this damn game!"

Adam looked frightened.

"Speak up!"

"They were loading lumber and barrels and barrels . . ."

"Of whiskey," whispered black shirt hoarsely into plaid shirt's ear.

"Why were you in Walkerton?" demanded the short man.

"My Fahdah's barn burned down two days ago. We travelled to Walkerton to buy beams from another barn."

"And these cars were being loaded right in town in front of everyone," sneered the tall, thin man.

"No," Adam seemed to shrink in size under the gaze of all seven men. "The old cheese factory spur line is not near the town. It is out by itself. Fahdah had to go by it to see the barn. The men loading the cars told him to go away."

"Let's go!" said plaid shirt rising from his chair. Black shirt leapt to his feet. "Out of the mouths of babes. Thought you could keep us here playing this stupid game while the whiskey was being moved out at Walkerton, didn't you?" Plaid shirt addressed Smitty.

"No such thing!"

"Come on." Plaid shirt made for the back door. "We're maybe too late already." The snoopers disappeared out the door.

"Get up Moore, we've got to go." Rocco's men stood.

"Gentlemen," protested Arthur. "I would appreciate an explanation as to where I'm going."

"They've already got a head-start," the short man said to his companion. "Perri isn't going to be happy if he misses that load. On your feet, Moore."

"Mr. Moore is not going with you," Caleb spoke.

"Look Moore, we're taking you with us."

Arthur started up.

"Sit down, Arthur." Caleb commanded.

The short man reached to his jacket.

"I would not pull that gun if I were you."

Caleb removed his right hand from his bandaged left. "I do shoot to kill." The barrel of a gun stuck out of the bandaged hand. "There is nothing wrong with this hand except for an itchy finger under this bandage. I want your gun on the table. I've had this pointed at you all night."

Smitty hid his surprise by saying, "Do as Caleb says. Arthur, remove that man's weapon. Caleb is an excellent shot."

Arthur placed a handgun on the table.

"How dare you come into my house armed," said Smitty. "Get out before I send Adam for the constable."

"Out the back door so I can see you at all times," said Caleb.

The pair walked stiffly past Caleb who kept his bandaged hand pointed at them. They disappeared out the back door.

Smitty grabbed their gun off the table and went after

them. He soon reappeared through the front door. "All four of them are off in the direction of Walkerton, I'll bet." He slapped Adam on the back. "Well done, young man. Off with you now. You know what to do next."

Adam nodded and slipped away.

"I'll get the suitcases," said Smitty. Caleb, you keep an eye out the window."

"This was a set-up wasn't it?" Arthur Moore looked from Smitty to Caleb. "I've been set-up but good, by the pair of you."

"You could say that," Caleb answered. "Now if you will just co-operate with us."

"I'm staying here."

"I don't think you are. You're not safe here. What if Perri's men come back? What are you going to tell them? Will they believe you weren't co-operating with us? Not likely?"

Smitty brought three suitcases downstairs.

"Our friend says he is staying."

"Now don't say that, Arthur. I'd have to physically put you in the car. I don't want to have to do that tonight. You carry the suitcases to the Stuttgard. I'll help Caleb to the car. Where did you get the gun, Caleb?"

"Gun?" Caleb removed a small piece of tubing off the still from his bandaged hand. "What gun?"

Smitty roared with laughter.

"I'll be damned!" exclaimed Arthur. "You bluffed those two."

"What did you do with their gun?"

"I've got it here." Smitty pointed to his pants pocket. "The bullets are here." He pointed to another pocket. "There'll be no accidents around this farm. Come on. We'd better leave before they get back. Are you coming of your own free will, Arthur?"

"Prudence is the better part of valour," said Arthur. "I believe I'll stick with you fellows."

The Stuttgard roared down the concession line, Smitty at the wheel. He stopped just long enough to throw gun and bullets into the Conestoga River at the bridge.

"I possibly owe you a debt of gratitude," Arthur conceded. "I didn't expect Perri would send two goons to get me. The telegram I received said he'd pick me up himself."

"If I hadn't made a promise to Mrs. Carliss, I would have let them carry you off. You shouldn't play with such dangerous people. You know, your disappearance would have solved a few problems."

"Problems?"

"Nothing to worry about," said Smitty "We'll be in Toronto before the sun rises. Erie said she would explain all when she saw you. She did give me a message for you. She said, tell Arthur . . . 'one of them can be equal to him.' "

"That doesn't make sense."

"Well, that's what the message was. Bill heard it too."

"Bill who?"

"Bill O'Grady. I understand you know him?"

"So that's what she's been up to. I knew there was a reason for her to come up here."

"It's a long drive," Caleb interrupted, "and I feel like talking. Do you want to listen, Arthur?"

Smitty laughed and gave the Stuttgard a little gas. A cloud of dust billowed behind the car as it sped towards Toronto.

Adam didn't touch a dish. He checked the lamps, locked the door, and scouted the barn once more. Calling the dog to his side, he left a note at both the front and back doors of the house. He and the dog disappeared into Smitty's barn.

When the snoopers arrived back at the Smith farm, they cautiously approached the house from the orchard.

"Look at this," exclaimed black shirt, retrieving a note from the big latch hole on the door.

"Why would they leave a note?"

Black shirt struck a match and read, "Margaret, gone to Collingwood."

Plaid shirt peered into the kitchen through the window. "Lamp's on. Dishes are on the table. The wife isn't back yet."

"I knew it. I knew it," roared black shirt. "It was a set-up. We chased after a load of bridge forms and kegs of nails in Walkerton, and they're in Collingwood loading the whiskey."

"They took the Stuttgard," observed plaid shirt. "It's a fast car. They're going somewhere in a hurry."

"What now?"

"We had better head for the docks at Collingwood. If we lose the whiskey there'll be hell to pay. We can't take a chance it is not being shipped out of Collingwood. Either these men have nothing to do with the whiskey, or they have more brains than I am giving them credit for."

When Perri's men arrived back at the Smith farm, they walked directly up to the front door and hammered on it.

"Wait," said the tall man. He pulled a slip of paper out

from between the door and the jam. He passed it to the short man, who read by the light of a cigarette lighter, "Margaret, gone to Kincardine."

"Kincardine," exploded the short man. "We've lost the shipment and Moore too."

"Maybe not. If we leave now, we might get to Kincardine before they get it loaded. Moore is with Smith. We'll have two birds in one net if we move fast enough."

"Who's to say they have anything to do with Perri's whiskey?" asked the short man. "Who's to say the note's not a plant?"

"All I know is the boss wants Moore," said the tall man. "They have Moore and we want him."

"I trust nobody. What if this note is for real? The Stuttgard's gone. They're making time somewhere. I'll bet it's to Kincardine. Let's go."

CHAPTER THIRTY-FOUR
BAY STREET

MARGARET FOUND IT DIFFICULT maintaining the posture and gait of elderly Mrs. Schmidt as she made her way along Bay Street, but she was careful to do so. She knew she must continue her performance until she reached the office of Carliss Enterprises's agent. Everywhere she looked, lean purposeful Torontonians were going about the city's business dressed in expensive suits and dresses. And, goodness, the women's hats! She could not imagine herself in such costumes, but felt conspicuous in her black Mennonite clothing, though she received surprisingly little attention from the people she passed. They didn't seem to notice anyone or anything, such was their hurry. Margaret tried to imagine them on the streets of Drayton.

It was a cool day and pigeons flew briskly to and from their perches on window ledges high above. Margaret followed the numbers on buildings up Bay, impressed by the polished brass plates and the fancy digits stenciled on the windows of huge oak doors. By her reckoning, the agent's office was only a half block further. She opened her bag of knitting and felt beneath the wool for the envelope containing the signed instructions for the shipment. *It will be such a relief to have Smitty and Caleb out of this business,* she thought. *It's a wonder I'm not as grey as one of those pigeons.*

"Margaret Smith," a man's voice called.

She turned to respond. She had relaxed her practiced old-woman stoop and was fully turned around before she realized what she had done. There was no returning to Mrs. Schmidt.

"I thought you might need an escort. The city can be a dangerous place for a woman alone."

The man looked as foreign as she did, dressed as he was in overalls and work boots. It was Erie's shadow, the man from the train. Before Margaret could react, he had her by the wrist. She tried to pull free from his grip. She was a strong woman, but he was much stronger. The people passing by seemed oblivious to her struggle.

"I'd stay calm if I were you," said the shadow, grabbing her knitting bag. "In the eyes of the law, you're as much a criminal as I am."

Margaret was about to launch a vicious kick, but stopped abruptly. It was true. What would the police do if they confiscated the papers and traced the shipment to Smitty and Caleb? Her heart sank.

The shadow guided her roughly into a narrow, blind alley between two nearby buildings and blocked her escape with his thick body.

"Now that you've joined the Mennonite faith, you won't want anything more to do with whiskey, will you? Let me deliver you from temptation." He gave Margaret a push backward. She stumbled and almost fell. For the first time she felt physically threatened. The shadow removed the envelope from Margaret's knitting bag and flung the bag down the alley. It struck her head as it flew by.

Reading the captured documents, the shadow said, "This is going to make me a very popular man. Yes, indeed. I won't be wearing these again." The shadow hooked a thumb in his overalls. "I think maybe I'll mail them to your bumpkin husband as a souvenir." He stuffed the papers in his pocket and advanced on Margaret. There was nowhere to run. She closed her eyes as his hand shot towards her. He seized her right hand and held it directly in front of her face, squeezing powerfully. Her eyes teared with the pain. What was he going to do? She had nothing to confess. All the information he needed was in the documents.

"You don't find one of these on a Mennonite," he scoffed.

Margaret opened her eyes to see her mother's cameo ring. It was small and so much a part of her that she had forgotten to remove it when she became Mrs. Schmidt.

"You were flashing it all over the place while you were knitting on the train," said the shadow. "You weren't fooling anybody but yourself."

So she was responsible for the failure of Smitty and Caleb's scheme. Her oversight had cost them the shipment and perhaps endangered their lives. At that moment she didn't care what the shadow might do to her. "Who are you working for?" she asked.

"Wouldn't you like to know," he said, releasing her hand. "Go back to the farm. Tell your husband and his pal to stick to milking cows. They're out of their league playing this field." He turned and walked out of the alley.

Margaret massaged her hurting hand, staring at her ring

in disbelief. How could she have been so clumsy? There was no time for an alternative plan now. It was too late. They had counted on her, and she had let them down—Smitty, Caleb, Erie, all the others involved around Maryborough and beyond. Smitty's instructions were for her to give up the papers immediately if she were caught. But she shouldn't have been caught. She had ruined everything. It was all her fault. Patrick said if anything happened, she was to go immediately to Bill's house. Dejected, she picked up her knitting bag and started walking.

CHAPTER THIRTY-FIVE

PARK AVENUE, TORONTO

A CITY WAS DIRTIER AND NOISIER than Erie remembered. She said as much to Bill as she stood beside him on his front veranda.

Bill, his arm around her, agreed. "It takes me one month to adjust to the city after I leave the bush. And it takes one month to adjust to the bush after I leave Toronto," he said. "Maryborough seems so peaceful, if one can ignore the antics of Patrick Smith and Caleb Gingerich." Bill laughed. "Those two are a pair of devils."

"The scheme Caleb hatched up this time was brilliant, but had its dangerous moments. Will he ever quit?" Erie asked.

"He'll have to," said Bill. "His ankle and foot are badly mangled. The doctor in Drayton was furious he wouldn't head right to Toronto. He declared the man would walk with a limp for the rest of his life if the bones weren't set properly by a specialist."

"Silly man!"

"Loyalty kept him in Maryborough. He wouldn't leave until Smitty was ready to leave with him."

"I'm going to miss those two," said Erie.

"What are you going to do now?" asked Bill.

"I'm going back to New York to help Ian with Carliss Enterprises. I'm not so sure now that I want to run the company."

"Do I figure anywhere in your life? Tell me now if I don't. You know I love you. I'll change my entire life for you if I must. I wouldn't ask you to join me in the bush. I'd even consent to work for Carliss Enterprises."

Erie faced Bill. "You do love me, I know. Give me one week, Bill. I must deal with Arthur. If it is any consolation to you, I am not going to marry him."

"I'll marry you," said Bill emphatically, holding Erie to him and kissing her forehead. "I'll wait here until I hear from you. If the answer is no, I'll bury myself in the bush forever."

"If the answer is yes?"

"I'd be the happiest man on earth."

"You make it so easy for me to love you," whispered Erie, putting her arms around Bill's neck and lifting her dark eyes to his face. "It feels so right to be in your arms."

Bill kissed her. When he pulled back to look into Erie's eyes again, he saw Margaret over her shoulder, standing at the bottom of the steps. A Ford taxi belched exhaust as it pulled away. Margaret's Mennonite dress was scuffed in spots, and she'd been crying.

Erie saw the surprise on Bill's face and turned around. "Margaret!" she exclaimed.

Margaret remained silent, looking up at the two of them.

Bill rushed down the verandah steps and put his arms around her.

"What on earth happened?" asked Erie.

Margaret clutched Bill tightly and said, "I was caught."

"Oh Lord!" said Erie, stunned.

Bill tried to help Margaret up the steps, but she chose to sit on the bottom one. He sat down beside her and attempted to comfort her. "The shadow?" he asked.

"Yes. He got the papers."

"Are you hurt?" asked Erie.

"No," Margaret said weakly. "He frightened me, but he didn't harm me."

"We have to figure out what to do," said Erie. She began to pace erratically.

"There is nothing we can do," said Margaret. "They're on their way to intercept the shipment right now. There's no way we can get there ahead of them. There's no time left. We can't exactly phone the authorities."

"There has to be some way," Erie insisted.

"I'm sorry," said Margaret. "It's all my fault."

"How did he know to follow you?" Erie wondered aloud.

"My mother's ring."

"Pardon?"

Margaret held her hand up for Erie and Bill to see. The hand was still shaking. "My mother's ring," she said again.

Bill chuckled. "That vain Mrs. Schmidt," said Bill. "She's been in the jewelry box again."

"This isn't funny, Bill," said Erie. "We must tell Caleb and Smitty."

"So they can join the shadow in Port Colborne for a

picnic?" asked Bill, giving Margaret a hug before leaning back against the steps.

Both women looked at Bill with great confusion.

"The whiskey is headed for Chicago via Windsor," said Erie.

"Yes," said Bill. "The whiskey is headed for Chicago via Windsor, but our competitors are headed nowhere via Port Colborne."

"If the man on the train took the instructions from Margaret . . ."

"Then we're home free," finished Bill.

"I don't follow," said Margaret.

"That makes two of us," said Erie.

"Your agent has already started to process the shipment as per your instructions," Bill explained. "The documents Margaret carried were fake; planted to put up a false trail if they were taken."

"But they were signed by Erie," said Margaret. "I saw them."

"The ones stolen from you were a good imitation, signed by Smitty," said Bill. "I had a set too, just in case I, or Erie, was the one the shadow chose. The real documents were always with the agent. Erie's signing them was merely a formality. I saw the shadow go after you Margaret. I couldn't warn you."

"And, what made Smitty and Caleb so sure that Margaret would survive an encounter with the shadow?" demanded Erie.

"Margaret had strict orders to give up the papers immediately if she were captured. Smitty made her promise. Margaret Smith has never broken a promise in her life. Once the shadow had the papers there was nothing to gain by harming Margaret. These men aren't violent as long as they get what they want. And he knew Margaret couldn't tell the police.

Besides, you've never seen Margaret with her Irish dander up. Patrick knew she'd put up a good fight if necessary. Still, it was risky."

"Risky!" Margaret sputtered. "I'll have a talk with Mr. Patrick Smith! I cried," she said, "because I thought my chances to start a different sort of life with Patrick were gone with the papers."

"How do you know so much?" Erie said, looking at Bill.

"My trip to Maryborough was at the invitation of Caleb and Smitty. One of the reasons I came was to protect you."

"You are in cahoots with them and didn't tell me?"

"I'm a minor partner. I was also to watch out for lovely old Mrs. Schmidt. Smitty and Caleb will join us later, when they're sure the shipment is over the border."

"How did they manage Arthur?" asked Erie suddenly remembering him.

"That's a long story," said Bill. "One best told by Caleb. I'll let him tell you."

"I've had enough excitement for a whole lifetime," announced Margaret, brushing alley dirt from her black dress and shawl. "I'm going to wash up and go find Anna. She's the only sane one among us. What are you two up to now."

"Wait a week," said Bill, pulling Erie closer to him.

Erie kissed his cheek and smiled.

CHAPTER THIRTY-SIX

JACOB'S PORCH

JACOB STOOD ON THE SLEEPING PORCH and looked over the valley. An owl hooted in the orchard. Smitty's dog barked in Jacob's woodshed. The stream trickled musically over its rocky bed. Hearing footsteps behind him, he turned to greet Miriam. "Ahs gehbd fruhshd dee hancht."

"Is a beautiful night, Jacob."

"She has gone, Miriam." Jacob looked over the valley again.

"She will come back," said Miriam, standing beside him. "But she was meant to be shared by many people, not only those of her faith. Erie is of the world, not of us."

"Doo hen drie kinah, Jacob; tsvay boovah oon ay maydahl."

"Ich hehn tsvay kinah, Miriam oon ah friend."

"Erie will not forget her fahdah."

"Nay," said Jacob, reaching for Miriam's hand. "She will come back to the valley."

"She will write, Jacob. And when she has children of her own, she will bring them here. She must. You have not lost your daughter again."

"I am sorry, Miriam." Jacob turned from the valley to his wife. "We must begin a new life. Can you forgive me the mistakes I made?"

"You are a good man and a good fahdah, Jacob. I forgave you a long time ago. I learned that love is strong. I did not stay because I felt duty to you or your family. I loved you, Jacob; and you did not realize it."

Jacob tenderly placed his arm around Miriam's waist.

"Is it too late? Can Miriam leave a legacy for this valley too?"

"Ah, Jacob, I hope. My arms ache for a child."

Overhead a brilliant fiery fragment of meteorite hurled above Rachael's valley, burying itself in the ground somewhere in Perth County.

"Is a good sign for us, Jacob. Patrick Smith would say so."

"Is so," Jacob said. "Is Rachael giving her blessing."

The End

BIOGRAPHIES

Erie Gingerich-Carliss married Bill O'Grady in April 1926. They lived in many parts of the world, but always spent their summers at *Seawind* with Anna. All four children born to them were taken to Rachael's valley during their sixteenth year and introduced to their grandfather. All were told of their unique heritage. Bill died in Toronto in 1976. Erie died in August 1999.

Anna Carliss moved from *The Dakota* in New York City to Camden, Maine in 1929. Although she never married Caleb Gingerich, he was her constant companion and mentor. He lived in a small cottage in Camden near the harbour. His bad foot made it impossible for him to work around horses. The monies from the scheme provided enough income he could live comfortably. With Anna's encouragement he began writing his memoirs which were privately published in 1947. Anna died during a visit to Fergus in 1954. Caleb died in Camden in 1957. Anna is buried between William Carliss and Caleb Gingerich in the shadow of Mount Battee.

Margaret and Patrick Smith, with the money from the sale of whiskey and home farm, bought a large house in Fergus, Ontario. Smitty returned to carpentry but was never happy unless he had some small diversion. Smitty drowned in Lake Huron in 1968 while attempting to save the life of a small child. Margaret moved to Toronto to live near her eldest son, a lawyer. She died in Toronto in 1972. Both are buried in Belsyde Cemetery, Fergus, Ontario.

Arthur Moore married Rivona Gilds in 1927. He invested heavily in the stock market and lost everything in the crash of 1929. He died in 1953, leaving no heirs. To his credit, he never told Erie's secret, if he indeed knew it.

Adam Gingerich left the faith and moved to Kitchener, Ontario. He married a German girl and they raised three children—two dark haired boys and a flaxen-haired girl. Adam died in 1981.

Abraham Gingerich stayed on the family farm and never married. He died in 1981, two days after his brother.

Miriam Gingerich had three children by Jacob, all beautiful girls. All grew up in the Mennonite faith, married and had large families. Jacob died in March 1965. Miriam died in September 1965. They are buried at their meeting house burial ground in Maryborough Township, Wellington County, Ontario.

Wild roses have completely taken over the abandoned Catholic Cemetery in north Wellington County where **Rachael Gingerich** lies buried.

GLOSSARY OF TERMS

Ah—ah neht hairicht da-ah moose feelah: He who doesn't obey must fail.

Ah gehbd fruhshd dee hancht: We will have frost tonight.

Brodh, booodah, kays, shmoh-gah dah: Bread, butter, cheese, taste good.

Doo hen drie kinah, Jacob; tsvay boovah oon ay maydahl: You have three children, Jacob; two boys and one girl.

Doo sin hoong-ahrich. Com. Ehsah: You are hungry? Come. Eat.

Grohs moodah's gvild . . . gha visah: Grandmother's quilt . . . for sure.

Ich hehn tsvay kinah, Miriam oon ah friend: I have two children, Miriam and a friend.

Kinah oon nahrah sawgah dee vawah hied: Children and fools say the truth.

Miriam id doh?: Is Miriam not here?

Miriam is vay gahdoo: Miriam is hurt.

"*Oon glawblich!*" *Mariam exclaimed.* "*Oonfahshdelndich!*": "Unbelievable!" Miriam exclaimed. "Very astonishing!"

Ouna is ows dee hiesley; crazy, crazy. Ouma hichd neht may fah-shdahnd we ah shdick fee: Grandmother is out of sorts; Grandmother has no more sense than a cattle beast.

See huhd hawah off dee tsoong: She has hair on her tongue.

Schvehts duhch kay blehch: Speak not like tin—means literally "make shallow talk."

Vah ich neht vays, mahct mich neht bays: What I don't know, doesn't make me angry.

Vah ich vays mahclt mich bays: What I know makes me angry.

Vah lhts is, is lehts oon vahs rehchtes, is rehcht: What is wrong, is wrong and what is right, is right.

Vah sich tsvelt dehs drit sich: What happens twice will happen thrice.

MORE BY PAT MESTERN

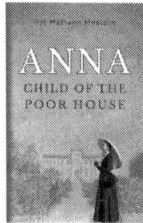

Anna: Child of the Poor House
Anna Ellington was born in the Wellington County House of Industry and Refuge, known as the "Poor House" near Fergus, Ontario, Canada. Later she was bound out to a wealthy family in Toronto. In 1904, Anna returns to Fergus as a beautiful young woman in search of her family. She hopes to learn why her mother ended up in the County Poor House. During her visit to the area she encounters several local characters and finds romance, mystery, wealth, intrigue and answers to many questions. Readers will never forget Anna and the folks that enter her life.

Vein of Love
Grieving the recent loss of her friend Harry, Ramona Ashdon's life converges with that of Don Chambers. As the executor of Harry's estate, Don's presence in Ramona's town doesn't seem unusual . . . until he starts asking questions about Harry that nobody seems to know the answer to. Determined to piece together the story of Harry's life, Ramona and Don set out across Ontario in search of the truth. What they discover will change the lives of everyone involved, forever.

Magdalena's Song
When a mysterious old man arrives in the rural Ontario village on the Saugeen River, the man's appearance is considered suspicious by a number of local residents, especially when the lives of some of the most influential villagers begin to unravel quickly after his arrival. Is Daniel the ghost of a gypsy who once loved a woman from the area? Is he a labour organizer with a very slick cover story? Whatever—or whoever he is, the village will never be the same after Daniel leaves.

Pat Mestern

Pat Mestern has always called the Upper Grand River Valley in southern Ontario home. The combination of its beautiful natural heritage and multi-cultural diversity—the Scots, Irish, English, German, Mennonite and Amish settled this vibrant area—plays a major role in forming the characterizations and settings  for her works of historical fiction that are primarily set in Canada. Traveling and writing provide her with endless ideas for scenarios, time periods and characters for those works of fiction that are set "away." She credits her upbringing, surrounded by books, music, good conversation and encouragement from family, for her love of history and the ability to write.

Connect with Pat at

www.mestern.net

Facebook: Pat Matttaini Mestern Author

Made in the USA
Middletown, DE
17 June 2022

67252929R00196